The King of Black Diamonds

INTERNATIONAL BESTSELLING AUTHOR

NICOLE S. GOODIN

THE KING OF BLACK DIAMONDS

BOOK ONE

ROYALS OF WESTLAKE

NICOLE S. GOODIN

The King of Black Diamonds
Published by Nicole S. Goodin

ISBN: 978-0-473-65171-8

Copyright 2022 by Nicole S. Goodin
All rights reserved. ©

First published October 2022
Cover design by Nicole Goodin
Images purchased from Shutterstock
Editing by Spell Bound

This book is a work of fiction. All names, characters, places and incidents either are products of the author's imagination or are used fictitiously. Any resemblance to events, places, or persons, living or dead, is purely coincidental.

The author acknowledges all song titles, song lyrics, film titles, film characters, trademarked statuses and brands mentioned in this book are the property of, and belong to, their respective owners.

Nicole S. Goodin is in no way affiliated with any of the brands, songs, musicians or artists mentioned in this book.

 Created with Vellum

To the bratty little highschooler in all of us.

This book has been written using UK English and may contain euphemisms and slang words that form part of the New Zealand spoken word.
Please remember that the words are not misspelled.
They are slang terms and form part of everyday, New Zealand vernacular.
I.e: I'm from New Zealand and sometimes we say weird things down here... please try and be cool about it.

PROLOGUE

Cullen

"The Westlake High Black Diamooooonds!" the announcer's voice booms across the stadium.

Another year, another championship title.

I'm not surprised we're here for another year running, and I never doubted the team for a second – it's no secret we're the best, but I still soak in the moment of victory.

Half the school crowds around us, cheering and screaming – chanting our team's name as we round out the season with yet another win.

Unbeaten all season long.

No other team has been able to say that for years.

We're legends, and we'll be celebrated as legends.

Bianca sidles up next to me through the crowds, her short-as-hell cheer uniform showing off her tanned legs.

I've got no doubt I could have those legs wrapped around me by the end of the night if that's what I wanted.

And maybe I will...

"See you at the party tonight?" She bats her lashes at me. That look, in itself, is enough for me to know I'm bang on the money.

I shrug, noncommittal, but I intentionally brush the back of my hand against her leg to keep her on the hook.

I don't know if I can be bothered with her drama or her bullshit, but I do like to have options. Never hurts to know you have a sure thing in the bank.

"I'll see you later, Cullen." She giggles and rushes off back to her friends.

It's almost too easy sometimes. It's pathetic really.

I'm fucking royalty around here.

The best fullback Coach Green has ever produced and a sure bet for team captain next year.

I'm the golden boy of Westlake High, and everyone knows it.

Nobody messes with me and my boys, and we're only going to be even more untouchable next year – our final year.

We're the biggest fish in a little pond.

Coach calls us into a huddle, and we fend off our supporters to get to him.

Pax is bouncing next to me; he's so jacked up from the high of the win.

He should be proud, he played like a king out there today – scoring three times off the right wing in spectacular fashion – and I'm not just saying that because he's one of the best mates I've got, I'm saying that because he's as talented as I am on that field.

Coach gets stuck into his usual, post-game speech, the man is so proud I can see tears in his eyes. We all start cheering and whooping – giving thanks to the man who's been with us every step of the way.

I don't have a lot of respect for many men, but Coach has always treated me like a son, and I respect the hell out of his passion for the game. He's the closest thing I've ever had to a father figure.

Jay, our captain for the season, is directly opposite me, across the huddle.

We make eye contact as the circle breaks, and he gives me one short, sharp nod and points at my chest.

I nod back.

It's *my* time now.

ONE

Berlin

"Can't you just home school me or something?" I pout as my dad shoves me out the door of our newly acquired house and locks it behind us.

"You must be the only teenager in history to actually want to be home schooled." He chuckles, ushering me down the front path. "And hell no – I value my sanity too much for that kind of shit."

The garage is still full of boxes of our crap, so we've been parking on the driveway. Which probably also means the windscreen is going to be all icy, because apparently this hell hole of a town really means it when it says winter.

"I could do online classes. No parental supervision required."

He ignores me this time and chucks his jacket into the back seat of his ute.

I stop next to the driver's door and cross my arms across my chest, covering the stupid school emblem for the fire pit of an institution I'm about to be thrown headfirst into.

"Just get in the ute, B, I'm not in the mood for your theatrics."

"I'm not being theatrical."

He shakes his head in amusement. "You were born theatrical." He opens his door, but I'm blocking it, so he slowly pushes the door wider and wider, shoving me out of the way in the process.

"Stand out here all day if you want, but I'm going to work, and you know I haven't got you a house key cut yet." He smirks, knowing he's already won this battle, and climbs into his seat, slamming the door behind him.

I weigh up my options, even though I know I've got jack shit up my sleeve this time.

I resist the urge to stamp my foot – but that's too sixteen of me – and finally give in to the inevitable.

I round the hood, take up my spot in the passenger side and scowl at my father. "I hate this place."

"You'll learn to love it," he assures me.

I raise a brow at him. "If you love it so much, why were you on the first plane out of here the minute you finished high school, huh?"

He narrows his dark eyes at me. I take after my father in a lot of ways; olive skin tone, hair so dark brown it's nearly black, and dark eyes. Apparently, I have my mother's figure, but I wouldn't know – given I haven't seen her since I was three months old. My memories are understandably a little fuzzy on all things related to Mummy dearest.

"Just go to school and try not to be such a bitch to everyone you meet, okay? It'd be nice if you made some friends here, so I don't have to listen to so much of your whining. Gotta share that shit around."

I flip him off as we drive down the street, heading towards the local high school.

Not many girls my age have the type of relationship I have with my dad, but then again, not many girls have only a nineteen-year age gap between them and their father either.

He tells me if I'm being a bitch, and I tell him if he's acting like an asshole, and in general, we co-exist well. It's been just me and him for my whole life, and sometimes it's like he's my big brother more so than my dad.

It's been a good seventeen years.

I virtually had no reason to complain until he made the genius decision to pack up all our shit, put us on a plane and move us back to this crappy country and even crappier town that he grew up in.

No seventeen-year-old wants to have their life ripped out from underneath them, *and* to start a new school during their final year, but here we are.

New country, new town, new school. *Love* that for me.

It takes all of ten minutes to drive to school, because *of course* it does – you can basically get right from one side of this place to the other in under half an hour. It's one of those bullshit tiny towns where everybody knows everybody, or at the very least, they know somebody who knows that person. There's literally two degrees of separation between every unfortunate bastard in this place.

Me included now.

"Remember that Sophia is going to meet you by the library."

"Yeah, because I bet that's where all the cool people hang out."

He chuckles. "Anyone who says they're cool, is in *no* way cool, trust me."

"Yeah well, you would know," I bite back as he pulls up to a stop in the carpark. I'm probably laying on the sarcasm a little thick lately, but I don't care. It's my defence mechanism.

"Out you get, diva. I've had my quota of sass for the day."

I swing open my door. "Thanks for the ride, old man."

"Try not to tarnish my good name, and be nice to your cousin, I can't be assed dealing with Derick telling me off because you were mean."

"Derick's a pain the ass," I reply, referring to my uncle – my dad's brother.

"Derick *is* a pain in the ass," Dad agrees.

"I'm *so* glad we moved closer to him," I say, sickly sweet.

"Yeah, yeah, get out of my car."

He gently pushes my shoulder.

The sooner I can get my own ride, the better. Getting driven to the front door by my dad is straight up embarrassing.

"I hate this," I say as I get out.

"Love you too, B."

I slam the door and watch as my lifeline drives away, leaving me in this fresh hell that despite my frequent and thorough protests, has become my new reality.

I sigh and turn towards the entry of the admin building. It's only three quarters of the year. I can get through *that*, and then I'll play it the same way Daddy dearest did and jump on the next flight out.

I pass under the 'Westlake High' sign and roll my eyes at the mention of this being the *home of the Black Diamonds*. If there's one thing I *have* heard about from my dad, it's their nationwide famous rugby team. *The Westlake High Black Diamonds* are 'champions' apparently. My dad was the captain and all-star full-back in his day, and I don't think he's shut up about it since.

The old man loves to relive the glory days.

I shouldn't complain, his pro-sport career hasn't been all bad for me – I've lived a privileged life for the child of a single father. And my dad, despite his short-comings at times, always made it work in whatever way was best for both of us.

He was good too. He played at pro level until injury took him out of the game about a year ago. My childhood was spent in stadiums, locker rooms and at press conferences.

I, however, missed out on the sport genes almost entirely. I run sometimes, but reluctantly and only because it's the only sport that doesn't require me to catch or throw anything, or worse yet – interact with other humans.

I spot a sign for the library and head off in that direction. My cousin, Sophia, and I aren't exactly close – we've seen each other maybe twice in the past five years, and we have fuck all in common from what I gather. I don't really know the girl. It's probably sweet or whatever that she offered to show me around, but I can't really picture us being fast friends.

Unlike me, she's short with almost white-blonde hair, and she's always got her nose stuck inside of some book. She's naturally stunning, but dorkiness kind of surrounds her.

I look around and low and behold, find her leaning against a wall, reading some ridiculously huge book.

Fuck my life.

I don't particularly care what anyone here thinks of me, but if I did, I can't imagine I'd be gaining myself any popularity points by hanging around with Sophia.

She glances up from whatever tale has her totally engrossed and spots me.

I lift my chin in acknowledgement and she waves me over.

I already have so much regret, but I walk towards her anyway. I've got my timetable on my cell phone, but I have no idea where any of the classes are, and without her help, I'll be wandering around out here in the cold for even longer than I need to. Being seen with the dork is the lesser of two evils.

"Hey, you find it okay?"

"Unfortunately," I grumble.

She smiles sweetly, and I almost feel bad for my shitty attitude. Almost, but not quite.

"Dad said that you weren't exactly excited to be starting here."

"You could say that. I hate this place. I miss the warmth of home."

She looks at me, an amused expression on her face. "I hate to be the bearer of bad news, but it isn't even that cold yet."

"Any chance you can drive me to the airport?" I joke – sort of.

She giggles, a soft girly laugh that I want to hate but somehow can't. She's cute.

"Show me what classes you have?"

I pull out my phone and bring up my timetable for her to look at. I'm mostly taking art subjects, but English, maths, science and physical education were compulsory, so I'm going to have to endure those too.

She glances over it, a little furrow in her brow.

She really is the sweetest little thing. Her dad, Derick, is eight years older than my dad, and a total knob – but she seems to have turned out okay – if not a little helpless.

Sophia would have gotten eaten alive at my old

school. Those bitches chew up and spit out pretty, preppy little things like her, and take pleasure in doing so.

"So, all of the art rooms are in that block right there..."

She points out the general direction of all the classes I'll need to find and informs me that we're in the same PE class, which, surprisingly, makes me feel slightly better about the idea of having to go to it – she sucks at sports too.

"Are you going to draw me a map of the cafeteria and give me a rundown of all the cool kids?"

"Of course." She points at a random girl as she walks past and talks to me in hushed tones "That's Gretchen Weiners, she's totally rich because her dad invented toaster strudel."

A laugh escapes me at the unexpected 'Mean Girls' reference. "Not bad, blondie. I love that movie."

Sophia looks pleased at my praise.

"Come on." She gestures for me to follow her. "I'll walk you to English. It's on the way to my Economics class."

We walk along together mostly in comfortable silence, with her pointing out the main things we pass. The cafeteria, the gym, the school hall, she asks me for my locker allocation and smiles when she realises we're right next to each other – alphabetical order and all that, I guess.

"Come on, we've got time to go by your locker before class starts."

"Go on, thrill me then," I drawl.

She leads me into a newer-looking building. She's prattling on about how my English classroom is upstairs, or some shit, but I'm not really listening. I've just entered 'the zone'. Every school has one – it's where the 'cool' kids hang out. I can tell by looking at them; they're your typical jocks and barbies. The guys are all brawn – brains yet to be determined, and the girls' skirts are at least an inch too short for the dress code – not that I can talk – and ninety percent of them have bleached-blonde hair and fake tans.

I like makeup and fake lashes as much as the next girl, but this is something else. One girl looks like she dipped her face in cake batter, glued a couple of tarantulas to her lids and then went about her day. The one next to her isn't much better.

"Jesus, it's like a bad YouTube makeup tutorial threw up in here."

"Shhhhhh," Sophia hisses, her eyes widening in shock.

"*What?*" I demand, "it's true, do you think they've ever heard the phrase 'less is more'?"

"Keep your voice down," she demands, the panic in her tone rising as we walk further into the building.

"*Why?*" I ask, confused.

She looks like she's about ready to run away. "Because I don't want any trouble."

Another way we're different, I think to myself. I personally don't mind a bit of trouble – it's exciting, but

Sophia looks about three point five seconds away from passing out.

"Whatever." I shrug. "Which way to our lockers?"

She looks around, then grabs my arm and tows me quickly to the far side of the space, the opposite side of the room to the lockers.

I pull my arm back and scowl at her. "You're weirder than I remember."

"We can't go over there right now."

I arch a brow at her. "And why not?"

"Because *they're* in the way and I'm too scared to ask them to move."

I follow her line of sight. That's when I *really* see them.

"For the love of all things holy, how old are those fuckers?"

"Shhhh, *shit*, you're going to get me killed."

"What in the name of Anabolic steroids do you call that?" I demand, ignoring her plea for silence.

"That's the rugby team," she hisses, "they're big guys, okay, just shhhh."

'Big guys' is an understatement. One of them must be six foot three, *at least*, and the two flanking him on either side aren't far behind. All three are built like they'd be able to decimate a small village with a base-ball bat.

Sophia's gaze lingers on the blond-headed one of the trio, and almost as though he knows she's looking, his eyes meet hers.

I can practically feel the heat radiating off her face as she's caught creeping.

Meanwhile, I couldn't care less about being snapped staring. I want to know exactly what I'm dealing with here.

These guys are surrounded by females, like flies hovering around a pile of shit.

These are clearly the *most* 'popular' guys. Every school has a clique, and it makes sense that this rugby-mad school would put its hot shot players at the top of the pecking order.

I can see why they've got girls all over them; credit where credit is due, they're hot. The middle one is especially good-looking. Physically he's got everything going for him – tall, broad shouldered, lean, dark hair flopping forward into his face and golden sun-kissed skin. It's obvious he's the alpha.

The other third of the trio has olive skin, dark hair and a good-looking rig from what these shitty school uniforms will allow me to see. He's got a huge smile on his face too, there's something about him that makes me think he's the life of the party.

Blondie, on the other hand, looks like being in this school is draining the life out of him. I can actually relate.

There's a tall blonde girl soaking up the attention of the alpha, at least three girls vying for the class clown, but the blond guy is sending out some serious 'fuck off' vibes, so the groupies are merely admiring him from afar.

It's an interesting mix.

"So, tell me why we can't go to our lockers right now?" I question my cousin, who is still staring at the ground with bright red cheeks.

"Because our lockers are right behind where *they're* standing, and there is no way in hell that I'm going to walk over there and ask them to move."

"Why not?"

"Because they're the top of the food chain, and I'm... *me*. I bet they don't even know my name."

I don't get it.

"Who gives a shit? Just go up and say excuse me."

She shakes her head frantically, eyes wide, like I've just suggested she peel her fingernails off one by one.

"I just stay out of their way. We *all* do. Those girls scare the shit out of me, and those guys are kings. I know you're new, but no one gets in their way, it's an unwritten rule in this school."

"Well, you suit yourself, but *I'm* going to go check out my locker."

"No, you're not. I've seen them make people's lives hell, just because they can, and for a hell of a lot less than asking them to move."

"Well fuck that shit, I don't bow down to bullies."

I step away from her, but she grabs me by my backpack and drags me towards her.

"*Berlin*, you don't know what you're getting yourself into. They're like royalty in this school."

"I don't care. It's just some beefed up rugby players who need taking down a peg or two and their harem of bimbos who I'm sure as hell not afraid of. I'm asking them to move, not shine my shoes."

I pull free of her grasp.

"Rugby is basically religion around here," I hear her whisper, shocked at my apparent audacity.

I glance over my shoulder at her and smirk at the blind fear written all over her face. "Well then, it's lucky I don't pray to anyone's god."

TWO

Cullen

"New girl, ten o'clock," Bry says under his breath, not loud enough for our female company to notice, but loud enough that Pax and I both turn our heads to see what he's seeing.

That's the best thing about having a mate who doesn't say fuck all, when he does speak, we listen, and I swear to God, the guy sees *everything*. Nothing goes on in this place without Bryson knowing about it.

I find her at the same moment Pax does.

"Dibs," he says quickly.

I ignore him as I take her in.

She's talking to some girl I recognise, but whose name I have no idea of.

She's hot – there's no denying that – but she's not my usual type.

Long dark hair trails down her back and her long, lean legs are on display in her too-short skirt.

"How the hell does she look like a supermodel in that ugly-ass uniform?" Pax whistles low. "New girl's got game."

"*What did you say?*" Liana demands, fixing her glare on him. The dude only has one volume, and it's fucking loud.

I shoot my best mate a grimace over her head. He's only gone and done it now.

Liana is queen bee around here and she's a total bitch to anyone who might threaten that title. I don't blame her; I'd kick a guy's ass if he tried to take my place too, but her jealous streak is unrivalled.

"Nothing, Li," Pax replies, grinning. "Just some harmless new chick. You can put your hackles down."

Liana is still scowling at him; I can tell without even seeing her face.

I watch her look around until she finds her target.

She's fucking crackers, but she has her uses.

She turns back to her girls, and they start all that hushed whispering bullshit, taking turns to check out the new girl in some kind of coordinated routine so no more than two of them are looking at a time. Within minutes, everyone knows there's someone new on the scene.

"Who's the little blonde chick she's talking to?" I ask quietly.

There's no reply for a few beats. Pax is even less observant than I am, so if I don't know, chances are, neither does he.

"Sophia Davids. You've taken classes with her for five years," Bryson informs me. There's a slight edge to his voice that wasn't there before.

Pax glances over at Bry, as confused by his reaction as I am. In Bryson world, that was basically him telling me to go get fucked.

I'm about to ask what that was about when Pax hisses, "Incoming."

I look up and see the new girl heading directly for us.

Liana has noticed too; she's taken up residence directly in front of me. Her hands skate over my chest as she vies for my attention.

I give her what she wants, look down at her and smirk.

"Are you coming over tonight?" she purrs in my ear, pressing her body closer to mine.

Fuck yes, I am. I've snuck in her window every night for the past two weeks.

"I'll be there," I growl, cupping her jaw.

"Excuse me," I hear a sassy voice say. "Do you mind?"

Oh shit. Here we go.

Liana snaps her head around, and I can't help but look too. If I know Li, which I do, shit is probably going to go down.

"What's up, new girl?" Pax asks, a huge grin on his

face. I swear the bastard is always smiling about something. Even when we had nothing, he was always smiling.

It's pretty fucking obvious why he's smiling now. New girl *is* next level.

I was wrong about her being hot, she's not just hot, she's *smoking*. Still not my typical type, but she's hot as shit, there's no denying that.

"Just wondering if you could possibly move this mass orgy to the side so I can get to my locker."

Pax explodes into laughter at the same moment that Liana shrieks, "Ex-fucking-cuse me?"

The new chick barely even gives her a glance, which with Liana, is hands down the most effective way to throw fuel on the fire.

"New girl's got the sauce. I like it." Pax chuckles.

"Oh, I'm *so* glad," she replies, sarcastic as all get out, but there's a hint of a smile playing on her lips that tells me she loves the banter.

"I'm Pax." He extends his hand to her, and she surprises me by taking it.

"Berlin," is her reply as she shakes his hand.

Berlin.

"Don't touch the stray, Pax, you'll bring home fleas," Becky, Liana's right-hand bitch, quips.

Berlin looks at her and smirks, condescending as fuck. "Oh, *honey*, is that the best you could come up with?"

Becky looks like she's just been slapped clean across the face.

Liana looks like she's going to burst into flames.

Pax looks like this is the best day of his life.

"*Damn*, ice queen in the house," he announces.

"Well, this has been fun, but if you could just scooch there, big fella, I'll finally be able to get into my locker and you can get back to doing... whatever it is you do."

She's talking to me now, I realise, and not only is she talking, but she's reaching around me to hurry me along.

This chick has got balls the size of coconuts.

Liana wraps herself around me tighter as I take a step to the side.

It's not lost on me that she's trying to mark her territory against the new girl with the big, dark eyes and fiery attitude. She may as well be pissing on my leg at this point.

It's obviously not lost on Berlin either.

"Don't worry, babe, I'm not interested in your man, you can stop sinking your claws into his flesh now," Berlin says, all *fuck you* attitude.

"Fuck off, fresh fish," Liana spits.

"That was a good one," Berlin replies. "Do you girls brainstorm your insults ahead of time?"

Li is *fuming* – I can see how close she is to snapping, and it's closer than I've ever seen.

"Come on, Cullen, let's go to class." Liana tries to make her voice seductive, but she's lost some of her confidence in this exchange – something I've never witnessed before.

"*Cullen?*" Berlin repeats, sassy as hell as she turns to really acknowledge me for the first time. "As in like *Twilight?*"

"Blow me," I retort.

She bats her lashes at me and intentionally looks me up and down. "Oh, I'd *love* to, but I don't think I'm worthy of the *privilege.*"

I hear Pax try and cover a laugh with a cough.

This fucking chick. I don't know what the hell it is about this fucking girl, but I'm not mad. I'll get even, she can bet on that. If anything, I'm intrigued, and that just made life at Westlake High a risky little game for the new girl.

She's going to have a hell of a time dodging land-mines while she's out here tossing hand grenades the way she is.

It's her first day and she's already making enemies – that's going to turn into an awfully long rest of the year for her if she doesn't watch herself. Liana might be a lot of things, but quick to forgive isn't one of them.

The girl holds a grudge as if the world is out to get her, while she sits at home in her ivory tower, racking up bills on Daddy's credit card. It's a deadly combo.

I look Berlin up and down one more time, not even bothering to speak, but telling her with my eyes that I've got her number on this one.

I get it. I see her. Sassy, mouthy little thing, acting all tough and unscathed. Well, we'll see about that. She won't be so arrogant when this school is done with her.

"We're out of here," I say, and just like that, everyone moves with me.

"Buh bye now," she calls after us. "It was an absolute pleasure."

Pax is grinning so wide it's virtually ear to ear as we walk down the hall, away from trouble. "I like her."

"Yeah, well you're the only one, ass hat," Liana replies.

"She's fucking *hot*," he carries on, poking the bear even further.

I shoot him a look that says, *dude, shut the hell up*, but I know I'm wasting my energy. Only time this big goof ever falls in line, is when he's on the rugby field or in trouble with his mother – or mine.

He can't stand Liana and he hates the fact that I'm hooking up with her, so I know the prick is going to take every opportunity he can to get under her skin in the hopes that she'll up and take her overdramatic ass somewhere else.

"You don't think she's hot, *right?*" Liana asks me.

I might mostly be at school for the rugby, but I'm no idiot, I know there's only one right answer here if I want to keep getting the *perks* Liana's been offering me, whether that answer is the truth or not, is irrelevant.

"She's got nothing on you," I tell her.

Liana is hot too, but there was something about that new chick that'd just make you stop and look.

Pax makes a gagging noise, which I dutifully ignore as I sling my arm around Li's shoulders, a smug, satisfied smile on her pretty face.

I glance backwards and for some reason, it pisses me off that the new girl isn't looking our way. In fact, she seems completely unfazed by our collective presence.

It's fucked up. She's not from around here, that was fucking obvious, but where she came from and what her game is, is anyone's guess.

Liana is babbling on about some shit now, and I want to listen, I really do, but my mind is elsewhere, thinking of how I'm going to get my own back on this Berlin chick.

No one comes into my school and calls the shots but me.

"*Cull.*"

"Cullen!"

"Huh?" I come back to the present and look down at Liana, who's scowling at me now.

"This is my class," she snaps, clearly pissed that she's having to tell me something I apparently should already know.

Like I give a shit.

I don't say anything but dip my head and kiss her hard before gently shoving her in the direction of the door.

Her pout disappears and she smiles coyly at me. "See you later, babe."

"Ew. Take your little PDA somewhere else... *babe.*"

I spin around just in time to see a head of dark hair walking into the classroom Liana just went inside.

Liana and Berlin have first period together. Liana is going to be fucking *fuming* by lunch.

Pax pisses himself laughing when he sees. "Oh, this is going to be a fun term. This girl just made things interesting."

"Fuck the new girl, Liana can handle herself," I reply as I stalk off down the hallway. Pax follows, Bryson too.

I hear Pax mumbling something about how he wouldn't say no to doing exactly that, but I ignore him. If he wants to put his dick in that attitude-filled chick, then he can have at it.

We all have first period physics together. I don't know how coach gets away with it, but he's managed to get us together for three classes this term.

"You're an embarrassment with that chick," Pax tells me when they catch up to me again.

"At least I'm getting some action."

"No amount of action is worth dealing with that bunny boiler. I'd rather let my dick shrivel up and fall off."

"She's not that bad."

"You just wait. She's going to burn the whole damn place to the ground when you end it with her."

"Who says I'm going to end it with her?"

Even Bryson laughs at that.

They're not wrong. I'll get sick of her shit before long and I'll end it. Chaos will ensue. The writing is all there on the wall.

"At least it's fucking entertaining for me. I might even lend her some matches." Pax smirks.

A teacher passes us in the hallway. "Language," she warns him.

"Sorry, Miss." He gives her a blinding smile, and I swear the woman blushes.

That guy gets away with absolute murder. Charming prick.

I shove him and he erupts into laughter. "Don't hate on me cos I've got more of the ole' razzle dazzle than you. We all have our strengths, bro."

"Try and go one day without getting detention or Ma will kill you. She already looks like she's willing to choose violence after that stunt you pulled with the lawn mower."

"Ma wouldn't touch a hair on her precious boy's head," he replies smugly.

The asshole is probably right too – he's got an uncanny ability to get out of slippery situations unscathed.

"We training after school?" Bryson asks.

"Fuck yeah we are," I reply. "In the gym by four."

Rugby training doesn't officially start for another couple of weeks, but there's a shit load of work to do before then. Weights, cardio, resistance training... you name it, I'm doing it.

"Don't bring your bitch of a girlfriend," Pax tells me as he ducks into the classroom and out of reach of the jab I throw his way.

Bryson just gives me a look I can't decipher and follows him in.

My phone vibrates in my pocket, and I pull it out to check the message before I go into the classroom. Last thing I need is it getting confiscated again.

Liana: Meet me at my place at 4.30 – my parents won't be home until 6 ;)

I groan. She's going to be pissed when she finds out I'm blowing her off for the gym, but Pax is right; she's temporary and there's *nothing* in my life that gets put before rugby.

Nothing and no one.

I shove my phone back into my pocket and head to my seat so I can start counting down the hours until the school day ends.

THREE

Berlin

"I can't believe it. The sun is actually out."

Sophia shakes her head in amusement at me. "It's not *always* raining here."

I raise a brow at her. "I've lived in New Zealand for three weeks and it's rained for at least two of them."

We're sitting outside with Sophia's friends Carissa, Mel and Laura. They all seem nice enough, a little boring maybe, but if I've learnt one thing about Sophia, it's that she definitely likes to play it safe and fly under the radar, so her friend choices track.

She just about had a heart attack this morning when I confronted those rugby boof heads and their skanky little groupies. I don't know what she was so worried about, it was fun. No harm, no foul.

If that blonde-haired bitch hadn't have scowled at me the way she did, I would have just gone about my business quietly. So, when you really think about it, she started it, not me. I'm not just going to stand by and say nothing while her and her bitchy little girlfriends stare and whisper.

Speaking of... I glance across the courtyard and watch them joking around and eating.

The three guys from this morning are there. If I had to guess, they're the playmakers – the ones holding it all together. They make the rules and everyone else just follows. They're surrounded by random girls and guys to form one big group. The trio of beefed-up kings with Cullen at the head, running point.

"Tell me about them," I say as I point.

Sophia looks in the direction I'm pointing and groans. "Why do I get the feeling you're going to get me into trouble again?"

I toss another chip into my mouth and smirk at her. "I didn't get you in trouble."

"*Yet*," she grumbles. "The day is still young and you're far more unhinged than I remember."

"I still can't believe you just rocked up to them and told them to move," Mel says. I can't tell if she's impressed or if she thinks I'm certifiably insane, but she's entitled to her opinion either way.

Sophia filled them all in as soon as we got to lunch. Apparently, what went down was 'a big deal'. This town is so sad.

"I think I'd die if Cullen looked at me, let alone spoke to me," Laura chimes in.

I refrain from rolling my eyes. Sure, he's gorgeous, but he's not God.

"To be fair, it was only two words. 'Blow me'." I laugh as I remember the look on his face when he said them.

Carissa fans her face. "I probably would have dropped to my knees."

I laugh louder at her unexpected comment. Maybe she's not as boring as I initially thought.

Her reaction is helping confirm my suspicions about this place and the pecking order.

Cullen is the classic, teenage heart throb that all the girls drool over. Got it. It's fair enough I suppose – he certainly looks the part... but he's just so cool, calm and collected... emotionless even. It's weird.

"Pax seems alright. Looks like he's the only one with any sense of humour," I offer. "What's his deal?"

"He's Cullen's best mate. Actually, they're virtually brothers. They grew up together. Their mums both got pregnant right out of high school. Cullen's dad was killed in a crash with a couple of their other friends, no one knows for sure who Pax's dad is, but I once heard my parent's talking about how it was an older married teacher from the school. But anyway, even though their mums had kinda hated each other at the time, they decided to move into a flat and raise the kids together. The boys were born about a month apart and they've lived together ever since."

"Seriously?" I gape. "That's some small-town shit right there."

"Seriously," Sophia confirms. "We even looked up their old yearbook once, Pax looks *just* like the teacher from the rumours. And as for living together... I don't think either of them had many other choices. Dad was friends with some of the guys that died in the crash – Cullen's dad was a good mate of his. He helps out Hannah – Cullen's mum, sometimes."

Jesus. That's a lot.

"Everyone thinks their mums are lesbians, but that's just the boomers being stuck in their ways. Apparently, Pax's mum was pretty much disowned by her parents when she told them she was pregnant, wouldn't say who the father was, and that she was going to keep and raise the baby. They kicked her out... so doing it with another single mum and her baby made sense."

"This having babies at seventeen shit better not be contagious." I shudder. "My dad was only eighteen when he knocked my mum up, so if you all tell me that your parents made you when they were graduating, I'm on the first plane out of here."

"Nah, ours were all older," Mel reassures me. "You're as safe here as anywhere."

Thank fuck for that. I'd have become suspicious of the water otherwise.

That's quite enough baby chat for me. I don't want to risk putting anything out there into the universe.

"Who's the blond guy with the 'I hate life' look on his face?" I ask them.

"Why don't you answer that one, Soph?" Laura suggests with a smirk.

Sophia's cheeks colour. "Why would *I* know anything about Bryson Decker?"

I scoff at her. "Oh, *please*, it's as clear as day that you've got a raging crush on the guy, so spill."

Her friends giggle. Sophia blushes even deeper red but starts talking. "Cullen is the captain of the team and Bryson is set to be his vice-captain, if the gossip is anything to go by."

Of course Cullen is the captain. I should have guessed.

"I don't know what to make of Bryson and no one knows anything much about him. He's pretty quiet, unless it's about rugby, but that's about it. Keeps to himself. One younger sister, his parents come to his games, he hangs out with the boys and that's pretty much all we know."

"I'm not even sure I've ever heard him speak off the field," Laura says.

"He sure is nice to look at though," Carissa adds.

"So, Cullen is the captain... and that blonde thing is his girlfriend?" I question as I watch her vying for his attention with some pathetic attempt at a hair flip.

"That's Liana. I don't know if they're official, but I heard they've been hooking up over the holidays. Cullen doesn't really do the whole, *girlfriend* thing."

"Charming."

"He's been linked to like, six of those girls over the past year or two, but that never seems to stop whoever is next in line. Pretty sure Bianca had her turn after the season ended last year."

It's hardly surprising to me. Girls like that flock to guys like him, morals be damned, legs be open.

"And what about Pax? What's the go with him and the ladies?"

I don't know the guy from a bar of soap, but he seemed like the only one who wasn't a total douche this morning.

"Pax is actually alright. He's got less of that broody alpha male shit going on than the other two, but he's still a womaniser. He's one of the best players on the team, but he's definitely not the most committed. I heard he nearly got thrown off the team one year because coach caught him getting drunk the week before the quarter finals."

"He seems like a clown."

All the girls nod and agree with my assessment.

"One time when we were younger, he streaked across the netball court in the girls' final, it was hilarious, but I'm pretty sure he got suspended for it."

I watch him as he throws his head back and howls with laughter at something one of the other guys has said. Whatever it was has obviously rubbed Liana up the wrong way. She flips Pax off and storms away from the group, with two girls flanking her and her 'boyfriend' looking like he couldn't give a flying fuck.

High school is *so* fun.

Pax waves her off, a huge smile on his face. It's obvious to me that he's not a big fan of the blonde his 'brother' is sniffing around.

I laugh as I watch Cullen shove Pax in the shoulder, effectively pushing him off the ledge they're perched on.

As he gets up, Pax notices me watching and gives me a big wave, his smile growing even bigger somehow. I wave back, my head shaking with amusement.

I can't help but notice the way Cullen's eyes narrow as he takes in the exchange.

Pax might like me, but Cullen certainly doesn't.

Like I give a shit.

"You're making quite an impression around here already," Mel says, and I can't be sure, but I suspect I might detect a hint of jealousy.

"This is nothing. You should see what went on at my old school."

"I think I'd rather not. I almost died twice today already. You stress me out," Sophia says dramatically.

I roll my eyes. She better buckle up, because I'm sure as hell not going to change, and if the 'fuck you' vibe I can feel rolling off the golden boy is anything to go by, him and his buddies won't be backing down.

I raise my hand and wiggle my fingers at Mr. Captain himself.

His frown deepens, but other than that, he doesn't react.

I huff out a laugh. *Pussy.*

"Oh Jesus Christ," Sophia mutters under her

breath. "You know, I told Dad you were going to get me into trouble."

"Relax. No one is in trouble." I smirk.

Yet.

"We have PE next, let's go before you start a war."

"Sure thing, Mum." I wink at her.

PE is the class I'm looking forward to the least, but I don't think I'll be able to get away with 'forgetting' my uniform on my first day, so I'll just have to grin and bear it.

We say bye to the other girls and head to our lockers to collect what is quite possibly the most heinous-looking gym uniform I've ever seen, and I've seen some shit.

Not even I can make this eye sore look good.

Sophia rambles the whole walk to the gym, all the way through getting changed, and she's still talking as we enter the indoor court, so it takes her longer to notice them than it takes me, but there they are, right in front of us, 'B one' and 'B two', throwing a rugby ball between them.

Sophia stops dead in her tracks when she finally sees the two guys – men, really, because they're literally huge – in front of us.

"You have got to be shitting me," she whispers.

"I shit you not," I reply.

She's clearly horrified, but I'm actually quite entertained by this unexpected outcome.

Pax spots us and a goofy grin spreads slowly across his face, like his day has just been made.

"This just keeps getting worse. Next, you'll tell me that Liana is the fucking teacher," Sophia hisses as she stalks off to the opposite end of the gym.

I can't help but laugh. I don't know what the hell has happened to this girl that she feels the need to avoid any type of attention or drama like the plague, but it seems to be a real thing for her.

Cullen turns to see what his buddy is looking at, and his lip twitches when he sees who's standing behind him.

"Why are you *everywhere*?" he demands, pissed.

"Guess you can't hide in a small town after all," I say, bratty attitude rolling off me in waves.

He takes a step towards me. "Shouldn't you be off sharpening your pitchfork or something?"

"Shouldn't you be off chasing the head cheerleader or something?" I fire back, feigning innocence as I bat my lashes.

"Clocked the cheer squad, new girl." He smirks.

"Start on the volleyball team then, perhaps?"

He's standing before me now, his arms crossed hard across his chest, a frown on his perfectly chiselled face. His eyes are insane. They're the lightest, crystal blue I've even seen – a stark contrast to his dark hair and hard features.

"You sure love a cliché, huh?"

"I guess you just bring it out in me."

It's a shame he's such a walking cliché himself, I wouldn't have minded looking at that handsome face all day.

He chuckles darkly. "You know I can make your life hell here, right?"

It's a warning. One that I dutifully ignore. Classic me.

"It entertains me that you think I give a shit."

"Damn, Ice, give my boy here a break." Pax sidles up to Cullen's side, his amusement clear.

"Correct me if I'm wrong, but I think *he* approached *me*."

"You've got me there." Pax chuckles.

I turn my full attention to the friendlier version of dumb and dumber. "Should I be concerned about the big guy here and his army of skanks coming after me?"

Pax laughs. Cullen growls. Literally growls, like some kind of animal.

"Dude, did you just growl?" Pax asks him.

Cullen doesn't say a word, just fixes me with his stare for a few long beats before turning away to retrieve the ball they've left discarded on the floor. He means for the eye contact to be intimidating, and it is, but it's also kind of hot.

Clearly, I've got some issues.

I raise a brow at Pax in question. He's a good-looking guy too, not as chiselled or harsh in his features, more boyish – it makes him come across as a lot less threatening than the company he keeps.

"Cull doesn't like change," he explains.

"And is that what I am? *Change?*"

He smirks and begins to back away. "Among other things, Ice... I look forward to the next encounter."

For some reason, I look forward to it too. It's probably not particularly smart of me, but I never said I was smart, so it is what it is. There's something about Pax that intrigues me, and there's certainly something about Cullen that makes me want to stir up shit.

It's potentially quite a deadly combination.

I scan the room until I find Sophia, hiding in the corner, looking like she's ready for the floor to swallow her whole.

Poor, sweet, little Sophia.

She's probably cursing the day I was born.

We get through the rest of PE, and the rest of the day without further incident, much to Sophia's delight. I'm not as thrilled by it, but I probably would have felt pretty guilty if I'd sent her into full cardiac arrest on my first day here.

I'll have to ease her into the chaos.

I catch a ride home with Sophia and Aunt Alyssa. I love Aunt A, she's a real good bitch. If I had a mum in the picture, I'd be stoked for her to be like Alyssa. She's quite a bit younger than Derick, and she's about the only thing that makes him tolerable. I don't know what she sees in him, but he's definitely punching.

She asks all about our day, and I'm a little jealous of how close Sophia is with her mum. She tells her all about how I 'stirred up shit' with the cool kids, and unlike her daughter, Aunt Alyssa thinks it's hilarious.

They drop me out the front of my house, and I'm a little sad we can't stay and have a little more girl talk, but I guess since I live here now, there will be plenty of time for that.

"See you tomorrow!" I call as I walk up my driveway.

"Re-evaluate your life choices!" Sophia calls through her open window.

I laugh.

Not a chance.

FOUR

Cullen

I'm fucking tired as hell. It was after midnight by the time I snuck out of Liana's room and back into my own last night. I'm going to have to cut that shit out when rugby training starts again.

I don't need the distraction, and I sure as hell need more sleep.

Li was pissed that I couldn't come over while her parents were out – threw a full-blown hissy fit – so I climbed in her window after Mum went to bed and Ma was at work.

I'm surprised that Pax didn't rat me out this time.

I reckon he'd love nothing more than to send me up shit creek without a paddle, if it'd get rid of 'that dick-humping leech' – his words – but for now at least, I'm not in trouble with either of our mothers.

Thank fuck. The only thing worse than being in trouble with your mum is being in trouble with two of them.

"Can we run some of those plays after school? Eli and Tonksy are keen," Pax asks me as we walk to school.

"Yeah, bro. I'm in. I need to get a five k run in after that too if you're down?"

"Fuck that, take Bry."

This is the thing that pisses me off about Pax. He's probably the most naturally talented out of all of us, but for some reason, he isn't giving it everything he's got.

I'd kill to have the effortless swag he has on that field. There's no doubt I'm a better player than him, but I work twice as hard as he does to achieve it.

We walk in the school gates, and I already can't be fucked sitting through a full day of classes. My teachers cut me a fair bit of slack, but falling asleep at my desk on the second day of term is probably pushing my luck.

"What have you got this morning?" I ask him.

"Maths, then drawing."

I nod. He's a real creative bastard. I can't draw or paint to save my life, but I'm pretty good behind a camera.

"You?" he prompts as we head for our lockers.

"Photography and accounting."

We each get the shit we need for our first classes and head off in our separate directions.

Photography is probably the best way to ease me into the day without me losing my shit. There's something calming about looking at the world through a lens. Cuts out the bullshit.

Li has been bugging me to take some pictures of her for my next project, but I'm off it. I've never photographed a chick on her own, and the last thing I need is her thinking she's special.

I get to class early and pull up in my usual spot down the back. You'd think after three years of taking an art subject, that the confused looks would have disappeared by now, but apparently not. There's always at least a handful of people that look at me like I'm a dumb jock who must have got lost on the way to the locker room.

Bianca – one of my prior hook-ups – comes in the door with Cece at her side. Ce is actually one of the only girls in that group with principles; the rest barely have a set of morals between them. Bianca is one of the worst. It's probably rich coming from me, I'm not exactly squeaky clean, but I'm upfront with these girls. I don't bullshit anyone. They know the score when we hook up. What they choose to convince themselves of isn't my problem... and convince themselves they do.

Girls love that whole 'I can change him' bullshit. They never can, but I've got to give them kudos for continuing to try.

A couple of guys I took the class with last term show up and take up their spots at the desks around me.

The bell rings and I look up from my camera. That's the moment she walks in.

Berlin.

She's with Carissa, a little red head who's been in some of my classes for a couple of years now. They're laughing about something and neither of them look my way as they take their seats and get their books and cameras out of their backpacks.

Berlin is seated right in front of me, with only a few rows of desks and chairs separating us.

I fight the sudden urge to throw something at her. She's really got under my skin.

The chick is a bitch. She's arrogant and cocky, and she needs to learn that no one does arrogant and cocky as well as I do.

Ms. Ainsley walks in at that moment, and I tell myself to chill the fuck out. I'm not getting into shit with her – Ms. Ainsley is one of the few teachers around here that I can stand.

She starts talking, but I'm barely listening. I already know what the assessment is for the term. It's portraiture. I'm too busy trying to figure out how I can tell Liana she's not going to be my subject, without starting World War three, to be listening to the ins and outs.

Some people start asking questions, and I zone back in.

I seriously need more sleep.

"We can choose to take photos of anyone we want?" Cece asks.

"Actually, no. Not this year." Ms. A shakes her head.

That gets my attention. Liana can't lose her shit with me if it's not my decision.

I sit back smugly in my chair, hopefully listening for the words I'm praying will save my ass.

"This year we're going to partner up within the class and shoot images of one another."

Day. Made.

I watch as Berlin and Carissa exchange a look. Cece and Bianca do the same. The silent exchange of a look between two females that understand each other without so much as a word needed.

Magical.

I know I'm probably going to get stuck with one of the dudes I'm sitting next to, but I don't give a fuck. I can take pictures of anything – even Louis' filthy mug if it comes to it. Anything is better than Liana.

Some of the shots I got at a game I was too injured to play in, line the gym walls. If I can make fifteen sweaty, filthy dudes look good, I can do anything.

Whispers start filling the room – everyone is trying to lock in their partner.

"Before you get too carried away making plans, you should all know that the partners will be randomly assigned by me – *not* selected by you. I've already got the list here."

There's a low murmur of displeasure throughout the room.

No one wants to work with someone they don't

know – it's about as fun as standing up and telling the class a fun fact about yourself. I'd rather take a rugby ball to the nuts, but it's whatever. I don't care who the fuck I have to point my lens at if it gets me out of doing it with Liana.

"We don't get to choose our partner? What is this hell hole?" I hear Berlin hiss.

And that's when it occurs to me. *She's* in the room – so there is *one* exception to my 'I don't give a fuck who' rule.

Fuck.

It'd be just my luck...

Ms. Ainsley ignores us all and starts reading out the names of the partnered-up students from a sheet of paper in her hands.

"Cece and Lindsey. Jack and Max. Steph and Alex. Sam and Kat."

The moment she says my name, I already know what's going to follow it. *I already know.* It's going to be Berlin. I'm going to be stuck with the one person in the room that I'd pay good money *not* to be partnered with. In fact, fuck that, I'd not only pay good money – I'd sell my soul to the devil for anyone else in the room other than the one that will cause me a shit storm of trouble, but this is my life, and this kind of shit always seems to stick to me.

"Cullen and Berlin," she says.

"Fuck's sake," I mutter under my breath.

Berlin freezes and sits up ramrod straight in her chair.

Slowly, ever so slowly, she turns in her seat, as though she can feel my eyes boring holes in the back of her head.

It's obvious by the look on her face that she didn't even know I was in the room before this moment, and now, just like that, we're partners. Stuck with each other for the next ten weeks.

Fuck my life.

I glare at her, and she offers the same in return, before turning back to face the front.

I'm going to have to spend countless hours in the presence of the new girl, and not only that, but our final projects will be completely covered with each other's faces.

What the fuck could go wrong?

Liana is going to flip a lid and Pax is going to die from laughter when this gets out.

"Alright, get together with your partner and try and work out some type of schedule for the term so you can both work together to get what you need. You've got ten weeks; the project will be due on the last week of term and they'll go on display in the arts centre for the final few days."

I'd rather shit in my hands and clap than get together with the new girl and make time to meet up, but there's fuck all I can do here. My hands are tied.

I contemplate asking Ms. A if I can swap out for someone else, but I already know she'll say no. She's cool, but she's a stickler for the rules.

Everyone buzzes around the room, moving to find their partners and start making arrangements.

I don't move an inch.

She can come to me.

Berlin and Carissa have their heads close together and they're speaking in fast, hushed whispers.

Carissa's eyes keep darting over to look at me, and then her cheeks flame red when she gets caught looking.

Berlin stands up abruptly, her chair skidding back a few inches.

"I don't give a shit, I'll handle it," I hear her say.

She picks up her shit off the table, slings her bag over her shoulder and stalks towards me, her hips swaying like the middle of the class is a god damn runway.

She's gorgeous, making her look good in photos isn't exactly going to be a challenge, but keeping my fucking sanity just might be.

She grabs the chair from the desk in front of me and slides it towards my table, sitting so she's straddling it.

She puts her shit on my desk as though she's got some right to be in my space.

The fucking audacity.

"Yeah, I'm not exactly thrilled about it either, big guy," she snaps.

"I had a slightly more colourful description in mind," I growl.

"You going to suck it up or are we going to have a

problem here?" she replies, brow raised like the brat she is.

Oh, we're absolutely going to have a problem here. I'm sure she's smart enough to have figured that out already, but just how much of a problem remains to be seen.

"I don't need your psycho bitch of a girlfriend trying to claw my eyes out."

"She's not my girlfriend."

"Whatever, golden boy, *don't care*, as long as we can get this shit done without any casualties."

"I can't make any promises."

She stares hard at me for a few long beats. "Then what about a truce?"

Her eyes are looking directly into mine, her stare unwavering. It's fucked. No one keeps eye contact with me.

"I'm listening," I finally say.

"For the project only, we don't make life difficult for one another. This class has a truce surrounding it."

"What about outside of this class?"

She lifts her chin defiantly. "Have at it."

I think about it for a few beats. I don't like it, but it might be the best I can hope for out of this shit show.

I hold out my hand to her and she takes it in hers and shakes.

I feel like I just made a deal with the devil. She looks like she thinks the same about me.

"Are you any good at this?" she asks, the assumption that she's already decided I'm not, thick in her tone.

"Not your problem if I'm not."

She rolls her eyes. "You make me look like shit and it'll be a problem."

Superficial bitch.

"You just worry about your photos, and I'll worry about mine."

"When do you want to get this thing started?" She pulls up the assignment briefing on her tablet screen. "It says we have to use various locations and lighting conditions, so it's going to need to be several days of shooting, probably at various times of the day."

Fucking spectacular.

Just when I think this couldn't get much worse.

I don't answer.

"After school tomorrow?" she suggests.

I shake my head. "I have to hit the gym after school."

Her gaze roams down to my shoulders and arms. "Yeah, you are looking awfully scrawny. Couldn't possibly miss pumping a bit of iron."

She's obviously got no idea what it takes to be the best. No one ever got to the level I'm aiming for by taking days off whenever they felt like it.

"After the gym then?"

"Maybe."

"That's *super* helpful," she replies, snarky.

"Give me your number and I'll text you when I've got free time."

"Rugby superstar, Cullen Carrington, wants *my* cell number. Dreams *do* come true," she coos, all dramatic sass and attitude. She's so God damn spicy.

"Can you do anything without being a smart bitch?" I demand.

"Nope," she replies, not missing a beat.

"Lucky me," I mutter under my breath as I slide my phone from my pocket, unlock it and hand it to her.

She taps her number into it and then hits call as she gives it back to me, before taking out her own phone and saving my number after it rings through.

There's no going back now.

We sit there in silence as the rest of the class talks loudly around us, neither of us really doing anything other than holding our ground.

"Where'd you come from?" I ask her, the question escaping me.

She's got a bit of an accent that doesn't sound like it's from around here, but somehow like it belongs at the same time.

She deliberates for a minute, debating how much to tell me, if I had to guess. "Australia. I grew up there," she finally answers. "My Dad is from here, we just moved."

I nod. Mystery solved. I don't ask anything else. The last thing I want is her thinking that I give a fuck about her or her life story – because I sure as shit do *not*.

She doesn't seem fazed at all about my response or lack thereof. She pulls out a black sketching book and flicks it open to a clean sheet of white paper. She sketches away on the page while I sit there, watching until the bell rings and it's time to go to my next class.

I get up from my seat, grab my shit and leave without so much as a word.

FIVE

Berlin

"There must be something to do in this town other than eat."

"Not when it's raining." Carissa sighs.

"At least the food is good," Sophia offers.

It's not bad – the American-style diner is actually pretty cool, but that's not the point. I wanted to do something, see something – *anything*, really.

"Who cares, can we talk about the fact that you have to work with Cullen for the next ten weeks, *pleeeease*. That's definitely the most exciting thing that happened today."

I roll my eyes. The people in this town really need to get a life, if me being partnered with the captain of the rugby team is the hottest gossip available.

"It's whatever. The guy thinks he's hot shit. I don't care. We made a deal not to fuck with each other for the project, but I already know it's going to suck. He thinks he's so busy and important."

"At least you know he'll have to make *some* time for it, since he needs to get some shots of you too," Sophia points out.

I nod. That is a good point. He can't just blow me off entirely, not without failing the class himself.

"I bet he smells so good," Carissa says, her tone dreamy.

I frown at her random statement. "Get a grip, woman."

Soph laughs at her. "You're so weird sometimes."

"*Maybe*, but you know I'm right, you can just tell when a guy smells good. And Cullen Carrington *definitely* smells good."

"I don't think sniffing him is part of the course requirement, so I'll just have to take your word for it," I reply.

"Oh, you'll find out." Carissa smirks, her tone full of insinuation.

I raise a brow at her. "What's *that* meant to mean?"

She sips her milkshake and eyes me over the top of her glass. "A pretty little thing like you? There's no way he's not going to make a move at some point."

"Oh *please*." I scoff. "Me and Cullen aren't happening. The guy is a tool."

Sophia and Carissa exchange a knowing glance. I

ignore them, instead shifting my focus to the bowl of fries in front of me. I don't argue with nonsense.

"He's a tool you sure seem to enjoy interacting with."

"And? If he's going to treat me like a game, then I'll damn well show him how to play."

Carissa looks like she wants to high five me. Soph looks like she wants to smother me with a pillow.

"Should we just go back to my house and watch Netflix or something?" I suggest. "Dad will be so happy to see I've got some friends; he'll probably shout us pizza for dinner later."

"I should probably go home and do some home-work," Sophia replies.

"It's only the second day, don't be such a nerd. Text Mel and Laura and tell them to meet us at my place in an hour."

She pouts but takes out her phone.

I'm being bossy, but I don't care; the girl needs to learn to live a little. I know full well she'll still do the homework later when she does get home, but at least she won't spend *all* evening being a loser. There's a time and a place for homework and the second day of term is not it.

"Did you have any of the other rugby boys in your classes today?" Carissa asks me as Sophia types out a message to the other girls.

"Pax was in my drawing class, but I didn't talk to him, he sat by the door – came in late wiping lipstick off his face."

"What about Liana or any of her minions?"

"Liana is in my Bio class, she glared and flicked her hair with a lot of aggression and frequency, but other than that, nothing exciting happened. I don't know which ones of her sidekicks were around, they all look the same to me."

"Did you say anything to Liana?"

"Nah." I shake my head. "I just flipped her off when I got sick of her staring."

"I love this." Carissa beamed.

"*I* don't," Sophia replied.

"Love what?" I question.

"That you don't give a shit about them. Those girls have made so many people's lives hell over the years, and they do whatever the fuck they want, and get away with it. I just love that you don't bow down."

She's looking at me as though I've done something revolutionary, just by not ass-kissing the cool kids. It's actually pretty sad when I really think about it. These poor bitches have been getting looked down on for years by a bunch of slutty cheerleaders, and not one of them figured out that they didn't just have to lie down and take it.

Sure, I go a little further than biting back – I probably bite first, but still. It's obviously a startling change of pace.

"Okay, the girls said they'll be there," Sophia pipes up.

"Cool." I nod.

I pull out my cell phone to give my dad the heads up.

Berlin: Old man, I'm bringing some friends over, be cool.

Dad: How the hell did you make friends when you're so entirely insufferable?

I roll my eyes.

Berlin: Be. Cool.

Dad: I'm not a regular dad, I'm a cool dad.

Clearly my family has far too much of a thing for *Mean Girls*.

I get to work demolishing the rest of the fries, then we pay and head out. Carissa is the only one of the three of us with a car, so we pile into her hatchback and head for my house.

Laura and Mel are just pulling into my driveway as we arrive, and my dad's car is there too – love that for me.

For someone who wants me to make and keep friends, I'm willing to bet he'll have absolutely no qualms in trying his best to embarrass the ever-loving shit out of me.

We walk in the front door, and I call out to my dad, there's no point in delaying it – I already know exactly how this encounter is going to go, I'm yet to be surprised by new friends meeting my dad, and I'm sure this time will be no different.

"Dad! I'm home."

He appears in the doorway. Grey sweats, tight white t-shirt, eating a bowl of cereal. I swear he does this shit to me on purpose.

I don't even have to turn, I hear the sharp intake of breath from my three new friends.

"Dad, this is Mel, Laura and Carissa." I introduce them quickly, and without pointing out which is which.

"Girls." He nods. "Did she pay you to tolerate her?"

They all giggle like the giddy schoolgirls they are.

I flip him off. "They're Soph's friends, they didn't inherit me by choice."

"Unlucky break," he muses.

Sophia goes over and hugs him, "Hey, Uncle Cole."

"Hey, sweetheart, how're you doing?"

They make small talk, and I decide to take the risk and see how the girls are holding up. Laura is bright red; Mel's jaw is on the floor, and Carissa looks like she just fell in love.

Wonderful.

I get it. My father is a handsome man.

He's young, in excellent shape, and he comes from an exceptionally good gene pool. Sophia's dad, Derick, is decent-looking too, but he's the slightly past it, dad-bod version of my dad. Dad was always the athlete of the family and that hasn't changed, even though he's retired from professional sport these days.

I'm yet to have even one friend that hasn't developed some type of unhealthy infatuation with him. It's *super* fun.

"We're going to watch a movie," I call over my shoulder as I usher the three quivering messes out of the room.

"Oh. My. God."

I don't even know which one of them spoke, but it doesn't really matter. I do *not* need to hear how 'hot' my dad is or listen to him being labelled a 'DILF'.

"Yeah, yeah, can we just *not*?" I flop down on the couch and grab the remote.

"Oh, but we *must*. How fucking *banging* is your dad?" Carissa gushes.

"Careful, he'll hear you and never let you live it down."

"I don't even care, I have absolutely zero qualms about becoming your new step-mum, no offense."

"None taken."

"Um, your dad is *Cole Davids*," Mel says, her jaw still pretty firmly on the floor. "He's a legend."

That gets my attention, I turn to look at her, forehead creased. "How do you know that?"

"*Everyone* knows that. Hometown rugby hero who went on to kill it overseas. He's kind of a big deal. Best fullback I've ever seen."

"*Ew*. Rugby chat." I grimace. "But I can't believe you've actually heard of him."

"I like rugby." She pouts.

"Well maybe you should actually go and talk to him then, as long as you just appreciate his talents and don't want to hump his leg?"

She smirks as she stands back up. "Maybe it's a little bit of column A, little bit of column B."

I grab her hand and pull her back down as she cracks up laughing. "Park it, perve. And keep that rugby legend shit to yourself, I don't want it going around the school."

Laura is still bright red. I don't even ask for her opinion; it's written all over her face.

"If you could all control yourselves for thirty seconds, maybe we could choose a movie?" I suggest.

"Maybe we just go back out there and stare at your dad for an hour and a half instead."

I don't even dignify that suggestion with a response.

Sophia comes into the room and slides into a spot on the couch. We might not have all that much in common, but right now I could not be more grateful that at least one person in the room isn't undressing my father with their eyes.

"Your friends are dirty whores," I inform her.

"That tracks," she replies, unfazed.

"They all want to do your uncle."

She takes the remote from me and starts channel surfing. "Gross, but not entirely surprising."

"You're no help," I grumble.

She chooses some new chick flick, rom-com situation, which I feel like I should complain about, but deep down, I do love a trashy romance.

I see my dad lingering in the doorway out of the corner of my eye.

"Don't do it, pops," I warn him.

He chuckles, and I swear to God, the girls go on heat. You can almost smell it in the air.

"A father can watch a movie with his daughter and her friends, can't he?"

"Not if he wants to continue to live in a non-hostile environment."

"Be real, B, your environment is always hostile," he says with a shit-eating grin.

"Sure feels incredibly hostile," Carissa stage whispers to me.

"Why don't you just worry about keeping it in your pants," I fire back at her.

"I might head out for a run," Dad says, clearly having heard the exchange. If the look on his face is anything to go by, he's finding it amusing.

"I think that'd be wise, old man. Try not to pull a hammy."

"My credit card is on the kitchen bench if you want to order food," he calls from the hallway he's backed out in to.

"Love your work," I yell after him.

"I wish I could talk to my parents like that. My dad is so strict," Laura says once he's gone.

"I swear my mum's full-time job is making sure I don't have any fun," Mel comments. She's looking wistfully at the doorway my dad was standing in.

"He is pretty cool; I'll give him that. But we have our moments. Apparently, I'm as stubborn as my mother."

"Where is she?" Mel asks me.

I can feel them all looking at me now; Sophia, because she already knows the answer, and the other three because they've clearly been dying to know.

"She's dead," I reply.

They're all silent.

"Don't go all weird on me. I didn't even know her. Her and my dad had a one-night stand right after he moved to Australia, from what I can gather. Turns out she was pretty big on the drug scene. She got pregnant with me, stayed clean for nine months and then just went ham on the gear once I was born. My dad got full custody when I was about five weeks old, and she had supervised visits until I was three months old. Then she overdosed. My dad was the one who found her, with a needle hanging out of her arm like the junkie she was."

"Jesus," Mel breathes.

"Right?" I agree. "At least she stayed clean while she cooked me, I guess, but still, silly bitch went straight back to it."

"So, your dad raised you on his own from five weeks old?"

I nod. "Sure did. He's kind of superman. I had a nanny and stuff when he was in the peak of his career, but we always travelled with him as much as we could. I feel like I was raised by teams of burly rugby players for half my life."

"So why don't you like rugby then? Sounds like it was a big part of your childhood," Carissa asks.

I always get asked this, and it's a fair question.

Most people assume I'd be head over heels for the game and everything it entails.

Couldn't be further from the truth.

"It's not that I have anything against the sport, per se, it's the culture. I'm not saying that every pro player is a dog, but a lot of them are... I've seen guys that are the biggest family men at home, then they'll go away and risk it all for a cheap thrill or an ego boost. And it's not only that, but I've also watched some of my dad's closest mates change before our eyes with concussions – they've never been the same. I guess I've seen the less glamourous side of the sport. The prescription med addictions, the injuries... Those guys miss things like their children being born, ya know? It's just not always all it's cracked up to be. And then when the players retire or are forced into early retirement like my dad, they're usually discarded and replaced with a younger, fitter model in the blink of an eye."

"Well, *damn*," Carissa says.

"It's a great game," I reply, "it sure as hell isn't the most important thing in the world, but since the best players usually have egos to match, that's what stops them from seeing that."

"So, no rugby player boyfriend for you then?" Sophia jokes.

I shake my head. "I think I'd rather stick pins in my eyes."

"I'm really sorry about your mum," Laura tells me, sincerity ringing true in her voice.

I shrug my shoulders. Every now and then I

wonder what it would be like to have a stable female figure in my life, but I think I'm doing alright without it.

"It's all good, I kinda hit the dad jackpot, so I figure you can't win 'em all."

"Mmm, mmm. Ain't that the truth." Carissa hums. The bitch is basically drooling.

We all crack up laughing at the look on her face, and for the first time since I arrived in this stupid town, I don't feel quite so lonely.

SIX

Cullen

"You've got to be joking me!" Liana hisses, trying and failing to conceal the absolute scene she's creating.

"Do I look like a fucking clown?" I drawl.

"You're making *me* look like a fucking clown, Cullen."

I refrain from rolling my eyes.

I knew this moment would come. She was always going to hear about me and Berlin being paired together for this project. To be fair, I'm shocked it took Bianca until now to spill the beans. I think the bitch was waiting for a good crowd, and she got one.

"How the fuck am *I* making *you* look like a clown? I didn't choose the pairs, Li. Chill the fuck out."

"Don't tell me to chill out. Out of every person in this school, you get paired with *that* bitch."

It's ironic, I'll give her that. I don't know that it warrants the complete and utter shit show that Liana is currently orchestrating, but she has always been bat shit crazy.

"It is what it is." I shrug, done with this bullshit.

"That's not good enough. Get your teacher to change it. Complain to the principal."

Now she's just plain pissing me off.

I don't know who the hell she thinks she is, but she won't be telling me what to do, that's for damn sure.

I feel my expression harden as I look down at her. "No."

"*What?*" she shrieks, "what do you mean 'no'?"

I know everyone is watching this exchange closely. I'm tempted just to bin it right here and now, but those pouty fucking lips of hers make me pause. I can picture them wrapped around my dick and the visual is enough to make me hesitate.

"Come and talk to me when you've calmed the fuck down," I tell her.

I turn away, heading for the car park. Bryson and Pax immediately fall into step with me, flanking me on either side. Pax is probably disappointed the show is over, but Bry will be nothing but grateful to get the hell out of here.

"Fuck you, Cullen!" she screams after me.

"You've already done that, sweetheart." Pax chuckles.

I punch him in the shoulder. He does nothing to kill the fire Liana gets going – if anything, he stokes it up more.

"*What?* That's some next level crazy, bro. I don't know what the hell you're thinking with that one. I'm all for getting your dick wet, but *shit*."

He's got a fucking good point, he really does.

I should just flick her. Rugby starts soon and I don't need the distraction, but it's convenient, for now at least, and there's a lot to be said for convenience.

"She'll calm down."

I already know she'll be back, she's a stage three clinger. She's probably already planning our wedding, which is going to be an issue for me when I do cut her. I've got no doubt about that.

There's just something about the crazy ones that gets me going.

"I thought her head was about to explode." Pax chuckles. "That was awesome."

"Dreams are free," Bryson mutters.

Bry is much quieter about his disapproval, but it's definitely still there.

"I dunno what the fuck she wants me to do. I'm not exactly stoked to be working with the new girl either."

"I'd work with the ice queen, *any* day of the week," Pax quips.

"She's all yours, bro."

The last thing I need is another crazy female in the mix. Working with her on this project is bound to be bad enough.

I rub my ear. I swear I can still hear Liana's fucking screams ringing deep down in there.

We pile into Bry's car and head to the local gym to smash out a weights session before heading home.

Me and Pax have been saving for the past year to go halves in a car – our mums can't afford to buy us one, but Bryson's parents are like next level loaded, so he drives a brand-new Audi and acts as our chauffer most of the time.

He drops us off at home after an hour of pushing weights and talking shit, and I'm so covered in sweat, it's literally like I've been swimming.

Ma is in the kitchen, cooking dinner when we walk in the door.

"Hey, Ma." Pax kisses her on the cheek.

"My darlings, you stink," she says as I kiss her other cheek.

I lift the lid off the pot she's got on the cook top.

I'm starving, so I'm glad she's the one in the kitchen. My mum sucks at cooking.

She swats my hand away. "It's spaghetti and meat-balls. You've got time for a shower."

"What makes you think I need to shower?" I chuckle.

"That insanely ripe smell coming off you was my first clue." She grimaces.

Pax chuckles. "Shot gun first."

He dashes from the room, presumably to take up residence in our shared bathroom.

I snag a carrot stick off the chopping board next to the sink. "Where's Mum?"

"She took a double shift at the hospital, said to tell you boys that she'll be home when you wake up in the morning."

I frown. I hate it when she works overtime like that. She's always worked too hard. My whole life she's hustled nonstop – they both have.

I've offered several times to get a part time job so I can chip in, Pax has too, but they won't allow it. Apparently, we need to focus on school, rugby and 'being kids'.

Ma obviously picks up on my unease. She gives my arm a squeeze. "She's got four days off after this. She'll get a good break."

I nod as I chew on the carrot.

"How's school going?"

I shrug. "Alright. Same old."

"Did Liana convince you to let her pose for your photography assessment?"

I groan. Pax and his stupid big mouth. The prick needs to learn when to shut the fuck up.

"Nope," I reply. "Ms. Ainsley assigned us partners."

Ma looks amused. She's met Liana once, when she turned up here unannounced and uninvited over the break. I was less than impressed. I don't think Ma was too taken with her either.

"I can't imagine that went down well. Who did you get?"

"This new girl. Berlin. She's a pain in the ass, causing trouble already, but I can handle her."

She gives me a look, but I don't bother asking for clarification on what it means. One thing I've learnt from essentially living with two mothers, is that some things are better left not understood when it comes to women.

I grab my cell phone out of my bag and check it for messages.

There are six from Liana over the past two hours.

I almost laugh.

Liana: I can't fucking believe this.

Liana: You better text me back, you have some serious grovelling to do.

I actually do laugh when I read that one. This chick clearly doesn't know me at all if she thinks I'll be doing anything that even resembles grovelling.

Liana: Maybe I overreacted a tiny bit

Liana: Can you just text me back?

Liana: Cullen!

She's so fucking needy.

There's one more message.

Liana: I'm sorry okay. Just text me back. I want to see you tonight.

I'm about to tap out a reply when Ma makes a comment that stops me in my tracks.

"If you're thinking about sneaking out to go and see that girl tonight, you might want to think again,

Cassanova." She's stirring the pot of sauce – she's not even looking at me.

I don't know how she does that. The woman has eyes in the back of her head.

"I don't know what you're talking about."

"*Of course* you don't, but I'm just saying, the roses outside your bedroom window didn't squash themselves now, did they?"

Shit.

Note to self – go out Pax's window from now on.

"Wouldn't know anything about it."

"Mmm hmm, let me just remind you about how your mother and I wound up living together with newborn babies, fresh out of high school."

I groan.

She laughs. "Yeah, well I hate to break it to you, but there were probably squashed roses outside of your father's bedroom window too."

I don't know how she isn't more bitter about the situation that led to two single mums raising their babies together. My dad was killed in a car accident before I was born, so obviously that tragedy is out of anyone's control, but Pax's dad has never been in the picture. Ma refuses to talk about it, and when I asked Mum once, she told me that maybe one day we'd get to hear the full story.

Neither me nor Pax have any fucking idea what that means, or what all the secrecy is about, but when I do hear the story one day, I fully intend to track that prick down and beat his ass for not taking responsibility for his child.

I'm sure as hell not planning on having babies any time soon, but one day, when I do, there's nothing in the world that could stop me from being in my kids' lives.

"All I'm saying is, be careful. And that some girls are more high maintenance than others, so maybe be extra careful."

I grunt out an "okay."

I hate having these kinds of chats with Ma and Mum. It's just not something I'm keen on. They sat both me and Pax down when we turned fourteen and gave us the birds and the bees talk, and the experience still haunts me to this day.

Scarred for life.

Pax chooses that moment to come back into the kitchen, and I praise the freaking lord for an excuse to get the hell out of this room and this conversation.

I love Ma, I really do – she's been as much a mother to me as my own, but there is no way in hell I want to talk to her about my sex life.

Where a teenage boy puts his dick is not dinner time conversation.

I bail from the kitchen and take my time showering. I still haven't replied to Liana, and I'm tempted not to at all. She made a scene today, and the last thing I want to do is deal with that shit on the regular. She needs to learn her lesson.

I could use this as an excuse to bin it, but I know I won't – not yet – not before Bry's eighteenth.

He's having a massive party at his place next Saturday night, right before we start back at rugby training, and I want to have a good blow out and a chill night, not have Liana causing drama and shooting me daggers across the room.

I shut the water off and grab a towel.

I decide not to reply. I'll let her be terrified of her own mess for five seconds. It won't kill her.

Me and Pax take our dinner to the lounge to eat it in front of the TV.

"You've got to work pretty close with the new girl on this photo stuff, huh?" he asks in between mouthfuls.

"Yip," I answer, unamused.

"You have to admit, it's pretty fucking funny." He chuckles.

I side eye him. "It's *something*."

"Oh, come on, man, she's not that bad, and at least she's hot. I'd rather stare at her face for hours on end then some ugly prick from your class. You only have to take her photo."

"If she doesn't try and cut my dick off first."

"Wear a cup. She seems kinda feisty."

Feisty is a fucking understatement. The girl has a chip on her shoulder the size of a truck.

"You got any other classes with her?" I ask him.

"Drawing." He nods. "Haven't talked to her

though. I was hooking up with Eve and ended up being late coming into class."

Classic Pax.

"That girl is bad news," I warn him. Eve is ten kinds of sideways.

"That's rich coming from you." He smirks.

Touche.

"Ma knows I've been sneaking out," I tell him.

"Course she does. Ma knows *everything.*"

I chuckle. Ma does know everything. Mum probably does too, she's just less vocal about it and not home as much either.

"I'll cut Liana after the party," I tell him.

"Whatever you say, bro." He puts his bowl on the ground and swings his feet up onto the couch.

"You want to run in the morning?" I ask, even though I know the answer.

"Not even a little bit."

"Training starts soon, you need to get your head in the game."

"I'll be ready."

If I know Pax, which I obviously do, he won't be ready. He'll probably still be hungover, if anything.

He's not actually that bad, his commitment is mostly there, but he's never given it one hundred percent.

I'm about to launch into a speech about him sorting his shit out, but he cuts me off.

"Don't even start, man. I know rugby is your whole

life, but it's not all there is to mine. I'll be there, I'll give it everything. But stay off my back about it."

Considering we're more like brothers than mates, we surprisingly never really fight these days. This is about the only thing we frequently disagree on anymore.

I also know when he's serious – which isn't often, but he is right now. He hates it when I give him shit about rugby at home. I know he'll tolerate it on the field, and at training, because I'm the captain, but not here.

He loves the game; he's fucking good at it too. I just can't get out of him why he doesn't take it more seriously.

I don't reply, we just fall into a comfortable silence watching TV before I call it a day and turn in for the night – still leaving Liana on read.

SEVEN

Berlin

I walk into my drawing class and the first thing I see
is Pax.

He's kind of hard to miss; he's a big guy, and he's
standing right in front of me, grinning in a slightly
deranged kind of way.

He says something, but I've got my AirPods in my
ears. I tug them out, being careful not to drop the stack
of drawing supplies I've been balancing in my arms.

"Huh?"

He smiles wider. "Morning, Ice. We're sitting
together."

I arch a brow. "Are you asking me or telling me?"

He reaches out and takes the pile from my arms,

and I'm so bewildered by what's going on, that I let him.

"That's not important. Come on, over here."

He walks towards a desk where it would seem he's already set up his own stuff and has saved me a seat.

I don't know what the fuck is going on, but Pax seems alright in my book, so I follow, albeit reluctantly.

"What's brought this on?" I question as I take my newly acquired seat.

"Did no one tell you? We're gonna be friends."

"Well, that *is* news to me."

He's grinning again and damn him, it's contagious as hell. I can't imagine this guy has got an enemy in the world. He's too likable.

"I didn't pick you for the drawing type." I nod towards his sketch pad, which is still shut, in front of him.

"I'm multi-dimensional. I have layers, okay."

That's a hell of lot more than can be said for the girls he hangs around with, but maybe he is somewhat of an onion. I guess I'll be finding out if this seating arrangement is going to continue all year.

"Show me some of these layers then." I tap the cover of his book.

He shoots me a sheepish expression.

"Oh, come on, now, Paxikins, if we're going to be friends, you're going to have to learn how to share."

He laughs. "Did you just call me *Paxikins?*"

I pop a shoulder. "Yeah, but I'm not sure I'll stick

with it, something more fitting might come to me yet, so don't go getting too attached."

I expect him to tell me that he can't be having that nickname floating around, that it'll fuck up his street cred or something, but he doesn't say shit. If anything, he seems quite pleased with it.

The dude is a real mystery.

"Go on." I nudge his elbow.

He shrugs, flicks open his sketch pad and starts flicking through the pages of his drawings from the year so far.

I feel my jaw fall open as he flicks to a charcoal sketch of a woman. It's *incredible*.

"Holy shit, you did that?" I ask, my hand coming to rest on his, stopping him from moving to another page.

He glances down at the page. "Yeah. That's Ma, my mum."

"She's beautiful."

"She sure is. Best lady I've ever met. Followed closely by Cullen's mum, who I call Mum too," he says before huffing out a laugh. "Unusual home life."

He flicks the page over and there's a drawing of another woman, who I can already tell is Cullen's mum. He looks a lot like her.

"I heard."

I trace the lines – pencil for this one – with my finger. "These are incredible."

"No sassy insults, huh?"

"Not this time."

He's beyond talented. Everything in here is amazing, but the one of his mum is easily my favourite.

"Is it your turn to share yet?" he asks.

"I don't have much in here yet, I got a new book when I started, but I did a few sketches the other day while your boy Cullen had an internal meltdown about having to work on a project with me."

The corner of his lip curves up into a smirk. "Highlight of the school year so far. Liana flipped a lid."

"I heard she made quite the scene."

"She's such a fucking bitch."

I bite back a laugh. I'd picked up on the fact that Pax didn't seem to be much of a fan, but it's still funny to hear him voice his displeasure so vocally.

The teacher walks in and puts a halt on any further discussion, but I notice Pax watching me as we're told to open our books and work on the floral sketches that we started the day before.

He nudges my knee with his under the desk. "Those are really good," he whispers.

I don't know what it is about this boy, but I like his praise. This is virtually unheard of for me; I don't want or need anyone's approval, but his is welcome.

It's a weird realisation that I'm going to have to file away and unpack another day, but maybe it wouldn't be so bad to be able to count him as a friend after all.

We draw in mostly silence for another half an hour, and the murmuring and quiet conversations start to pick up around us. Pax seems to take that as his indication to start questioning me further.

"Tell me about your family, since you already know about mine."

I don't look up from my drawing. "It's just me and my dad. My mum passed away when I was a baby, back in Australia, and it's just been me and him ever since. My cousin Sophia goes here, so when we moved to New Zealand, Dad enrolled me here. My grandparents live about half an hour away."

"That sucks about your mum."

I could tell him that it's no big loss – that she was a no hope, druggy loser, but I don't know this guy well enough to spill all that. For all I know, he's got ulterior motives for this 'friendship'. I know I've pissed off his mates, so it wouldn't be that much of a shock if he was playing a double agent.

"Could be worse. My dad is pretty cool."

"What does he do?"

I sigh. It's a simple question, but I wouldn't mind a rugby head like Pax, *not* knowing exactly who my dad is, but I opened this can of worms.

"He's just got a job at the regional rugby union. He'll be coaching there."

That gets his attention. "No shit? What's his name?"

I pause for a moment. I know he's going to have heard of him. This town, this school. It's a sure thing.

I sigh. "If I tell you, you have to keep it to yourself, deal?"

I know it'll get out eventually; his name is still on record boards in the gym. His team photo is probably tucked away somewhere in some display cupboard, but the longer the cat stays in the bag, the better, as far as I'm concerned.

"Weird request, but I accept your condition."

He looks so eager to find out, I hope he won't be disappointed.

"Cole Davids."

He blinks twice, momentarily shocked. "As in, superstar fullback, Cole Davids?"

Definitely *not* disappointed.

"The one and only."

"Westlake High legend, Cole Davids?"

"Yip." I nod.

"Holy shit, your old man is the guy Coach uses as a folklore tale to inspire us all."

"No shit?"

"I've seen tapes of his old school games. He was the man even back then." His voice is giving serious fan girl vibes.

"I *won't* be telling him that. His ego is big enough."

"It's not ego if you can back it up, baby." He grins.

I laugh. My dad says something similar. Rugby boys and their inflated confidence.

"Well, he's old and washed up now, so bad luck for him."

He's not actually all that old or all that washed up, but it's fun to give him shit about it anyway.

"You should ask him to come in and train with us when the season gets underway. That'd be epic. Most of the guys would probably jizz in their pants."

I grimace. "That was a visual I didn't need."

He chuckles.

"And no way. It's bad enough being the new girl starting during the final year of high school, I don't need my dad romping around like king dick, making even more of a scene."

He looks at me, amused. "You *do* seem like the type to try and avoid a scene," he says, sarcastic as fuck.

I flip him off.

"Anyway, *whatever*, that's my dad. It's just me and him, no siblings," I say, ending the line of questioning.

He nods, his attention back on his sketch.

"Have you got any brothers or sisters?" I ask him, returning to my drawing.

"Nah, just me and Cull."

"You guys are pretty close, huh?"

"Yeah, we're brothers, maybe not by blood, but I've never known life without him."

I have to admit, that's pretty cute. It must be kind of cool to grow up with your best friend.

"Is he all good? He seems like he's always in a mood."

He chuckles. "He *is* in a mood most of the time. He takes life too seriously sometimes, but he's not as bad as he seems."

"I'll take your word for it."

"Criticism is a bit rich coming from you, Ice. You've been here all of five seconds and you're already stirring up shit."

I shrug. "I do what I do well."

"I think you and Cull probably have more in common than you think."

"I doubt that, but as long as we don't kill each other during this project, it'll be all good."

He chuckles again, and something tells me that he's looking forward to watching the shit show unfold before his eyes.

We sketch in silence for a few minutes, he's drawing a rose that's so realistic, it's hard to believe that it's not really there, laying on his sheet of paper.

"Why do you wanna be my friend anyway? You trying to piss off your brother?"

He looks at me, right in the eyes, amused by my outburst. "I dunno, there's just something about you, new girl. Don't go making me regret it, okay?"

He goes back to his drawing, and I feel myself blush. I don't know what the heck is going on.

I don't blush. Ever. I'm not a blushing kind of girl. But here we are.

I mentally slap myself and keep my head down until I've got my shit together and my face back to its normal colour.

This fucking school, these stupid, beefed-up rugby boys – it all needs to chill the fuck out. It's messing with my head.

The bell rings and Pax walks with me to the building that houses all the lockers. He's easy company to keep, and I'm grateful to have someone to walk with for a change.

He's talking my ear off, so I see it before he does.

I almost roll my eyes, it's *so* typical.

My locker has been defaced, with lipstick if I had to guess. The words, 'stay in you're fucking lane bitch' are scrawled across the metal door.

I'm so completely unthreatened that I laugh. The silly twat needs to work on her spelling. How embarrassing.

It's obviously Liana or one of her minions, no points for guessing that – the girl has watched one too many teenage dramas on Netflix.

Pax is still talking, totally oblivious to what I've seen. I tap his arm and point at my locker. "Look."

He follows my finger with his eyes until he sees what I'm seeing.

"Nah *fuck* that," he growls, striding ahead of me.

I just laugh and follow after him.

"Do people actually do this shit here?" I ask him, amused.

He turns around to face me, and his expression is anything but amused. He looks absolutely ropable.

"This isn't fucking okay."

It's cute that he's so pissed, but I couldn't care less.

"Chill. It looks like it's just lipstick."

"Shitty fucking girl bullshit is what it is."

"That too." I shrug. "But your temper needs some serious attention."

He pulls his bag off his shoulder and starts rifling through it, presumably to find something to clean the mess off with.

"Don't." I grab his arm. "Leave it."

He frowns at me. "What? *Why?*"

"Because it's funny," I offer. "And I don't care. Whoever wrote that wants me to be humiliated. They want to watch me scrub it off. Screw that."

Students have filed in around us now, the hallway is bustling. Some people are pointing and whispering as they notice my new artwork.

I smile and wave to them.

"So, you're just going to leave it there?"

I shake my head and rifle through my bag, pulling out my own lipstick. I scribble 'your*', next to her spelling fuck up. "Talk about embarrassing."

Pax watches what I'm doing and then slowly smirks. "You know what, you might be kind of a genius."

"If there's one thing I know, it's high school politics... *And* whether to use 'your' or 'you're'."

"Those bitches will shit the bed if they don't get the reaction they want."

"I know." I unlock my locker and get out the books I need for maths. "But they're going to have to try a lot harder than that if they want to rattle me."

"You're made of some tough shit, Ice."

"Hardly." I roll my eyes. "You seriously think anyone out here is going to be getting upset over some lipstick and the word *bitch*?"

"I've seen *way* worse. No shit, girls crying like toddlers over gum in their hair."

That's hilarious. This shit is child's play compared to what I saw and dealt with back home. Girls were next level there, guys too. When shit went down, it went *down.*

"Well not this girl." I slam the locker shut and turn around.

I lock eyes with Cullen, he's over the other side of the hallway, Liana hanging around him like a bad smell – as per.

His gaze shifts to my locker for a few beats and then back to my face. I swear I see a small crease in his forehead, but it's gone again just as quickly as it came.

I cut to Liana, and she's looking at me now, a smug smile on her face.

I laugh. This pathetic little girl really thinks she's one-upped me here.

She wants to play, shit, I can play, but it'll be a hell of a lot more exciting than this basic-bitch stunt.

She presses up to her tip toes and whispers something in Cullen's ear. He looks like he's barely listening. His expression doesn't change as he looks between me and Pax.

I blow them a kiss as soon as she's looking in my direction again.

Pax pisses himself laughing. "Why do I get the feeling I'm going to have to stop that bitch from clawing out your eyes one of these days?"

I turn away from them to face my new friend and roll my eyes. "Oh *please*, it insults me that you think I couldn't handle her on my own."

He chuckles and shakes his head. "You scare me."

"I think your fear is well placed."

"I have to go to class. Try not to get into any brawls until I'm available to watch."

I snort a laugh. "Your compassion moves me. You could take bets, make some cash."

"Not just a pretty face, eh?" He smirks as he walks backwards, towards Cullen, still facing me. "See ya, Ice."

"Buh bye, Paxikins," I call after him.

EIGHT

Cullen

"I'm sorry, okay, can we please just forget it and move on?"

"Fuck's sake, Li, I told you to stop going on about it already. We're good. Chill."

She pouts. "You say that, but you've been cold towards me all day."

Truth is, I've barely tolerated her all day, and the less I give her, the more she demands. I'm about at the end of my patience. That whingy tone she's using is sure as shit not helping.

"Let it go," I growl. "And stop looking for trouble with the new girl. I have to work with her. You drawing on her locker doesn't fucking help."

"I don't know what you're talking about."

"Whatever, just leave me out of your petty bullshit. I can't be fucked."

Part of me would enjoy watching those two girls go at it – one outs in the parking lot style – but I've got more important shit to worry about right now. Rugby, scholarships, professional offers, not getting anyone pregnant – I never got to meet my dad, but I don't really want to repeat any of his mistakes.

"I make no promises." She smirks.

There's something about the look on her face that makes me think she's already done something else. That some fresh carnage is about to rain down on me in God only knows what way.

"*Liana*," I warn her.

She scowls at me. "Are you trying to protect *her*?"

I don't even reply, I just pull her in and kiss her hard. It's the easiest way to shut her up, and the only way to stop me from doing my scone entirely.

She moans into my mouth and the sound alone makes my cock twitch. At least she can do that for me.

She looks dazed as I pull away.

"I'll see you later." I make an escape before she finds her voice again. I don't know how much more of it my ears can take.

I've got PE next with Pax... *and* Berlin.

Fuckin' hip, hip, hooray.

"I hope your afternoon is... eventful," Liana calls after me. I don't know what the fuck that's meant to mean, and I don't want to either, but something tells me I'm about to find out, whether I want to or not.

"What's the *She Devil* up to now?" Pax asks as he swings his bag over his shoulder and falls into step next to me.

"Anyone's guess."

"Why'd coach call training after school?"

"He wants to round up all the boys so I can name my vice-captain."

"Surely it's gonna be Bry."

The fucked-up thing is that it should be Pax, but I can't trust him to give it one hundred percent of his energy. He's right though, Bryson is the next in line and I'll be naming him as my right-hand man when we meet after classes.

"Yeah, I asked him last week."

"You might have to get him drunk, so he actually talks at practice."

I chuckle. Bryson is a man of few words, until you get him on the piss, and then you can't shut the guy up.

We call his drunk persona *Darren* – he's like a whole other man.

"Remember that time he got smashed from that bottle of rum Smithy stole from his dad?"

"Do I remember? That shit scarred me for life. I saw way more cock and balls than I bargained for." Pax laughs. "Dunno what it is about him and getting nude when he's on the rip, but it happens way too often."

We stroll into the gym and head straight for the locker room, reminiscing about all the times Bryson has outdone himself on a night out and then woken up and gone straight back to virtually being mute.

It's not until we've changed and headed back into the gym, that I realise there's something going down in there.

One guy's wolf whistling while others are staring with their tongues almost hanging out. Some of the girls are laughing. A couple of Liana's friends look shocked.

The crowd moves around me, and that's when I see her, because *of fucking course* it's got something to do with *her*.

"Holy shit, Ice," Pax whispers.

She's wearing her PE uniform, but there's fuck all left of it. Her shorts are cut so short that her ass cheeks are hanging out the bottom, her top is slashed across her mid-section, and there's a slice cut right across her tits too.

What fuckery is this?

She's standing there without one ounce of humiliation. Can't exactly blame her, she looks like a walking wet dream and every father's worst nightmare, all rolled into one.

"What in the fuck is she wearing?" I demand.

"I don't know, but it's *something* and I'm sure as hell not mad about it."

It's something alright. More accurately it's *nothing*. That outfit is leaving very little to the imagination.

"You're insane, new girl," Pax calls out to her.

She notices us then and she smirks before walking towards us, all sass and attitude.

Ah fuck.

I don't know why, but my brain tells me to bolt.

"What the fuck are you up to now?" Pax asks her, his tone full of amusement. He's enjoying this, as are the rest of the heterosexual males in the room, I'm sure. "You do realise you're only wearing half of the dress code, right?"

"Am I?" She feigns innocence. "I hadn't noticed."

I don't say anything, but I look. She might be a pain in the ass, but *damn*, the girl is *banging*, and I've got exceptionally good eyesight.

"You might have to suggest your little girlfriend gives up her dreams of being a fashion designer," Berlin says, talking to me this time.

I frown at her comment. I don't know what the fuck she's talking about, but she doesn't falter as she sidles up even closer. "Between you and me, I don't think she's got the potential. Little heavy-handed on the scissors."

It clicks. *Fuck my life*. Berlin thinks Li did this, and she's probably right too.

"What the hell? *Liana* cut up your shit?" Pax demands, and he sounds *pissed*. More pissed than I've heard him sound about anything in a long time.

Berlin pops a brow. "I didn't see her do it, but it doesn't take much to figure out now, does it?" She turns abruptly and points out one of the viewing windows that separate the gym from the foyer, it takes me a minute to figure out what she's pointing to, but then I see it. Liana and Eve, huddled together with their phones out filming.

Berlin is on the money – Liana has definitely had a hand in this.

Berlin waves to Liana, and I see the girl I'm 'dating' visibly balk. If I had to put money on it, Li was hoping to see Berlin get upset when she found the clothes, maybe run out of the gym in tears or some shit – definitely not put it on and walk around like a bad bitch. I doubt the footage she's videoing is going to scratch any of her petty bitch itch.

I don't get this chick. She's not even pissed off. If anything, she's loving it. Most girls would have cried or ran to a teacher when they found their gym gear all chopped up to shit in the changing room, but not this girl. No, she put on that hacked-up uniform and came out here looking like fucking fire.

Berlin struts around us, shaking her ass and popping her hip, and I swear to God, I see steam coming off Liana. All the guys start cheering as Berlin works the room, drops it low and flicks her long dark hair around.

Pax bursts into laughter when he realises what's going on – that Liana is being played and *beaten* at her own game – and that Berlin doesn't give two shits.

I don't know what pisses me off more – the petty bullshit Li is playing, or the fact that Berlin is so totally unshakable. This girl is like nothing I've ever encountered. It's fucking unnerving.

"Miss Davids, do you care to explain what on earth is going on here?" our PE teacher demands, her voice thundering over the noise of the chaos – putting a stop to the little show going on in front of us.

Berlin looks at her, all wide eyes and fake innocence. "I just found my uniform like this, Miss. I don't know why someone would do that to me."

Miss Oliver eyes her up and down. "I can appreciate that you've been mistreated here, but was it *really* necessary to actually put the uniform on while it looks like that?"

"I'm just giving the people what they want, Miss."

Some of the boys whoop and holler.

"Take it off, Berlin," Miss Oliver warns her sternly.

Berlin reaches for the hem of her shirt, and fuck me sideways, she's going to take it off right here and now.

"IN THE CHANGING ROOM!" Miss Oliver shouts hurriedly when she reaches the same conclusion I just did.

Berlin grins, shrugs her shoulders and skips off towards the changing rooms. The blonde girl I saw her with the other day, Sophie or something, looks absolutely mortified, like she'd quite happily lay down and die if she thought she could get away with it.

"My office, Berlin," Miss Oliver yells after her.

"I'll be waaaiiiitiiiing," Berlin replies in a sing-song voice.

"I knew I liked her for a reason," Pax says, his voice hushed as we all watch the drama leave the room, a bunch of hype and boners in her wake.

I shoot a look over to where Liana was filming from, but she's gone.

As a general rule, I don't give a *fuck* what that girl – or *any* girl, does, but if she's going to mess with people, she needs to up her game. She's about as subtle as a freight train and I can't have that shit coming back on me – not with a pro rugby career right around the corner.

"Has this got anything to do with you, Mr. Carrington?" Miss Oliver asks me – I've got no doubt she saw Liana out there too. The teachers in this school seem to be as clued up as the students are about who's dating who.

I shake my head quickly. "Not even a little bit, Miss. *Trust me.*"

She eyes me suspiciously but leaves it alone. Thank God for that. The last thing I need is coach getting wind of this garbage in the staff room and giving me shit.

"Get warmed up, everyone," she tells us.

"That was pretty fucking epic, bro. You gotta give credit where credit's due; she killed that," Pax says once the teacher is out of ear shot.

"I'm staying the hell out of this one, but if crazy does it for you, then have at it."

"Your girlfriend is the one who chopped up her clothes. Don't go getting all high and mighty with me." He bounces the basketball that's found its way into his hands.

He's not wrong. I'm going to have to have a word with Li over this shit. If she wants to stir up trouble, she can leave me out of it. I'm not impressed by trash fires.

"You reckon she's going to get in shit?" he asks, tipping his head in the direction of the door that Berlin walked out of.

"Don't know, don't care."

He chuckles. "Whatever you say."

I don't know what the fuck that's meant to mean.

He jogs off, dribbling the ball, and throws an easy layup, the ball swooshing through the net clean. He's such a natural athlete.

I'm not exactly uncoordinated, but there is something about Pax that makes me think he could pick up any sport and exceed all expectations within about a week.

Class ends, and I drag my feet to last period. I count down the minutes until school ends for the day and then haul ass out onto the rugby fields to meet with coach and the guys.

We held trials a month ago and picked our team. It's virtually all the usual suspects that played last year, plus one surprise player, a year nine boy, fresh-faced and all of about thirteen years old. Never seen anything like the kid. Never heard of a year nine making a championship first XV team either, but here we are. If he keeps this form as he gets older, he'll be an All Black one day. He's built like a brick shit house, and he probably hasn't even hit puberty yet. He'll spend most of this season on the bench, but it'll still be a hell of an experience for the young prop.

"Coach." I hold out my hand to shake his as I approach.

"Good on ya, boy," he replies, firmly gripping my hand in his.

"We all set for Monday?" I ask him. It's the first day of team training and I'm chomping at the bit to get started.

"Slight issue with the coaching staff, but I think I might have found a solution. Leave it with me."

"Where is the big man?" I question, referring to Mr. Janson, Coach's assistant. He's also the school groundskeeper. He's a huge fucker, absolutely massive mountain of a man, and I'm over six foot three, so that's saying something.

I saw someone else on the mower yesterday, and now that I think about it, I haven't seen Jano all term.

"Ah look... unfortunately son, his wife has fallen ill and he's taking leave to look after her. We're not sure when he'll be back, if at all. Things don't look so great for her."

That actually guts me. His wife is a good sort. Made us all cookies last season after the games. A real sweet woman.

"Shit. That sucks."

He nods his head in agreement.

Coach is the only member of school staff I'll swear around. He's heard it all on that field – doesn't even bat an eyelid anymore.

"It's not a nice situation. He's happy for me to round up someone else to help me out with you boys for now at least, so I'll do my best to get that locked in next week."

"I'm happy to help out with anything I can. I can step up more, I can –"

"You do too much already," he interrupts me. "Just keep showing up to classes and don't get into any trouble and the rest will take care of itself."

I nod.

I know exactly why he's saying this. I was only year ten, but I remember the stories about the captain at the time getting expelled for bunking too many classes and getting caught with booze on school grounds. The vice-captain stepped up and they still managed to win the comp, but it was a fucking circus.

Coach doesn't need to worry about me. I make all my classes and maintain a top percentage grade average. I'm no idiot. I just come across as not giving a flying fuck about anything but rugby.

The timing of this talk only reinforces the fact that I'm going to have to put Liana in her place though – her bullshit is the last thing I need coming back onto me.

All the boys turn up one after another until we're all there. I announce Bryson as my vice-captain, and the guy even smiles and says a few words. It's a fucking miracle.

I can't wait to play ball this season. Finally, it's *my* time.

NINE

Berlin

"I'm really not sure why *I'm* the one in trouble, I didn't cut up my own uniform."

Miss Oliver seems like a half-decent sort of woman. She's probably about forty, maybe mid-forties and she's a total fox – I'll be stoked if I look like her, at her age, but she's killing me with this uniform shit.

"I'm aware of that, Berlin, but the issue is the little performance you put on for the other students, it was inappropriate, especially given how little you were wearing."

I shrug a shoulder. I'm sure it didn't exactly line up with the school's code of conduct, but I doubt defacing of public property does either.

"Maybe, but at the end of the day, I didn't do

anything wrong. I put on my gym gear and came into the gym."

She raises a brow at me.

"Okay, fine, I danced around a little bit, but you saw those girls filming me, right? They wanted a reaction, and I wasn't about to give them the one they were looking for. I've dealt with plenty of girls like that and if you show them weakness, they'll eat you alive. They're like sharks when they smell blood in the water."

I actually think she agrees with me and my assessment of high school politics, but she's not going to say that out loud. She's got to be all professional and shit. I know how these things work.

"I *did* see them, and I know they were both meant to be elsewhere, in their respective classes, but there's no other evidence at this stage to show that they were the ones who cut up your clothing, and you know how the saying goes... innocent until proven guilty."

I roll my eyes, and I don't try to hide it even a little bit. "I'm sure if someone searched through their phones, they'd see pretty quickly who was responsible, but you know what, I don't even care. Can I go and get on with the rest of my day now?"

She eyes me warily. "Of course you can, but I am going to have to take this to the principal. We take bullying very seriously here. I'm sure he'll also have questions about the borderline nudity."

"I'm sure he can see that on Liana's phone too, if he really wants to," I pipe up with a smirk.

She gives me a look that indicates she doesn't think

I should push my luck, pulls out a late slip and scrawls something onto it before handing it to me.

"Off you go to your next class, Berlin."

I give her a wide smile and take it from her without a word.

There's only one class left, which I get through without issue once my teacher sees my note and removes the scowl from her face, and then I'm on my secret mission.

Cullen is still being a complete and utter prick about organising time to do our photography project together, but there is no way in hell I'm going to let this boy get the better of me. I'm going to take his photo whether he knows about it or not.

I heard some of the rugby team talking about meeting on the fields after school today – from what I hear, Bryson is about to be named the vice-captain of the team by Cullen, so that really ought to get the big guy's motor running. Maybe he'll even crack a smile as he announces one of his best friends as his side kick.

I skirt around the edges of the fields, sticking to the tree line, just in case they're already out here, but I'm in luck. It's just the coach setting out some cones.

I pick my spot and get settled with my camera and my zoom lens.

I don't have to wait long. Cullen is the first to arrive – it seems he's very conscientious when it comes to this team.

I snap a few pictures of him as he talks to the coach, and a few more as the players start to arrive. I don't know if he even realises it, but they all gravitate towards him. A circle loosely forms around him, and even though some of the guys are having their own conversations amongst themselves, they're still hyper aware of Cullen. If he were to start speaking at any moment, I'm sure he'd have them hanging off his every word.

Bryson turns up with another guy I don't know and then Pax turns up a few minutes later, wiping what looks to be red lip gloss off his mouth.

I huff out a laugh as I watch Cullen giving him shit about it through my camera lens.

I focus back on Cullen and just like that, he's in captain mode and every single set of eyes on that field is on him. Hell, I'm hanging on every movement of his mouth, and I can't even hear a thing he's saying.

There's just something magnetising about the guy.

I snap picture after picture, and I don't miss the moment he says Bryson's name. All the guys whoop and cheer. I shift to look at Bryson for a moment and click a few pictures of him smiling – something I'm yet to see until now.

He can show emotion after all.

I've got no use for these shots, but Sophia can put them in her wank bank or whatever.

The coach takes over and rallies the troops, and together they all start jogging around the field. I shuffle a little farther back into the tree line. The absolute last thing I need today is to get caught looking like a weirdo peeping Tom.

I expect Cullen to lead the pack – he easily looks the fittest, but he doesn't. Instead he drops back, farther and farther until he's bringing up the rear with some big dude that I assume is a prop, based sheerly on the size of the guy.

They all turn well short of my hiding spot, thankfully, as they make their way around the field.

I get some really good shots. Cullen's face shows a lot more expression when he's out here doing what he clearly loves. He drops that stone-cold bullshit act he's got so well perfected. He's a bit more human with grass under his boots.

They all huddle for a bit, and some of them start throwing balls around in a slick, synchronised drill that they've obviously done a thousand times before, while the rest sprint shuttle runs.

It doesn't seem like a full-scale training session to me, but they're all hyped nonetheless.

I'm done with my picture-taking-borderline-stalking, for today at least, and I'm about to pack up my camera when I hear a stick crack behind me.

"What on earth are you doing?"

I clutch my chest and nearly drop my camera in fright as I spin around to see who's just successfully snuck up on me.

It's Sophia.

"Jesus Christ, Soph, you almost gave me a heart attack."

"I'm not cut out for tramping," I hear Carissa grumble as she emerges from the bushes behind

Sophia, looking like she's been dragged through the thing backwards.

Sophia rolls her eyes. "I'm not sure you can call walking through five metres of bush 'tramping', but whatever."

"Is that a fucking spider?" Carissa shrieks.

I laugh as she freaks out trying to get some leaves out of her hair.

Sophia looks up and sees the rugby team across the field from where I'm sitting. A smug smirk crosses her face. "And what exactly might *you* be doing?" she asks me again. "When you said to meet you at the back of the fields, this isn't exactly what I had in mind."

"What? No concern that I'm going to get us all into trouble this time?"

She narrows her eyes at me. "I think you've already covered that base today, don't you? And besides, when you're really up to no good, you seem to be in much closer range," she accuses.

Shit, it cracks me up when she gets all up in arms about me doing what is sweet fuck all when it comes down to it. I'd be wearing way less on a beach in summer than what I wore into that gym today, but she looked like she was about to pass out from the whole experience.

To be honest, it only makes me want to take it further and see what it'll take to really crack her. She *is* a Davids though, and when push comes to shove, we're made of some pretty tough shit. I just don't think she knows it yet.

"You look like a creep sitting under here with a camera," Carissa informs me.

"I'm just getting some shots of Cullen. He's being a dick about setting up times to work on our photography projects, and I don't want to risk failing the class, so I'm taking matters into my own hands."

"I guess that's fair."

"Still, it's giving me stalker vibes," Sophia replies.

I laugh and stuff my camera back into its case and into my bag. "I can live with that."

My phone vibrates in my pocket, and I slide it out to see who's calling.

It's Daddy dearest. Lucky me. No prizes for guessing what this call is about.

"Old man, what can I do for you?" I drawl.

"You can start by telling me why some girl is cutting up your gym gear."

I roll my eyes. Teachers are such fucking snitches.

"Honestly, I think she's just a grade A bitch, but could be shoddy parenting. I haven't had time to make a thorough enough assessment."

"*B*," he warns me.

"I don't know what you want me to tell you. The girl just doesn't like me, but I don't care. I'm going to need new gym gear though, so that's unfortunate, but I think you can probably afford it."

Sophia looks like she cannot believe the way this conversation is going – she would one hundred percent have been the kind of girl to give Liana the crying reaction she was after, and her parents probably would have gone in for mediation or some shit.

Carissa is holding back a laugh.

He sighs. "You'd tell me if it was anything more, right?"

"I would indeed, but trust me, this is nothing I can't handle."

"Do you want me to push for them to get the footage from her phone?"

I shake my head. "Nah, don't worry about it. She's not completely stupid. I'm sure she'll have it locked down, but she's an attention whore, so she'll slip up somewhere and incriminate herself, and it'll be so much more satisfying if she digs her own grave."

"You scare me sometimes, you know that?"

"I should hope so."

"Alright, kiddo, I'll give your principal the slip and leave the drama in your very capable hands then."

"I think that's wise. Last thing I need is you coming around here and killing my street cred."

"Yeah, I'm sure you're a real badass."

"Toodle-loo, old man."

He just chuckles before hanging up the phone.

"You're not even in trouble?" Sophia asks, her expression bewildered.

"God no. I've done way worse than partial nudity, and he's barely broken a sweat. He knows he can trust me to ask for help if shit gets serious."

"I wish my dad was that cool." She sighs.

"I wish my dad was that hot," Carissa chimes in.

We both look at her.

She grimaces. "That came out wrong."

"I fuckin' hope so." I snigger.

"You know what I meant."

"Are you done being a freaky little perve?" Sophia asks me.

I stand up and brush off my skirt. "I am indeed. Let's go."

TEN

Cullen

I don't know why the fuck it bugs me so much that Pax seems to be friends with the new chick, but it does.

It pisses me off to absolutely no end if I'm being honest with myself.

The more time I have to be around her, the more she winds me up. She's sassy and outspoken and the girl just gives absolutely no fucks about what I think.

I don't think she cares what *anyone* thinks.

I need to find a way to put her in her place, but I'm waiting for my moment. Good things take time and I'm going to hold out for the perfect opportunity to take her down a few pegs. That's what I'm telling myself anyway.

I watch across the hallway as Pax howls with

laughter at something she's just said to him. Some bull-shit private joke between the two of them I'd say.

Berlin's locker is still covered in writing. Liana denies her involvement, but I'm not fucking stupid. I recognise the handwriting – she's just pissed because it didn't have the desired effect. It seems nothing has – the girl cannot be rattled.

I'm pissed too, but it's got nothing to do with lipstick or bitchy pranks and a lot to do with the fact that I can't get her strutting around the gym with her ass hanging out, out of my head.

Berlin does a little dance and Pax pisses himself laughing again. I feel my lip curl up in agitation.

I don't even know why the fuck I care that they look like they're getting more and more friendly by the day.

I don't know what the hell is wrong with my mood in general. I'm like a fucking girl.

Thank God it's Friday. I need to get out of this place; it's messing with my head, big time.

"Are you picking me up tomorrow night?" Liana tugs on the collar of my shirt to get my attention.

I shake my head and finally pull my eyes from Pax and Berlin. I try to focus on the blonde in front of me. The one I'm meant to give a fuck about.

I shake my head. "Bry is picking me and the boys up earlier in the day to help set up. I'll meet you there."

She looks pissed off with my answer, but she doesn't say shit. Leaving her on read for a whole day last week was the best call I've made in a long time –

she's still on her best behaviour – with me at least. It should see me through until after Bry's party and then I can end things for good.

"I'll get ready with the girls and see you there then."

I nod. I couldn't really give a fuck what she does or where she does it, but at least I'll have the option to get laid if I want it.

Some of the girls start talking about what they're going to wear, and I zone out, my gaze wandering back to Berlin and Pax again.

Bry nudges my arm and I glance over my shoulder at him.

I raise my brows in question.

"You look like a jealous prick."

I scowl at him. "Jealous of *what*?"

He shrugs. "Him. *Her.* Fucked if I know, but you look like you're about to kick off." He's looking at Berlin and Pax while he speaks.

Bry is usually bang on the money, but he's wrong here. I'm irritated, not jealous, but he's right about one thing, my body is tense, like I'm ready for action. That fucks me off more – now it's affecting me physically.

I force my muscles to relax, but I don't answer him. I don't even know what I'd say.

The bell for class rings. I've got English with Pax and Bryson. Only a couple more hours in this place and it's the weekend and we'll be on it for Bry's eighteenth.

I haven't blown the cobwebs out in forever – it's long overdue and the boys are all hissing for a big night before we put our heads down and become the champs for another year on the trot.

Liana is still talking about nail polish or some shit, so I make the most of the opportunity to get out of there. I don't even stop to get Pax, just give him a chin lift as we pass, me leading, Bryson at my side.

Pax reciprocates the gesture but makes no move to leave. Berlin gives me a sassy smirk.

Fuck him, he can walk on his own for all I care.

"That chick makes for an interesting dynamic," Bryson says.

Interesting is one word for it – it's not the one that I would have gone for, but whatever.

"She's trouble," I growl.

He makes a noise but doesn't reply, so I look at him, glaring. "*What?*"

He shakes his head, and if I'm not mistaken, he looks like he finds something funny. "Nothing. Just thinking about how you have a knack for attracting trouble."

"Go fuck yourself," I fire back. "That chick has nothing to do with me."

The prick actually chuckles.

"You got the shit for tomorrow night?" I ask him, looking to change the subject, fast.

Bryson isn't technically eighteen until tomorrow, so I know he hasn't bought the alcohol himself, but his parents would have hooked it up. They're too busy and important to sit around worrying about shit like underage kids drinking. They probably just told him to make a list for the butler to buy. Fuck, I'd be surprised if they're even home at all tomorrow night. They basically leave Bry and his sister Carley alone to do whatever the fuck they want and dole out huge amounts of cash so they can get it done.

My mum calls it borderline child abuse, but I think it's pretty epic.

"Yeah, got enough piss to sink a ship and a fuck load of pizza coming at ten to start soaking it up."

"Tonksy bringing some of his shit?"

He just shrugs at me. Bry is about the only one in the team who doesn't partake in the odd recreational drug use. I dabble, but never touch the shit during the season, and Pax is another story entirely.

Some of the guys smoke weed in the weekends, but I'm not into that vibe. I've got other ways to relax. If I'm going to get on the gear, I want to go up, not down.

I take my seat as Pax bounds in the door; he's like a fucking over excited dog sometimes. Massive golden retriever energy. He bumps into a table on his way past and earns himself a glare from the teacher.

He flops down into the seat next to me and shoots me a goofy grin but doesn't say anything even though he's clearly got something to say.

"*What?*" I snap.

He chuckles. "That chick *really* has a way of getting under your skin, huh?"

"What chick?" I grind out the words from between clenched teeth.

I already know who he's talking about. We all

fucking know, because he's right. She does get under my skin.

He just laughs again, louder this time.

"I invited her to the party tomorrow," he says, and I swear to God, I almost clock him.

"*Bro*," Bryson says. I can't tell if he's annoyed or amused.

"What?" Pax shrugs, looking totally unfazed. "You told us to invite anyone we want. She's my friend, so I invited her."

"Some things just go without saying," I growl.

The dickhead laughs.

"What the fuck is your problem, Cull? You don't like her, so what? No one said you had to. You've got your girl, and Berlin hasn't fuckin' done anything except run her mouth. Liana is the one who needs a leash, so unless there's some other reason you're throwing your toys out of the cot, maybe you should get the fuck over it. It's got nothing to do with you."

That pisses me off, and not because he's wrong. Because he's *right*. I've got no real reason to feel this way, there's no logic, no reason. It's fucked.

I *do* need to get over it. I need to find a way to stop that dark-haired chick from getting under my skin.

"You're a shitty brother," I tell him.

"And you're a spoiled man-child."

I flip him off.

"You're only mad because you have no reason to explain why she's got you all stressed out and you know it. For once you're not in control and that drives you fucking insane."

"Boys, open to page ten please," the teacher says loudly, looking directly at us.

I shoot Pax a scowl and open my book.

I'm half glad that we got interrupted, because if I'm being totally real with myself, I have no idea what I would have said.

It's pretty God damn hard to argue with the truth.

<hr>

THE BASS THUMPS heavy around me. If I danced, I'd be dancing now.

I'm halfway through my sixth or seventh beer, and I'm settling in nicely to what is shaping up to be a mint night.

Bry's house is absolutely packed; most of the school is here along with half of his fancy-ass neighbourhood.

His sister Carley and all her mates have taken over the top story for the time being, but I know how that'll go, they'll all be mingling down here and trying to land themselves an older guy soon enough.

Liana is here with her girls, and surprisingly enough, she hasn't caused one bit of trouble for me so far. She's looking good too. I need to sneak her away to find an empty bedroom before too much longer.

Hell of a night.

It's still young though, plenty of time for drama, and I'm uber aware of the fact that the new girl hasn't shown her face yet – hopefully she won't at all, but I can't deny that my attention turns to the front door every time someone comes in it.

Pax ambles over to where me, Bry and a few of the other guys are lounging around, watching the girls dance, and drops into the seat next to me, a bottle of beer hanging from his fingertips.

"Where's your new best friend?" I ask him, salty as fuck.

He chuckles. "She'll be here soon, Romeo. Chill out."

"She better not cause any shit."

He rolls his eyes. "The only one who's been causing shit is your leech of a girlfriend."

"*Not* my girlfriend," I point out.

He just shakes his head. "You're getting pretty good at lying to yourself, Cull."

He turns his attention to Bryson, who, if I'm not mistaken, is right on the verge of turning into Darren. "She's going to bring that little blonde that you think we don't all notice you watching," he tells him.

Bryson just lifts his hand and flips Pax off, a lazy smile on his face. *Yip.* He's toast.

"Daaaarrrreeen!" the boys all call out in chorus, cheering and whooping.

Me and Pax erupt into laughter. I fucking love it when Bry lets loose.

"Ice," I hear Pax say, his voice filled with warmth.

Before I can even question him, he's out of his seat and weaving through the masses of people. I look ahead, already knowing who I'm going to find waiting for him.

There she is. And *fuck*... for a girl who isn't my type, she sure looks a lot like one who is.

She's wearing a skin-tight, bright red dress; it's short as fuck, and her long dark hair is in waves around her face.

She looks like absolute sin. Pure fucking trouble, and if I can't pull my eyes off her quick, that's exactly what I'm going to find myself in.

Bry kicks my shoe, and it breaks the spell. I look over at him and he's grinning lazily at me. He takes a long pull of his beer, his eyes locked on me, making me wait for whatever it is he wants to say.

"You're so *fucked*," he says, the drawl that only comes out when he's pissed, causing his r's to roll.

He's slumped in his chair, relaxed as hell.

I can't even be mad at this fucker with a mug like that. I just laugh at him. "Have another drink, Darren."

I down the last of my beer and grab another one, cracking it open. I get to my feet and push my way through the crowd, being careful not to look in any direction but the one I know I'll find Liana.

She's got on a leather mini skirt that barely covers her ass and some blue top that isn't much more than a triangle of fabric and a few strings... high-as-hell shoes that I don't know how the fuck she hasn't broken an ankle in yet.

I catch sight of her and move farther in that direction. People scatter to get out of my way, I don't even have to shove.

I wrap my arms around her middle when I reach her, and she looks up at me, her eyes glassy, no doubt from the pink, sugary drinks I watched her carry in.

She's a fuckin' light weight. She's probably only had two or three.

She throws her arms around my neck and slams her mouth against mine.

It's sloppy as hell, but fuck it, I've got a buzz on now and drinking always makes me horny as fuck.

I pry her off me and grab her hand, pulling her behind me, out of the huge main room and into the hallway. We pass Pax, Berlin, and her friends on the way, but I don't even look at them.

I want to make it clear that I don't give a fuck.

Maybe then I'll start believing it too.

I open the first door I find and gently shove Liana inside the room, closing the door behind me.

"What the fuck is that bitch doing here?" she demands, looking a hell of a lot more sober all of a sudden.

I don't answer. I can't be fucked. I back her up against the door I just shut and kiss her until she melts against me.

I don't know what's going on, but I feel this sense of urgency, like I need to forget – I need to lose myself for a minute.

She pulls back, gasping for air. *"Holy shit,"* she pants.

I don't give her a chance to say anything else, I just claim her mouth again, with even more intensity this time.

I forget all about the girl in the red dress and lose myself in the one in front of me.

ELEVEN

Berlin

"I'm *next level* good at beer pong. Maybe we should put money on this," I brag to Pax as I round the table to take up position at the opposite end to him.

He shakes his head in amusement. "You want to put Daddy's money where your mouth is, Ice?"

I shoot him the middle finger and he laughs.

"Actually, I've got a better idea, let's play doubles." I smirk to myself, my genius plan unfolding in my head.

He notices my cunning expression and lifts a brow in question – he knows I'm up to something. He's scary in tune with me, but I like it – saves me having to spoon feed him everything all the time.

"You sure you want to play a game like that, with elite athletes like us?" he says, bragging.

I roll my eyes – hard. "Oh, *please*... do I need to remind you that you're small-town rugby players, *not* royalty?"

He chuckles.

"Me and Soph, versus you and Bryson," I wager.

Pax smirks knowingly.

"Oh no, no, no. I don't play ball sports," Sophia argues.

Pax howls with laughter. "I don't think throwing a ping pong ball into cups of beer counts as 'ball sports', blondie."

"And I don't care, you're on my team," I argue with her.

"Let's fuckin do it." Bryson gets up from his spot on the couch and sways his way over to the table we've set up, all swagger and masculine energy.

He's half cut, but he's actually talking, so this might just work.

Sophia hasn't ever admitted to me that she's into the guy, but it's so obvious, she doesn't need to say the words. Even a blind man could see the way she watches him. She drinks in his presence, it's crazy.

"You're up first, Darren," Pax says as he hands Bryson a ping pong ball.

I shoot him a questioning glance, but he just chuckles and shakes his head. I'll have to remember to ask him about it later.

"Come on, Sophia," Bryson pleads. His voice caresses her name, and hell, it even gets my motor running a little. "For my birthday."

I look at Soph. Her jaw is just about on the floor. I'm starting to think this might be the first time he's ever spoken directly to her.

It has the desired effect though. She gets up from the stool she's perched on, and the poor bitch, I can actually see her legs shaking as she walks towards me.

Pax has a huge grin on his face, as though this whole thing really tickles him.

"I don't even know how to play," she tells me in that weird fast, hushed yet yelling way people do when they're aggressively unhappy about something but don't want to make a scene.

"You throw the ball in the cup; it's not exactly rocket science."

"There is no way I'm going to be able to get that to happen. I'll probably miss the whole table."

"Have another drink," I tell her. "I've got to be the right level of drunk to really come into my prime."

"Stop being a pussy and just get on with it," Carissa tells her.

She doesn't look happy, but she takes the drink that Carissa is holding out towards her and chugs the whole thing.

I can't imagine that Sophia has ever really drunk much before, so this should be interesting. Thankfully, the girls are all staying at my house tonight, so it'll only be my dad that has to bear witness to whatever level of trollied we are when we walk through his front door.

He's got a pretty high tolerance for shit; I had a bit of a rebellious phase back in Australia, so I'm sure he will have seen worse than anything that this evening could possibly offer, but you never know. Doesn't hurt to keep him on his toes.

Laura offers Sophia a thumbs up before downing another of her drinks and cheering loudly.

I actually think I might have totally misjudged these girls. Throw a couple of cans down their throats and it's all go. I guess sometimes it really *is* the quiet ones after all.

"A good game's a fast game, boys," I taunt Bryson, who is chewing Pax's ear off about something, while making a whole heap of hand gestures.

I swear this dude is a real mystery, can't get him to speak normally, can't get him to shut up now.

Bryson barely looks towards us, just reaches his arm out and throws the ball.

It lands swish in one of the cups.

"Ah *shit*," I mutter. Maybe this wasn't such a great idea after all.

"I'm going to *kill* you," Sophia whispers.

I can't help but laugh. She might not know the rules, but she already knows this is bad.

Pax throws his ball, but thankfully it narrowly misses a cup – I think Sophia would have passed out on the spot if they'd made two in a row.

I grab the cup and down the beer from Bryson's successful shot.

"You want to start?" I ask her.

She shakes her head frantically, pure fear in her eyes.

I shrug and toss the ball. Much like Bryson's shot, it sails effortlessly into a cup.

"Boom," I say, nonchalant as hell, as though I had absolutely no doubt it was going to happen, rather than it being an absolute fluke.

Carissa, Mel and Laura cheer, as do a bunch of people I don't even know.

"Alright, I see how this is going to go, Ice." Pax points his finger at me before fishing the ball out of the cup.

"I told you I was good," I say with a shrug.

"Let's see how good your teammate is," he challenges.

I give him a look that says, 'bring it'.

"You're up, Soph." I nudge her.

She looks like she's about to puke. Bryson gives her a blinding smile and I shit you not, her step falters. This girl has got it *bad*.

"Keep it together," I whisper.

"I'm trying," she hisses.

It'd be pathetic if it wasn't so cute.

I don't know what the fuck she's going to do if this guy ever kisses her – probably go into cardiac arrest or some shit if I had to guess.

She's standing there like a deer in the headlights. I can't be sure, but I think she might be having some type of stroke.

"Throw the ball," I prompt her. "Elbows behind the table."

Her eyes widen in panic, but she throws it. There's

no way it was ever going to go in, but it hits the table near the side of the triangle of cups, so it's not a complete embarrassment.

We volley back and forth, lots of near misses and a few epic shots. Even Sophia lands one and does a victory dance before remembering that she's got quite an audience.

We've made up a handshake and everything. The shit talk has escalated with every shot made.

We've amassed quite the crowd to watch our little battle, but somehow, I still don't miss the change in the air when Cullen sidles up to the table.

I don't bother looking at him, so I don't know if he's bought Liana over here with him or not, but either way, I don't care. I'm going to win this game whether they're here to witness it or not. He made it abundantly clear earlier that he didn't care about even glancing in my direction, so I'll happily return the sentiment.

Each end of the table has got one cup left to land a ball into, and it's our turn to throw. Either of us make this shot and we win. Game over.

There's been some flirting between Soph and Bryson, but nothing they're going to be able to tell their grandchildren about one day if I don't find a way to up the stakes.

"What do you say we make things more interesting?" I suggest loudly, causing the chatter around the table to die down.

Pax smirks at me. "What have you got in mind, Ice?"

I think for a minute, a plan forming in my head.

"Winning team gets to choose," I offer. "Your imagination is your limit."

"Absolutely not happening," Sophia cuts in, giving me the most brutal death glare I've ever received in my life.

"Chill," I tell her, "I've got this."

The look on her face makes it plenty clear that she does not agree with my assessment of the situation.

"Careful, new girl, your mouth is writing cheques your reputation can't cash."

I don't have to look to know who that voice belongs to. Cullen fucking Carrington. The golden boy himself.

I turn my full attention to him for the first time, and fuck my life, I shouldn't have. He looks good. *Too good.* Ripped jeans, scuffed-up Docs and a tight black t-shirt never looked so appealing. His dark hair is falling over his light eyes and *shit*, I've never seen anything like it. He makes being bad, look *so* good.

He's a total prick and he wears it too well.

"Who said I can't cash them?" I challenge.

He gives me a slow head-to-toe appraisal, and I hate to admit the way I can almost feel his eyes travelling over my exposed skin.

He's clearly had a bit to drink, he's not as staunch or composed as he normally is. He also hasn't got a blonde hanging off him. Firsts all round tonight.

"Maybe you should have brought your camera," I tell him as he continues to stare, totally unhurried and unashamed.

Some people start laughing but he doesn't seem to care, nor does he look away. He finally looks at my face again after taking his sweet time with my body.

"You done?" I ask, popping my hip.

"Maybe."

"Well unless you've got something to contribute, run along and find yourself a barbie to play with."

He just smirks and gestures for me to go ahead.

I give Pax a look, trying to convey that I want us to work together to stitch up Sophia and Bryson.

"If we win," I say, loud enough for everyone to hear, "you two have to go skinny dipping in the pool, right now, with an audience."

They look at one another, shrug and nod. "Deal," Pax tells me. "And if *we* win, you kiss me, and blondie here, kisses Darren."

I hear Sophia virtually choke on her drink.

"Deal," I say, without even consulting her. It probably makes me a shitty cousin and an even shittier friend, but I don't care. She needs to get out there, and I'd sure as fuck rather kiss Pax than have to go naked swimming with everyone from school watching anyway.

I glance over at Cullen, and he looks *pissed*. I don't know what or who has rubbed him up the wrong way now, but he's not my monkey and it's not my circus, so I don't give it another thought.

"I think I might pass out," Sophia says.

Well shit, she does look kind of pale.

"Get it together," I whisper.

"I'm not drunk enough for this," she replies.

That's easily fixed.

"Mel, can you pass me my drink?" I call out quickly.

She reaches behind her and grabs my drink from where I left it on the countertop and hands it to me. I've only had a couple of sips, it's pretty much full, but Sophia grabs it and chugs about two thirds of it before I can stop her.

She's going to be utterly shitfaced at this rate, and I'll have to deal with a lecture from the old man while she pukes on his tiles.

I make a mental note to get her some pizza after the game is over. This is nothing a bit of grease can't soak up.

I pull the bottle from her hands and down the last of it before she can.

"Hit it," I instruct her as I put the ball in her empty hand.

She takes a deep breath and throws. I hold my breath as the ball sails through the air. I want to win, I *really* do – seeing the boys get their kit off for a midnight swim would be entertaining as hell, but I also really want to lose, so that Soph can finally get a kiss from the boy she's been pining over forever.

She's a bit of a book nerd loser and this might be her only shot – I don't even mean that in a nasty way, but she loves books, she's quiet as hell until you get to know her, and she has absolutely no balls, so it's time someone gave her a nudge.

I don't know if Pax received my subliminal messages, or he just made a good guess, but either way, it's the perfect set up for me – win or lose.

The pounding music, the people yelling and singing, it all fades away as the ping pong ball sails towards the cup.

It hits the rim and bounces out.

The air releases from my lungs. Sophia cusses.

"You're up, Ice," Pax says. He's looking at me with a shit load of expectation. He knows as well as I do that we need to hook these two up and that there's never going to be as good of a chance as there is right now.

I could throw the game, but my pride won't let me.

I aim, and throw. It's a perfect shot, it goes into the cup, and swirls around the rim, picking up speed.

Sophia squeals with relief, but it's short-lived; without missing a beat, Pax leans forward and blows into the cup, causing the ball to pop back out.

Half the crowd goes nuts cheering and jumping around as he smirks at me.

"Unlucky." He smirks.

"What the fuck?" Sophia yells. "Can he do that?!"

I shake my head in disbelief at his play. It's not all sewn up yet, but it could be very soon.

"Afraid so," I tell her, impressed by my new friend and his skills.

"No one told me that rule." She pouts.

I roll my eyes at her. "Oh *please*, you've had your hands full just throwing the ball and trying to stay upright simultaneously. We didn't need to add *exhaling* into the mix."

She flips me off, but the corners of her mouth are curved up ever so slightly. She doesn't fool me – she's loving this really.

Pax grabs the ball off the table and catches my eye for a long moment before turning his attention back to the cup at our end of the table and throwing.

It sails over the lip, barely missing.

So quickly, before I can even register what's happening, I see another ball flying towards the cup before landing directly in the beer with a splat.

Game over.

"Ah shit," Sophia mutters.

My eyes flash up to the other end of the table, and I see Bryson, his gaze firmly on my cousin.

"We win," he states – the absolute picture of control. I can't help but think he's been toying with us this entire time. I'm not even sure he looked when he threw that ball.

Pax starts whooping and hollering, jumping around with the cheering crowd.

I pluck the ball out of the cup and down the beer before Soph can even think about doing it herself. She's had more than enough.

Her attention is elsewhere, though. I'd be willing to bet she can't even see anything but the blond boy striding towards her.

He stops right in front of her, cups her jaw and whispers something to her. She nods her head, eyes wide as saucers, and then he's crashing his mouth to hers in a kiss so intense I almost feel like I should look away. I don't – because it's hot, but I probably should.

Every fucker is cheering, and I can hear Sophia's friends – *my* friends – because I think that's what they really are now, screaming over everyone.

"Yes, girl!" I join in. "Geddit!"

"Good game, Ice," I hear from behind me.

I turn to face Pax and smirk. "Not bad, Paxikins."

He chuckles. "Looks like you owe me a kiss."

I step closer and tip my chin up to look at him. "A deal's a deal, I guess."

He's a good-looking guy, there's absolutely no denying that. I'm sure he has girls falling all over him, but when I look at him, I'm not entirely sure I think about him that way. But it's just a kiss, and I'm no piker.

I grab the front of his t-shirt and pull his face closer. His lips meet mine, hesitantly at first, but he takes control quickly.

I hear something smash behind me, but I don't turn.

His hands find my waist and tug me closer as I wrap my arms around his neck.

Him and Bryson won this bet fair and square, and while it feels a little like I'm kissing the wrong guy, the boy knows how to kiss, and I'll damn well give him his money's worth in return.

We finally break apart. Pax has a huge grin on his face – nothing new there.

"Not bad, new girl. Not bad at all."

I pretend to be offended. "I'm a lot better than *not bad*."

He chuckles.

I step away and hold my hand out for him to shake. "Pleasure doing business with you. I look forward to the rematch."

He shakes my hand, his eyes never leaving mine. "You and me both." He grins.

I must have had too much to drink throughout the game, my head is starting to spin a little bit.

I turn around and find Soph standing with Mel, Laura, and Carissa, her face flushed and her eyes bright. Bryson is a few feet away, still watching her. Cullen is nowhere to be seen.

Yay.

"You good?" I ask her, trying and failing to hide my amusement as I approach them, a slight sway in my step.

"I'm *so* smashed," she whispers. "But, seriously... Best. Night. Ever."

TWELVE

Cullen

The party is still in full swing around me, but I'm not feeling it as much.

I can't put my finger on what the fuck is wrong with me, but ever since I saw Pax hooking up with the new girl, I've been in a shitty mood.

I know I've got no right and there's no logic to it, but here we fucking are.

Liana has been MIA for the past hour. She's probably up to no good, but I'm glad she's not hanging around for once. I don't have the patience for her right now.

I sip my beer and watch people coming and going from the spot I've claimed on a lounger by the pool. A few have stopped and tried to talk to me, but the 'fuck off' attitude I've given everyone has stopped it from going on for long.

"Cull!" My name rings out over the music. There's no mistaking that voice, I've been hearing it my entire life.

"Yo!" I yell back to Pax. "By the pool."

I see him approach the pool fence. "What the fuck are you doing out here in the dark like a loner?"

"Sitting."

"*Why?*"

"Because I fucking wanted to sit."

He studies me hard for a few beats, before a shit-eating grin appears on his face. "I fucking *knew* it."

"Knew *what?*"

He points a finger at me. "You like her. You're into Berlin."

"Like fuck," I bite back.

"You're fucked off because I kissed her and now you're sulking."

"Go do one."

He chuckles, smug as hell. "I fucking *knew* it."

I open my mouth to tell him to fuck off, but he cuts me off.

"Doesn't matter right now anyway, we've got a situation and I need your help."

"What kind of 'situation'?" I sit up a little straighter.

The boys better not have been fighting again. I'm sick of that shit. One more brawl from my team and I'll be benching the pricks.

He rubs at the back of his neck, his expression sheepish. "You know that little blonde thing that Bry's into?"

"Yip." I nod.

"She's like next level smashed, and Ice isn't looking so great either."

New girl.

"What the fuck has that got to do with me?" I snap.

"I need your help to get them home. Bry's passed out on the couch, so he's no use."

That sounds about right. At least he's not running around nude for once.

I hold up my beer to him. "I'm not driving anywhere."

"Jed has his van and he's sober, I just need help getting them in there and out at the other end."

I grind my teeth together. Part of me, a big fucking part if I'm honest, wants to already be out of my seat and tracking Berlin down to find out for myself that she's alright, and get her out of here.

I could justify wanting her to leave so she's not going to stir up any shit for me with Li, but that's not it.

That's not even close to being it.

I'm torn between my urges and my ego.

"Come on, bro, you owe me for not snitching on all your late-night sneak-outs."

Jesus Christ.

"Fuck's sake. Where are we going?" I say as I stand and make my way to the gate.

I follow him inside, through the living room and into the entrance.

There's five girls piled up. I know Carissa, but I can't remember the names of the other two, and then there's a totally smashed blonde – Sophia I'm pretty sure it was – curled up on the floor, and a drunk-ass-looking new girl.

She's leaning against the wall, purely out of necessity by the looks of it.

At least she's semi upright. The blonde, not so much.

"What the fuck did she drink?" I demand, looking Sophia over.

Carissa looks up at me from where she's kneeling next to her wasted friend. "She didn't even drink *that* much. Like she's had a bit, but not *this* much. I don't know what happened. She was fine one minute and then absolutely wasted the next. We fed her pizza, but she spewed it all up."

Fucking charming.

"Did she take something?"

There's not exactly a shortage of gear at this party, but I wouldn't have picked the little nerd lying in her own vomit to be the drug-taking type.

"No way," Berlin slurs. "She's clean *squeaky*."

I glance over at her. I can only assume she means 'squeaky clean'.

"Did *you* take something?"

"*Nope*," she replies, popping the 'p'.

"You sure?"

"I know drugs, *okay?* And I didn't take *any* of them."

She's even sassy when she's off her head.

I'll worry about her later. Right now, something has to be done about Goldilocks here. She needs to get to bed, ASAP. No story, straight to sleep.

"Are you sure she didn't take any drugs?" I look deliberately at the rest of the girls as I point at Sophia.

"She's never taken drugs before. She drinks a little bit, but I've seen her have more than what I saw her have tonight," one of the other girls says.

"They were playing beer pong with me and Bry. You saw her, she was sweet. Then half an hour later she... *wasn't.*" Pax shrugs at me.

I frown but don't push it further. She looks like she's about two lines deep on a bad trip.

Jed comes through the front door, looks at us all one by one and points behind him. "Van's out front." The poor cunt looks like he's seriously concerned about getting vomit through his ride.

"Let's get this show on the road then," Pax says. "You got Berlin or Sophia?" he asks me.

I look at Berlin, immediately decide that's a bad idea, and then crouch down next to Sophia. I scoop her up off the floor and into my arms. Thankfully, she's not actually bathing in puke, but she definitely has some stuck in her hair. It's pretty rank.

She's totally lights out. She doesn't even open her eyes as I carry her out of the house and across the front lawn.

I almost make it too. I should have known it wouldn't be that easy. Nothing ever is.

"Where the fuck are you going?" I recognise the shrieking voice instantly.

"Fuck off, Liana," I hear Pax say behind me.

"Go fuck yourself, loser," she fires back.

"Cullen, what the fuck!" she yells after me again. "Where are you going?"

I turn around, still with the girl in my arms. "Kinda got my hands full right now, if you want to save the hissy fit for when I get back, that'd be fuckin' great."

She looks at the girl I'm carrying, then at my face, too shocked to speak.

Pax brushes past me, a slightly stumbling Berlin on his arm. She's cooked her book in one way or another, but she still manages to flip Liana off as she departs the party.

All class.

We somehow manage to get all five girls into the van. Sophia is snoring softly now, I don't even bother putting her down, I just climb in and keep her on my lap.

Berlin recites her address and looks proud of herself for remembering it. Her and Pax have squeezed into the front seat like a couple of little kids.

Carissa looks like she's starting to find this whole situation funny.

"Don't you dare," I warn her as she pulls out her phone and points it at me.

"Oh, come on, hot shot, we both know I need photo evidence of this to embarrass her tomorrow."

I scowl at her, but she takes a photo, flash and all, anyway.

"Is your dad going to kill us?" Carissa asks Berlin.

"He's not gonna be happy about *that*." She throws a thumb over her shoulder in the direction of me and Sophia. "Uncle Derick is a diiiiiiick. Dad is gonna hear alllllll about it if he finds out," she says between hiccups.

"She's your cousin?" I ask her, surprised. Maybe that explains her sudden appearance in this town in particular.

"Yuuuup," Berlin replies.

"If anyone needs to spew, you better give me time to stop," Jed warns us all.

"I fucking love this!" Berlin yells before turning the volume up high as fuck.

The van fills with some god-awful chick song.

Pax howls with laughter as Berlin sings at the top of her lungs, using her hand as a mic. Jed looks like he's falling for her charms too. I don't remember seeing the guy ever smile like that before. She holds her fake mic out to him, and he even sings along for a few lines. Pussy-whipped prick.

My eardrums endure the torture for the entirety of the song before Pax reaches over and turns the volume back down. "Your dad will end you if you rock up with that shit cranking."

"That one!" She points out the front window, and Jed pulls into the driveway.

Pax climbs out and slides open the door to the back.

"You girls got it from here or what?" I ask.

Berlin is trying to climb out the front and failing spectacularly.

Pax rushes to grab her before she lands on her face. She pisses herself laughing. He grins like a loon.

"I think we might require further assistance," one of the girls says as she watches the encounter with wide eyes.

I sigh. The absolute last thing I want to do right now is carry this chick inside and put her to bed, but it looks like that might be what has to happen if I want to get the fuck out of here.

I hope to fucking God that Berlin's dad is a deep sleeper because I'm going to dump and run if some irate old dude comes out, flipping his lid.

"Someone get the door unlocked," I say.

Carissa climbs out and rushes ahead. She wrangles the keys from Berlin and goes and opens the door for us all.

At least one of them can make shit happen.

I cart Sophia up the path, not even bothering to be careful not to jostle her; the chick is well out to it. I don't think she'll be prying her lids open until morning, and I don't envy her when she does.

She's going to feel like she got hit by a truck.

Berlin is dancing around, twirling and stumbling as Pax tries to keep her upright.

I might find it funny if I wasn't so over this circus.

"Shhhh," she tells him as they approach the front door.

"I'm not the one making the noise, Ice," he replies, clearly amused, as we all file inside.

"Where's this one sleeping?" I whisper.

"Ummm, maybe in... here." Berlin points to a door and flicks a light switch, but it lights up the entire staircase that leads upstairs instead of the room she's pointing to.

She looks around in confusion for a few moments. "Whoops."

She flicks the switch again, and then the other three, about ten times each. The place is flashing like a God damn strobe light.

"Jesus Christ," I mutter, "cut it out before someone finds out they're epileptic."

"I-dunno-howta make-the-lights-go." She holds up her hands in confusion, her words running together.

Another light turns on, but it's from upstairs this time.

"B? Is that you?" a man's voice calls from upstairs.

"Fuck's saaaaake," I groan.

Pax makes eye contact with me and grins like the cat that got the cream. I don't know what the hell he's so excited for. I'm fairly certain we're about three seconds away from meeting Berlin's dad, and that's not something I'm keen on.

The girl in my arms is getting progressively heavier

by the second, and I'm about *this* fucking close to just laying her on the floor and getting the fuck out of here.

"B?"

"Old maaan!" Berlin calls back. "We wake ya?"

He appears at the top of the stairs, shirtless, rubbing his face.

The girls – the conscious ones at least – are all staring with laser fucking focus. I can't even blame them. Berlin's dad is a unit.

"I think you probably woke up half the town," he replies, groggy.

He slowly makes his way down the stairs. Pax nudges me with his elbow – he's all hyped up about something. It's not until Berlin's dad makes it to the bottom of the stairs, and notices the girl I'm carrying, that I realise what's got Pax all jacked up.

This is fucking Cole Davids.

Berlin's dad is *Cole Davids*.

I'm in Cole David's god damn house.

"Jesus Christ, B, what the fuck happened to her?" He points at Sophia.

"She's white girl wasted... but be *chill* – she jus' needsa nap."

"With all due respect, Sir, I think she might need more than a nap," Pax chimes in.

Cole looks at him, and then at me. "Who are you two?"

Pax beams at him. "I'm Paxton, everyone calls me Pax, and I'm a big fan."

He holds out his hand and Cole takes it. Poor dude looks half asleep and a little bewildered.

"Any chance I can put her down? My arms are killing me," I interrupt Pax's little man-crush moment.

Cole eyes me up and down and then walks into the room that Berlin was trying and failing to light up.

He flicks a switch *inside* the room and points to a large leather couch. "I think a non-absorbent surface might be the way to go."

"Not jus'a pretty face, eh, old man," Berlin slurs from somewhere behind me. I swear she's getting more incoherent by the minute.

I hear Carissa mutter something about his body as I finally put Sophia down. Thank fuck for that; my arms and shoulders are screaming at me.

Who needs to do weights when you can just carry around drunk chicks?

Cole puts a blanket over her; and the other girls, his daughter included, all flop down in various spots around the room.

"I'll get her a bucket," he tells Berlin.

She salutes him.

"We'll be having words tomorrow," he warns her.

"Mmmmmm hmmmm."

He indicates with his head for Pax and me to follow him out.

"Later, Ice." Pax smirks before leaving the room.

I follow as Berlin yells something intangible after him.

Cole shuts the door to the room the girls are in.

"Did they take drugs?" he asks, his eyes carefully assessing both of us.

I shrug. I'm not prepared to pretend I know anything about this chaos. I'm just the delivery boy.

Pax shakes his head. "I don't think so, Mr. Davids. They just got smashed all of a sudden, Sophia especially. But I was with them all night and they didn't take anything that I saw. They didn't even drink that much."

Cole looks at him, probably weighing up if he can trust this random dude he doesn't even know. He nods his head once.

"Who are you?" He turns his focus back to me.

"Cullen, Sir." I hold out my hand to him.

"Like *Twilight!*" Berlin's voice comes from behind the door.

Fucking bitch.

He takes my hand, ignoring his daughter, and shakes it firmly.

"I'm a big fan. You're pretty much my idol," I tell him.

"You play?"

I nod. "Yes, Sir. Fullback, same as you."

He nods his head a couple of times, giving nothing away.

Pax is pretty much bouncing next to me – I swear the guy is about thirty seconds away from jizzing in his pants.

"Right, well if you'll excuse me, boys, I've got a bucket to find." He points towards the front door.

We stumble our way out, partly because we're both half cut, but mostly because we're both tripping out from meeting one of our heroes.

We clamber back into the van and Pax starts gushing to Jed like some little schoolgirl with no composure.

"I can't believe her dad is Cole fucking Davids," I mutter to no one. "Who the fuck is this girl?"

We drive back to the party, Pax not shutting up for one second of the drive. I don't even comment. I'm too deep in thought.

The absolute last thing I needed tonight was for the new girl to become even more interesting and intriguing... but that's exactly what's happened and it's a real problem.

THIRTEEN

Berlin

I groan as I open my eyes and the sunlight smacks me clean across the face.

I blink a few times, trying to figure out where the hell I am.

"Turn off the sun," a groggy voice next to me says.

Mel.

"I second that motion," I grumble.

My head is pounding, and my mouth is so dry it feels like someone has been in there with a vacuum cleaner.

I haven't even lifted my head up yet and I already know I'm going to have the hangover from hell.

"What did we *drink* last night?" Sophia says. I can

tell, just from hearing her voice, that she's at least as hungover as I am, if not worse.

"I don't know what the hell you had, but I feel alright," Carissa says.

I blink against the harsh light a few more times, groaning as I make out the living room. Apparently, we couch camped last night.

Carissa looks like she's been awake a while, she's sitting up with the TV on.

"I've been better," Laura admits.

I manage to get myself into a sitting position, and it's simultaneously better and worse at the same time.

"What the hell did I do last night?" I rub at my temples. "My head feels like it's about to explode."

Carissa points at the coffee table in the middle of the room. "Your dad put those there last night. I'd recommend taking a couple."

There's a packet of paracetamol and a jug of water with five glasses.

"That man is a *saint*," I mutter as I crawl across the floor to get them.

"Did I drink my body weight in alcohol?" Sophia half whimpers.

I fill her a glass of water and grab a couple of painkillers. I awkwardly crawl them over to her and her bucket, which thankfully, is empty.

She takes them from me, both grateful and looking like she's on death's door.

I can relate.

"The game of beer pong was the beginning of the

end," Carissa says. "It was pretty much all downhill from there."

I think back over the night and she's right. I can't remember anything much past the game. I remember we lost. I kissed Pax, Soph kissed Bryson, and then things start to get a little bit blurry.

I remember singing in a van, but I don't know who was driving. I remember yelling something about *Twilight...*

Oh god.

"Pax and Cullen were here, in my house, weren't they?"

"Oooooh *yeah*. They sure were," Laura replies.

"They met my dad?"

She nods. "I think Pax got a hard on."

"Don't blame him," Mel mutters.

I groan and lower my head to the floor.

Cullen Carrington knows who my dad is, and that is bound to end badly for me. Knowing my luck, *everyone* at school will know by Monday morning.

"Alcohol is the devil."

"You're telling me. I feel like I've spent an hour in a tumble drier," Sophia complains.

Carissa spends the next fifteen minutes talking us through the events of last night. I recall a few snippets here and there when she prompts me, but Sophia can recall nothing whatsoever after kissing Bryson – it's actually kind of concerning.

"Maybe someone spiked your drink?" Laura suggests.

"I don't even think I had a drink of my own once we started that game," Sophia replies. "I just drank some of the beer."

We're all quiet for a bit.

"Wait... that drink of Berlin's," Mel says.

We all look over at her.

"Remember? Right before the final shots, Berlin asked me to pass Soph her drink, it was sitting on the counter behind us? She smashed most of it and then Berlin drank the rest. It was already open..."

"And then next thing you're passed out." Carissa points at Sophia. "And you're pretty cooked." She points at me. "You have to admit, the idea tracks."

I still think it's super unlikely that anyone at that party would have the desire or the sleuth skills to put something in my drink without any of us noticing, but I have to admit, it's possible.

"We should get your sister to run bloods." Mel looks at Laura.

Laura shrugs. "She probably could."

"I think you guys are getting a bit carried away, it's just a game of beer pong gone too far," I argue.

"Maybe, but I don't recall seeing her drink anywhere near enough alcohol to explain why she was passed out, being carried around by Cullen."

Sophia pales. "Noooo, he did *not* carry me."

"Oh, but he did." Laura giggles.

"I've got a photo." Carissa reaches for her phone.

Sophia covers her face with a pillow.

"Maybe you *should* get a blood test. At least you'd

have a good excuse if someone roofied you," I suggest. Talk about humiliating. Especially for a wall flower like Soph.

I hear my phone ding with an incoming message. I find it tossed on the floor next to my shoes.

Pax: You and your girls alive, Ice?

"It's Pax. He wants to know if we're back from the dead."

"Tell him you need another kiss to revive you."

"I'm going to ignore that comment."

Me: I think I need someone to bring me a Powerade… and the will to live.

Pax: That bad, huh?

Me: Worse. Thanks for getting us home. Hope we didn't fuck up your night.

Pax: Are you kidding? I got to meet my idol. Best night I've ever had.

I roll my eyes and toss my phone onto the couch.

"I need to pee," Sophia announces.

"Me too," Laura agrees.

They both move with about as much enthusiasm as roadkill, but they get out the door without tripping or spewing.

"So, what's the deal with you and Pax? You looked pretty close last night."

I shoot Carissa a look. "I've told you. We're just mates."

"Oh yeah, I *always* kiss my friends."

"It was a bet."

"Such an unfortunate loss."

I throw a pillow at her, and she laughs.

It's a fair call. There's definitely been worse consequences for losing. I got off lightly.

"Hey, I tried to win that game and you know it, but I'll admit, I was more than okay with losing if it meant that Sophia finally got to hook up with Bryson."

Carissa throws the pillow back at me. "How self-sacrificing of you."

I flip her off.

Laura rushes back in the door. "Ah, guys, she's started puking and it's not pretty."

Carissa rushes out of the room after her, but I stay put. I know one thing about myself, and that is that I'm not built for cleaning up spew. It'll only result in more spew coming out of me – and therefore twice the mess.

"I'm there in spirit!" I call after them.

***

"I'M SORRY, what the fuck did you say?" I gape.

It's lunchtime Monday and I swear to God, I still don't feel one hundred percent.

Sophia feels about fifty percent, if the state of her is anything to go by, but given the words Laura just said, that isn't surprising.

Laura nods her head furiously. "Yip. She had *Ketamine* in her system."

Sophia's jaw drops open. "*Ketamine?* Is that actually a thing? I've only heard of that in movies. Isn't it like horse tranquiliser or something?"

"It's definitely a thing," Laura tells her, "My sister does *so* many drug tests at her work, and she was just telling me the other day that it's becoming a real problem in this town."

"I'm going to go out on a limb here and say that you didn't go down the k hole willingly?" I ask Sophia.

She shakes her head. "Down the *what*? I don't even know how you do that?"

All the girls look to me for answers.

Naïve, innocent little girls.

"Like, do you smoke it or what?"

"Jesus Christ, someone really *did* drug you."

"I reckon they were trying to drug *you*," Soph argues. "I swear, the only drink I had that came from out of my sight, was yours."

"Why would someone want to drug me? I don't even know anyone in this hell hole."

"Yeah, you haven't ruffled any feathers at all," Sophia says sarcastically, with a roll of her eyes.

"Liana and her friends might hate me, but I don't think they're the kind of girls who have got ketamine on hand, do you? And Cullen isn't exactly my biggest fan, but he helped get us home. Why would he try drug me and then help us get back safely? It makes no sense."

"This is high school. *Nothing* makes sense," Laura points out.

"Preach."

"What do we do now?" Sophia asks nervously.

I don't blame her for freaking out – in fact, I'm surprised she's not completely losing her shit about this. She just had what I presume was her first ever experience with drugs, and not only that, but she did so unwillingly. Thankfully, nothing worse happened.

I don't even want to think about what could have gone wrong.

This whole 'having real friends' concept is a weird one for me; I'm used to being surrounded by people with ulterior motives – people who want something from me and are out for everything they can get, but these girls, they're different.

"I don't know... do you think we should get your sister to test the rest of us?" I never thought I'd be suggesting that, but this has changed everything.

Laura nods. "That's a good idea, then maybe we can start putting together what the fuck happened and who's responsible."

"People were videoing the beer pong game on their phones. There might be something somewhere that we can look at," Mel suggests.

"That's actually really smart," I tell her.

We make plans for after school to all go around to the lab where Laura's sister, Tiff, works and get her to run a drug screen on the rest of us, then we all head off to class.

Soph and I have PE, and I've never been so unenthused about something in my life. I've got a brand-new uniform after the other *incident*, but I swear to God, if someone tries to make me catch a ball or swing a bat today, they're probably going to cop some shit.

We walk in silence, looking every bit the hungover pieces of shit that we are.

I sigh in relief when I see on the board that we're doing classroom theory today, but that relief is short-lived when my gaze wanders past the board and into the teacher's office.

I don't know what the fuck my dad is doing sitting in there, joking around with a couple of the teachers and coaches, but my gut tells me that it's not going to be something I like.

I stare for the longest time, and eventually he looks up and sees me. He waves his hand, but I can't even bring myself to wave back.

"What. The. Fuck." I mouth the words to him.

He chuckles and gets up out of the seat he's in, excuses himself, and then he's standing in front of me.

"What are you doing here?" I hiss, glancing side to side to make sure no one is paying attention.

It's bad enough that Pax and Cullen both not only know who my dad is, but have met him. I don't need the rest of this rugby-mad school getting the memo.

"Nice to see you too, B." He smirks.

"Hey, Uncle Cole," Sophia says.

"Don't you say hi to him," I tell her off, scowling.

She grimaces.

"Why are you here, old man?" I demand.

"I ah... I've been meaning to tell you that I kind of

got a second job." He looks sheepish as hell, and I don't like it. Not one little bit.

"I swear to God, if you tell me you're working at this school, I will put myself on a plane faster than you can say 'teenage runaway'."

"I'm not *technically* working at the school."

I narrow my eyes at him.

"I'm helping coach the rugby team."

Oh, mother of all things holy. Just when I thought this couldn't get any worse, my own father goes and hits it out of the park.

"You'd *better* be kidding."

"Afraid not, kiddo, it was jacked up through the rugby union, and it's only temporary while the assistant coach they had nurses his wife back to health. I'll be out of here before you know it."

"You're going to need nursing back to health once I'm done with you," I threaten through clenched teeth.

I can't fucking believe this. Every single student is going to know exactly who I am and who my father is before the day is through. My life here, as I know it, is over.

"Relax, B. It's just some coaching – you know that's what I'm actually good at, right? The Black Diamonds are on course to be champs for another year running. I'll barely even have to help out. I won't even be here during school hours."

I'm under no illusion about where my father's strengths lie – he's outstanding at his job, just as he was as a player – my beef is with my high school life turning into more of a shit show than it already is.

The second bell rings, indicating that we're now late to class. I point a warning finger at my dad. "This *isn't* over."

He crosses his arms over his chest, his posture staunch, but his expression amused. "Never dreamed it would be."

"Un-fucking-believable," I mutter as Sophia drags me off to class.

FOURTEEN

Cullen

"Jesus Christ, just end it already before I say something to that girl that we'll both regret."

"Just leave it alone," I snap at him, even though he's hit the nail on the head.

Liana has got to fucking go. She made such a scene about Berlin and her friends on Saturday night when I got back to the party, that Bryson's sister ending up kicking everyone out and shutting the whole thing down. Fucking Bry slept through the whole ordeal.

Lucky bastard.

I've been ghosting Liana ever since, but that hasn't stopped her from calling and texting non-stop. Me and the boys laid low at lunch, just to get the fuck away from her. I'd been hoping she'd take the hint and be too proud to keep chasing me, but I've obviously massively overestimated how little dignity she really has.

I toss my phone, which is still ringing, into my gym bag and signal for the team to follow me on a lap around the field. It's the first official training of the season, and I'm not going to let some blonde with sociopathic tendencies get into my head.

Not now. *Not ever.*

I was always going to end it, but she's pressed the fast forward button on it.

"I don't know what the fuck she's so wild about. You were the one necking with fuckin' Berlin in the kitchen, not me."

"I was wondering when you were going to bring that up." Pax grins.

"Why the fuck would I bring that up?" I demand.

"Because you just did?"

"Fuck off, Pax."

He laughs and holds up his hands in defence. "You started it, bro, not me. Don't shoot the messenger or whatever."

"Seriously, stop talking."

"It'd make all our lives a lot easier if you just admitted you're into the new girl."

"I'm *not* into the new girl."

"Alright." He shrugs. "Don't say I didn't give you the chance."

I don't know what the fuck he means by that, but I

don't like it. I don't want her, but I don't want him kissing her either. I don't know what the fuck I even want, but now is not the time to worry about it.

There's a shit load of chatter amongst the boys as we cruise around getting warmed up. Everyone is pumped to be back here doing what we love.

I look across the field and see coach walking towards the equipment that Bry and I have brought out. There's a big, dark-haired guy at his side and it takes me less than five seconds to realise who it is.

Cole Davids.

I also know exactly what is about to happen here. Coach is going to tell us that Cole is our new assistant coach. I don't even need to hear it, I already fucking know.

On the one hand, I'm stoked – Cole Davids is a legend – he's literally the guy whose games and plays I watch on repeat to try and learn and get better. I've idolised him ever since I got a taste for rugby. But on the other hand – he's the fuckin' new girl's dad, and the last thing I want is a connection to her family. In fact, the last thing I want is a connection of any sort with her, and between the photography bullshit and now this, I'm seriously concerned.

Bryson elbows me and tips his head towards where Coach and Cole are standing, waiting for us.

"Yip, I see it," I reply warily.

Bryson was lucky enough to swerve the trip to Berlin's house in the early hours of Sunday morning, but he's heard all about it.

I actually think he was a bit gutted he wasn't more sober – I don't know if that's because he wanted to be the knight in shining armour for Sophia, or because he missed out on meeting a legend of the game – but regardless, he'll at least get to do the latter, by the looks of it.

We pull up in front of Coach, and he nods his head at me. I step forward.

"Cole Davids, this is Cullen Carrington, the captain and fullback."

I look at Cole, trying to gauge whether or not he's going to rat me out for being out on the piss at stupid o'clock with his daughter and her mates over the weekend.

Surprisingly, he doesn't, just takes my hand and shakes it firmly as though it's the first time we've met.

I can hear the boys humming with excitement behind me. For most of them, this is probably the most successful player they'll ever meet, let alone be coached by.

"And this is Bryson Decker, Cullen's vice-captain."

Cole shakes Bryson's hand too.

"Mr. Davids is going to take over the role of assistant coach for the season, boys, so let's show him the respect he deserves and a warm welcome."

This is big. It's definitely got the potential to be bad news for me personally, but for the team, it's the opportunity of a lifetime. We've never had the chance to work with someone of Cole's calibre.

"It's an honour, Sir. I think I speak for the team

when I say that we're grateful for the opportunity to have you."

"Call me Cole." He nods at me once before looking around at the rest of the guys. "It's a privilege to be here, boys. Feels like only a couple of years ago that I was standing where you all are, wearing that jersey."

The fact that he's been in the exact position I am right now – captain of the team and star fullback – sends tingles down my spine. If I could have half the rugby career he's had, I'd be a happy man when all was said and done.

He goes around shaking each and every player's hand, asking them what position they play and how old they are. Seems like he genuinely cares too.

I'm impressed.

"I can't fucking believe I get to call him by his first name." Pax bounces.

I chuckle. "We all do, bro, chill."

"Got no chill."

Truer words have never been spoken.

I have to admit, even I'm pumped. This has put me in a good mood, despite all the Liana and Berlin bull-shit. This could be exactly the push I need to take my game to the next level.

It further cements the fact that I'm done with Li effective immediately. I need to get my head in the game – no more distractions. This is it.

Cole wanders over to me, Pax, and Bry when he's done with the rounds and tips his head to the side, indicating for us to follow him.

"I don't think I thanked you two for looking after the girls over the weekend. I know Berlin can be a bit of a handful, but you seemed to have it under control, so thank you."

"It's nothing. She's a good friend to me – I've got her back," Pax tells him.

Cole nods his head at him, and then at me, before turning to Bry. "Sounds like you throw one hell of a party."

Bryson clears his throat, unsure of how to respond. "Ah, yes, Sir. One last blowout before the season starts," he reassures him.

"Oh, to be eighteen again, eh?" Cole smirks knowingly. "And seriously, call me Cole. 'Sir' makes me feel like I'm eighty."

He's definitely not eighty. In fact he still looks like he's in the prime of his life. His wife must be a total fox.

"Let's get this thing going, boys. Not going to make finals by gossiping and standing around," Coach yells out.

I smirk and toss the ball in my hands to Pax. "Let's go, boy."

I'M BUZZING FROM TRAINING, at least I am until I see the blonde waiting for me in the carpark.

"Fuck's sake," I mutter. "This saga never ends."

"Want me to get rid of her?" Pax offers.

I shake my head and offload my bag to him. "I gotta

cut this shit now. Take my bag? I'll run home after. Blow off some steam."

He nods his head and slings my bag over his free shoulder. Him and Bry walk off in the opposite direction, towards Bry's car.

Lucky bastards.

She watches them walk away but doesn't make a move to walk towards me. She just stays right where she is, leaning against the hood of her shiny white Jeep, waiting for me to come to her.

I can't be fucked with this shit a moment longer. I'm done. I'm done with the games, the bullshit, the drama. I'm done with *her.*

"What are you doing here, Li?" I ask as I reach her.

She rocks forwards onto her toes, as though she's going to hug me, but I stop too far away, not allowing any contact.

"I wanted to talk to you, and you've been avoiding me all day." She pouts at me, and at one point in time that look would have turned me on, but not anymore.

"I've been avoiding you because you're fucking insane."

"*Excuse me?* You disappear from the party with that bitch and all her friends and *I'm* the one who's insane?" She takes a step forward.

I exhale heavily. "You know what, Li? I don't care. I just don't fucking care about any of it."

She recoils like I've physically slapped her.

"Are you breaking up with me?" Her voice is a harsh whisper.

Jesus Christ.

"No, I'm not *breaking up* with you, because we were never together, Liana. Jesus Christ, grow up. We fucked for a while, we're not in a relationship."

"*Cullen.*"

"I don't want to see you anymore. Get that through your head."

She looks broken, and for a moment I almost feel sorry for her, but then she steels her spine, and this evil look comes into her eyes.

That's the Liana I know.

"You know what? I don't give a shit, Cullen. You're not even that good of a fuck. She can have you." She flips her hair over her shoulder, and I almost fucking laugh. She's a walking cliché. She spends more time watching stupid Hollywood chick flicks and scrolling Instagram than she does in the real world.

"Can you hear yourself? You're acting like a jealous bitch over some chick I'm not even interested in."

"Funny how you knew exactly who I was talking about without me having to say her name though, huh?"

I want to rip my hair out at this point. *Of course* I know who she's talking about, because ever since Berlin set foot in this fucking school, Liana hasn't *stopped* talking about her. She's lost the plot.

"I'm done, Li. And we can do this the easy way or the hard way. You want to go full public blow up – then bring it, otherwise, I'm good with just getting the fuck on with it and not making shit awkward for everyone."

She's seething. I'm surprised she hasn't lunged at me yet and tried to rip my throat out.

"Fuck you, Cullen."

I'm done here. I can't even tolerate any further conversation with this bitch. I'm out.

I don't know how I've tolerated her this long – she's got fuck all between the ears. If brains were dynamite, I doubt she'd even have enough to blow her own head up.

I walk away, in the direction of home. I've got a twenty-minute run ahead of me to clear my head.

"Fuck you!" she screams after me.

Ironically, that's something she'll never do again, but I don't even care enough to turn back and point that out to her. I just want to get the hell out of here. I need less crazy in my life, and I need it by yesterday.

I break into a run. I can hear her screaming after me, but I've got no fucking clue what crap she's spewing, and I don't give a shit.

I hope to God that by tomorrow she'll have cooled down and won't start World War three, but with a girl like Liana, it could go either way.

I've been running for about five minutes when Bry's car pulls up next to me, with a grinning Pax in the front seat.

"Get in loser, we're going shopping."

It kills me that I know the movie he's referencing, but after being forced to watch it about a hundred times, I pretty much know the whole thing off by heart.

"Why are you still here?"

"We wanted to watch the show... And make sure she didn't stab you or something."

"She wasn't happy," I tell him as I stop jogging and climb into the back seat.

"You should have heard her screaming down the phone after you took off. Think it legit burst my eardrums from across the car park. 'Wasn't happy' is an understatement."

"At least it's done."

Pax and Bry exchange a look that makes it pretty fucking clear they don't agree with my assessment of the situation, but I don't give a shit. I've said the words, what she does next is up to her, but either way, it's done. Dead and buried. Over.

I hear a message come in on my phone and I brace myself, expecting it to be a string of abuse from Li, but it's not. It's from Berlin, but I don't know which name I want to see on the screen of my phone less.

Berlin: Alright, golden boy, if you don't make a time for us to take these fucking photos, I'm going to sneak into your house at night and take pictures of you while you sleep.

I think she's joking, but I'm still not sure how crazy that bitch is, and I don't really want to find out. I'm elbows deep in crazy already, and it's starting to feel like wading through shit with lead boots on.

Cullen: Tomorrow, 5pm at the gym.
Berlin: Sir, yes, Sir.
I drop my phone to the seat and rub my temples.
Fucking chicks, man.

FIFTEEN

Berlin

"*B*, I let that booze fuelled night you and your friends had the other night go. You owe me," my dad tells me, attempting some type of authority figure voice.

"That is *not* the same thing."

"It's only rugby coaching, what does it matter?"

"It *matters* because it's social suicide."

He huffs out a laugh at me. "Doesn't count. I'm not a teacher and I'm not some dorky kind of parent. I'm hot shit. If anything, I'll probably boost your social standing."

"Oh, dear God," I say with a roll of my eyes, "it's such a mystery why you're still single, with an ego like that."

He full-on belly laughs. "No woman could handle this anyway."

I make a gagging sound.

Truthfully, I've often wondered if he would ever settle down and find someone to share his life with. Not that I'm not great company, because I *obviously* am, but I don't plan on sticking around home forever. The idea of him all alone in that big house makes me feel a little bit sad.

He's dated over the years, and we've always had a very open line of communication about the women in his life, because let's face it, it was always going to sound better coming from him than it would if I read some gossip column about which sports stars were sowing their wild oats. But still, none of them have ever really been a permanent fixture in our lives.

Maybe now that we're back here in the Hicksville town he grew up in, he'll have more luck at finding *the one.*

"That kid Pax sure seems to think a lot of you," he says absently as he drives me across town.

"Huh?" I ask, distracted by an incoming message from Sophia; something about our drug test results.

I quickly close my screen. The last thing I need is my dad getting wind of this potential drugging situation. He might be pretty relaxed as far as parents go, but I know for a fact that he'd burn the place to the ground if he found out about this.

"Pax, that's his name, right? The one who brought

you girls home the other night. He plays on the right wing."

"Yeah, Pax, he's a good buddy."

"Just a buddy?"

I nod my head. "Yes, old man, he's a friend. We have a couple of classes together and he's one of the few rugby meatheads that I can actually stand to be around for more than five seconds."

"Rugby meatheads like Cullen?"

I groan at the mention of his name. I may have paid the price with my hangover on Sunday morning, but I knew I wasn't going to get away with the fact that I'd had the captain of the rugby team not only escort me and my friend's home, but physically carry in Sophia – according to reports anyway – my memory is still a little fuzzy.

"Precisely." I nod.

"He doesn't seem so bad, you know. Reminds me of myself at his age. Filled to the brim with ambition and drive."

'Ambitious' and 'driven' aren't exactly the first two words that spring to mind when I think of Cullen, but hey, the old boy can have his opinion, he's entitled to it.

"Mmm hmm." I raise my brows at him. "What'd you think of Bryson?"

"Jury's still out," he replies quickly. "It's hard to make an assessment when you can barely get two words out of the kid."

He's not wrong there.

"Sophia's basically in love with him."

He chuckles. "Likes the quiet ones, does she? Pity you haven't got more similar tastes."

I flip him off, although he has a point; my last boyfriend turned out to be a bit of a nightmare.

We pull into the school carpark and as per, I'm less than thrilled to spend another day in this cesspit.

"You're leaving now, right?" I ask warily.

"Yes, my darling daughter, I *am* leaving. I'll be back for training after school."

I swing open the door and get one foot out before informing him that I have to meet up with my photography partner at five, to work on our project.

I slam the door before he gets a chance to ask me any questions I don't want to answer. He's going to have a field day when he finds out his star player is going to be the main subject of my photos. I can hear the smack talk already.

I sling my backpack over my shoulder, and I've barely made it five metres before I'm hijacked by Sophia and Carissa and dragged to a private spot under a tree.

"Did you get my message?" Sophia demands.

The girl needs to chill. She's breathing so heavily you'd think she just sprinted up six flights of stairs after smoking a pack of ciggys.

"Oh yeah, Dad was right there so I didn't read it properly though. What the fuck is going on?"

"Laura found this." Carissa shoves her phone under my nose and hits play on a video.

I watch the semi-grainy footage – someone's been

skimping on buying a decent phone – of us playing beer pong. I watch myself throw the ball. It sails through the air and directly into one of the boys' cups. Pax groans and throws his head back in dismay.

"Yeah, okay, so what?"

"Look in the background. Blue top," Sophia tells me, her tone urgent.

Carissa hits play again, and this time I ignore the game in the foreground and instead look for what they're seeing.

It takes a few seconds but then there she is. *Liana.* You can't really make her face out clearly, but it's pretty obviously her. Blonde hair, blue top.

She enters the frame, looks around for a few seconds and then her arm reaches out towards the bench. Towards a drink. *My drink.* She pulls her hand back just as quickly and then she's gone. Not one single person seems to have noticed what she just did.

The video ends.

"That *bitch.*"

"Your drug test showed Ketamine too, B. Everyone else was clear, so that must be what that stupid cow put in there, and we both drank it. It's too much of a coincidence not to be it."

"That motherfucking psycho put *horse tranquiliser* in my drink?"

They both nod.

"Oh, she's *dead.* She didn't just fuck with me, she fucked with you too. She could have killed you." I look at Sophia.

I knew something fucked up had gone on, but I never dreamed for a minute that Liana would be that much of a sociopath.

"She could have killed you too, imagine if you'd drunk that whole thing on your own." Sophia shudders.

"I think we need to go to the police," Carissa whispers. She looks rattled, and rightly so. This isn't just some harmless prank. This is some next level shit.

I vastly underestimated the lengths this bitch would go to, but that's okay, because she's underestimated me too. She wants to play – we can play.

I want to go and smack her head in, but I won't – the punishment has to fit the crime, and she's going down. A broken nose isn't enough.

"We will." I nod, a plan hatching. "Just not yet."

"Why the hell not?"

Her concern is totally valid, but when it comes down to it, it's not enough for her to get the blame. Kids around here are taking ket all the time, for 'fun', some shitty footage that shows a whole heap of nothing, isn't going to get us anywhere.

"Honestly, I don't think we've got enough evidence. They're not going to be able to lock her up over a video you can't even make her face out in, and some drug tests done by your sister. If we go to the police and it's not enough, then we've played our hand. I think we should wait. We'll make her think she's gotten away with it and then when she least expects it, we'll show her who's the fucking one to fear around here."

"*Berlin*," Sophia groans. "We should let the police handle this. This is serious, she *drugged* us."

"I know, I know, but she's getting desperate. She's going to lose control, and when she does, everyone is going to be there to see it. Just *trust* me. We lose nothing by waiting a little while. We're one step ahead now, and it's going to stay that way. I bet she'll brag about doing it at some point and then she'll have no way to get out of it. We just need to be patient."

"You're *insane*," she mutters, but she doesn't argue like I expected her to, which makes me think that maybe she'd like to see some revenge served first hand after all. That, or she's learnt there's little point in arguing with me when I've got my mind set on something.

"I think she's right," Carissa says.

Sophia glares at her.

"*Hey*, I want to see her go down too, but Berlin's right; it's not enough, and then she's gonna get away with it. If we wait, we still have the evidence we have now, but we might be able to get her to confess. I want her to go all the way down, not just get a scare."

Sophia sighs deeply.

I shoot Carissa a grateful look. I don't know if I'm doing the right thing or not, but I have to trust my gut, and it's telling me to pick my moment.

"Just keep your eyes open and let the drama unfold," I reply. "Should be easy around here, especially with a girl like her."

"You know, *everyone* is saying that Cullen broke up with her," Carissa says as she looks at me expectantly.

"Huh... Well, if that doesn't brew up a shit storm, I don't know what will."

"What do we do now then?" Sophia asks, her expression making it clear she's afraid of the answer I might give.

"Now, we wait."

***

CARISSA WAS right about the breakup situation. It's all I've heard about all day. If it's not girls in the bathroom plotting to seduce Cullen now that he's back on the market, it's dudes making crude jokes in class about how they'd 'tap that' if Liana would let them.

It's all very *daytime TV soap opera*. The people in this town seriously need to get a life if this is the most exciting thing they've had to talk about all year.

Liana wasn't even at school today.

It amuses me to think that she's probably at home, licking her wounds and crying into a tub of ice cream with a fluffy pillow on her bed or something equally as pathetic.

It made biology far less exciting though – I've come to rely on her death glares to spice class up a bit.

What a day.

And it's not even over yet.

"Goooooodluuuuuuck!" Sophia yells out the window of Carissa's car as they drop me off back at school. It's just before five, and I've got to meet the man of the hour to finally get something done on this project.

Me and the girls went for a milkshake to kill the time after school and then shot home so I could ditch the bullshit preppy uniform. They've been making suggestive comments all afternoon about me and Cullen hooking up.

They obviously don't know how to read a room, because that is *not* the vibe that either of us are working with here. We'll be lucky if we survive this shoot without killing each other.

I roll my eyes and wave them off before slipping inside the empty gym and shutting the door behind me.

I stroll around for a bit, looking at all the team photos and trophies in the cabinets and on the walls.

I can't hear anyone else around, and it's kind of eerie being in here alone, but I keep aimlessly strolling. I see Cullen, Pax, and Bryson in last year's team photos, the trophy raised above some guy's head. They're also in the year before that, and the year before that too. I'm about to see if I can figure out how long they've been playing for the first fifteen, when my eye catches on a huge portrait photograph on the wall to my right.

Actually, there's not just one, there's at least a dozen. They line the entire hallway that leads around to the boys' changing room.

They're incredible. Some of them are close-ups of player's faces, their skin sweaty and covered in smears of dirt; others are farther back, like the kicker lining up a ball on his tee. Every element of the game is covered as I explore further, and not only has the photographer captured the essence of the sport, but they've done it with immaculate attention to detail and an eye for angles that I have to work really hard to nail.

"New Girl."

His gruff voice behind me stops me in my tracks.

"Golden boy," I reply.

He doesn't speak again, so I turn to face him, exactly as he wants me to.

"Well, well, well, if it isn't the talk of the town himself," I drawl as my eyes make an involuntary sweep of his body.

He looks good; the guy rocks a black t-shirt and blue jeans like the god everyone around here makes him out to be.

"People in this school need to learn to keep their mouths shut."

"Finally, something we agree on."

"Why are you lurking around in the hallways?" he asks.

I glance over my shoulder at the photographs behind me. "I was looking at these. They're amazing."

He just nods his head slowly but doesn't comment on them.

I'd actually been looking to see if there was one of him here. His boys each have a shot up on the wall, but I hadn't seen his yet.

"Let's get on with it, I've got other shit to do tonight."

I roll my eyes.

Must be tough being so important.

"Are you sure queen bitch didn't break up with *you*? If that's all the tact you've got, I wouldn't exactly blame her."

He narrows his eyes at me but doesn't respond, just turns and walks away, leaving me with little option but to follow. So, I do.

I follow him out the front door, and he turns in the opposite direction to the fields, instead leading me out towards a grassy, wooded area with big, tall trees.

He pauses to speak to me over his shoulder. "There's a stream down there. Is that all good with you?"

I nod. "Lead the way."

I follow him to the stream, and I have to admit, I'm surprised how pretty it is down here. He doesn't strike me as the kind of guy who comes to picturesque spots like this. It makes me wonder how he found it.

We unpack our gear in silence and take a few test shots, making adjustments to our cameras to get the lighting right.

I crouch down and get a few shots of a small but particularly brave bird hopping around near us.

"Do you ever use film?" I ask him without glancing in his direction.

I secretly love film cameras. I still use an old black and white film camera whenever I can. I haven't got around to setting up my dark room at the new house yet; I need the old man to section off a corner of the garage for me, but I used it all the time back in Australia. Digital is far more practical, but there's just something about dipping a sheet of photo paper into developing chemicals and watching the image emerge before your eyes that I can't give up.

I've actually used my film camera to photograph Cullen; he just doesn't know about it.

"Not since the school shut down the dark room. I like the feel of film shots, they seem more authentic somehow, but I haven't got anywhere to process the film or develop the prints, so digital it is."

I stand up but avoid looking directly at him. It's probably the most he's ever spoken to me, so I don't want to spook him.

I couldn't really give a fuck if this super star jock likes me or not, but we've got some hours ahead of us with this project, and if we can manage to be civilised and have conversations without totally rinsing each other, then that'll probably make the whole experience a hell of a lot more manageable.

"Why'd they close the dark room?"

"Some shit about keeping up with the times."

"That sucks. I usually have a set up at home, I'm just waiting on my dad to whack up some plywood walls in the garage at the new place."

"Really?"

I look over at him, and he's staring at me, his camera casually held at his side in one large hand.

I nod. "Yeah, I still used a lot of film back in Australia, so Dad let me have the basement. The house here doesn't have a basement, so he's going to black out a corner for me to use."

"That's epic. Your dad seems like a good dude. The team is lucky to have him."

"He's the best."

This interaction is starting to make me feel uncomfortable. I'm used to being ignored or shrugging off his insults. I don't know what to do with whatever the hell this is.

"What's your mum like?" he asks.

I feel a lump forming in my throat. This isn't a conversation I ever thought I'd be having with him.

"Ummmm... no idea actually. She died when I was a baby."

I'm fiddling with the dials on my camera to avoid looking at him, but I can feel his eyes on me.

"My dad died before I was born."

My eyes flash to his face in shock. This isn't new information to me, but the fact that he's telling me has taken me by surprise. It's only just occurred to me now, hearing the two things side by side, that we both have one living parent, and one not.

"I guess we do have something in common after all," I say quietly, Pax's comment making its way into my head.

The silence stretches, but there's something there – thick in the air between us that wasn't there before.

He looks like he wants to say something, or do something, but he does neither.

"I think that's enough sharing for one day."

"Agreed," I say quickly. "So, how do you want to do this?"

He pauses for a minute, then steps forward, his cool composure back in place. "I'll shoot you first. Go over by that tree."

"*Please*," I prompt him, raising a brow.

"Please," he replies eventually. The way he says it makes it seem like he's enjoying it about as much as swallowing acid.

"Do you want me to do anything in particular, or...?"

"I'll put you where I want you."

The tone in his voice catches me off guard. I don't know what it is about those words and that husky delivery, but I feel them right down deep in my belly.

There's something about the way he said it that makes me think I might like him doing with me what he sees fit a little too much.

I mentally slap myself. I have got to get a grip before these outrageous teenage hormones of mine get out of control.

Sure, he's hot, but so is half the population.

I set down my camera and walk over to the tree he pointed out. I can feel him close behind me, and when I turn around, he's right there.

He doesn't speak, just presses my shoulders backwards until I'm leaning against the trunk.

"Arms up."

"Excuse me?"

"Put your arms above your head."

"Why?" I demand.

"Just do it."

I don't move, because of course I don't. I agreed to a truce, not to being his puppet.

He grabs both of my wrists and pins them together in one of his hands.

The breath rushes out of me as he steps so close there must be only mere millimetres separating us, and holds my hands up above my head, pinning me there against the tree.

"You need to learn to do what you're told."

His voice is husky, raspy, like being this close to me is affecting him the same way it's affecting me.

He should know better. I rarely do what I'm told, but I hate my traitorous body for wanting to lean into his touch instead of pulling away from it.

I feel my face heat as I realise that while I can't stand him, part of me *wants* him anyway.

Our eyes meet, and it's like I can see my own thoughts mirrored in his. His neck flexes, bringing his mouth just ever so slightly closer to mine.

Fuck. This is not good.

A tiny lift of my chin and our lips would meet. It's taking every ounce of my self-control not to make that move.

He's fighting the same war I am; his jaw is clenched – his body tense. I move a millimetre.

I make a mental note to tell Carissa that she was right, he *does* smell good.

"You're a complication I don't need, new girl," he growls.

My head is spinning. I don't know what the fuck to do. I can't think of anything to say, and I honestly can't recall a time this ever happened to me.

I'm out here ready to risk it all like some type of moron.

All of a sudden, he pulls away, and it's entirely too late and too soon at the same time.

I close my eyes for a minute, my breath heavy as I try to regroup. His camera is at his face before I can even speak and he's clicking away, taking photo after photo of me. I drop my hands and run them through my hair, trying to forget he's there.

Jesus Christ, what is wrong with me?

"Sit," he orders.

I don't sit. *Obviously.*

I raise a brow at him in challenge.

The shutter clicks.

"Berlin. *Sit down.*"

The sound of my name in his sexy voice has my stomach flipping.

I step in front of the root he's indicated for me to sit down on, but I make no move to lower myself onto it.

He drops the camera back to his side and stares at me hard.

I stare right back, an air of defiance surrounding me.

"Oh, fuck it," he growls before striding towards me.

I don't know what I'm expecting him to do, so when

he wraps his free arm around the small of my back and pulls my body against his, I gasp.

He swallows the sound of my surprise with his lips, crashing against mine. He kisses me, hard, fast, urgent.

I melt into him, my mouth complying without permission.

His fingers dig into my back, and I welcome the feeling of my body melded against his. I want him closer, tighter... he's everywhere.

My hands are gripping his biceps, and I have no idea how they even found their way there, but I'm not complaining.

He stills, his breathing ragged as we stand there, as close together as we could possibly be.

"Shit," he mutters.

Shit indeed.

He steps away roughly, giving me some much-needed space... and perspective.

I don't know what the fuck just happened, but I know one thing for sure; it's not going to result in anything good.

We're playing a game made for fools right now, and in a game like that, there are never any winners.

"Fuck!" he half shouts as he runs his hand roughly through his hair.

I don't say a thing, I just watch as he walks away from me, striding over branches and leaves, to his bag.

He picks up his shit and leaves me standing here without so much as a backwards glance.

SIXTEEN

Cullen

Two week later

"You've been a real cunt these past couple of weeks, you know that, eh? If you weren't my brother, I'd have punched you square in the face by now."

I don't know what the fuck us being brothers has to do with anything – it's never stopped us from getting into tussles before. We've thrown punches over the stupidest shit and then forgotten about it five minutes later.

I probably wouldn't even blame him for resorting to

violence at this point. Maybe a smack across the jaw is exactly what I need. Knock some sense into me.

Everything is all fucked up. My head's a mess.

It's been fifteen days since I kissed Berlin by the stream, and pretty much all I can think about doing is kissing her again.

That, paired with Liana acting chill since the 'break up' – has me way off kilter.

I'd been expecting a dumpster fire of a tantrum when Li finally returned to school, but instead I was greeted with a quiet 'hi' and a small smile in the hall-way, followed by chatter of her being away to visit her grandparents, rather than at home plotting ways to kill me and dispose of the body undetected.

This shit isn't right – I can smell a rat a mile away, but I'm too off my game to do anything about it.

The only time I get any clarity and peace is when I've got a rugby ball in my hands. Thank fuck this drama can't seem to touch me there.

I haven't spoken to Berlin since that day, not that she goes out of her way to talk to me anyway when I see her in PE and the halls, but I've been cutting photog-raphy class, just to be safe. I know I'm going to have to turn up soon – any more ditching and Coach is going to hear about it.

"Cull? Are you even fucking listening?" Pax punches my shoulder, pulling me from my thoughts.

"Nope," I admit.

"Just tell me what the fuck is going on. I know it's

got something to do with Ice. She's avoiding all things Cullen like the plague."

"It's got nothing to do with your little girlfriend. Chill."

"You're a shitty liar."

It irks me way more than it should that he doesn't deny she's his girlfriend.

Fuck's sake.

I'm a mess. I don't know what the fuck is wrong with me.

So, I kissed her... who gives a fuck? I've kissed plenty of girls and not moped around like a little bitch about it afterwards.

"Learn when to leave shit alone, Pax."

"Nah, fuck that," he snaps, sounding more pissed than I can ever remember hearing him. "I don't know why the fuck you're acting like a little bitch, but either cut that shit out or drop me a clue about what the hell is going on, because I'm not dealing with another night of this bullshit moody crap."

I want to tell him to fuck off again, but I know by his tone I've pushed him too far. For the first time in a long time, he's done with my shit, and honestly, so am I.

I'm way up shit creek without a paddle, and maybe Pax has one hidden somewhere I don't know about that I could use to get me out of this mess.

"I kissed Berlin."

The words hang in the air between us for a few beats. His face is unreadable – even to me.

"Okay," he finally says, jaw clenched.

Okay?

"That's it? Okay?"

"I don't know what you want me to say, bro."

He's fucked off with me; even more so now than before by the looks. I don't get it. He wanted to know what my problem was – I told him, and now he's even saltier.

"You're the one who had to know, so I thought you might actually have something to say," I reply, my tone filled with venom.

"I've got *plenty* to say." He glares at me.

"Then fucking say it," I snap, my own voice rising an octave.

He looks like he's about to explode.

"Did you ever consider that maybe, just fuckin' maybe... not *everything* is about *you?* There's a whole fucking world outside the Cullen show. Did it ever occur to you that maybe *I* like her?"

I'm too stunned to speak.

"I asked you, Cull, I asked you over and over if you were into her and you said *no,* every single *fucking* time," he continues.

I don't like this. Don't like one thing about it. I hate the idea that she's something to me, but the only thing worse than that, would be her being something to him.

"*Are* you into her?" I ask, not really wanting to hear the answer, but needing to know one way or the other.

He exhales heavily, his angry mask slipping a fraction.

"No. Maybe? I dunno. *Fuck.* I think she's cool as

hell, and she's one of the few girls around here I actually give a shit about, so I don't want to see her get screwed over by you or anyone else. I dunno how or what I feel for her, but the fact that it never even crossed your mind to ask me is a pretty clear message that you don't give a shit either way. *That's* the real fucking problem here."

Well fuck.

"I *knew* you liked her, Cull – it was clear as day from the first time she gave you that sassy attitude, but I asked you... you wouldn't fucking admit it, and she's *my* friend now, and I won't stand by while you treat her like she's some interchangeable bimbo like the rest of them."

My ego wants to go him, real fucking quick, but my brain is screaming at me that he's hit the nail on the head, and I'm a prize jerk for it.

I don't even know what to say, but it doesn't matter, because he's not done serving me the reality check I've had coming for days.

"What if I *did* have feelings for her? What if I still *do?* You know we're close, and it never occurred to you to ask, because all you care about is what the fuck is going on in *your* head. Same old Cullen Carrington shit. Always looking out for number one, and fuck everybody else, eh?"

He drops the set of dumbbells he's been using for curls and shoots me one last, disappointed look before stalking out of the gym, leaving me alone.

Fuck.

I throw my drink bottle against the wall. Hard.

I'm fucking raging.

And not at him – but at myself.

COACH HAS GOT the boys running warm-up drills like a well-oiled machine. This might only be a pre-season game today, it doesn't count for anything other than bragging rights, but the crowds have turned up in droves.

St. Marcus' is our biggest rival team – we beat them in the final last year, and the year before that – so no one wants to miss seeing the game that could start the grudge match of the year.

They got close to beating us once last season, and I don't want to see it happen on my watch.

I fucking love this game, but I have to admit that right now, half an hour before kick-off – I'm feeling the nerves. This is a championship team I'm leading here; I should be able to take us all the way to the top, but sometimes I wonder if I'm really made of the right shit.

It's like Pax said to me two days ago – I look out for number one – and that's not going to work for me anymore. I'm captain now – I have to figure out how to lead. I have to put fifteen guys first instead of just one.

Not talking to my brother isn't going to work for me either – we've barely exchanged two words since he gave me a tune up. I'm stubborn as hell, but for once, that wasn't the main factor. I needed time to think and get my head on straight, and try and make sense of all the shit swirling in there before I tried to explain it to him.

We've never gone into a game on bad terms, and I don't plan on starting today. I've got to fix it before the starting whistle.

I hand the ball off to Eli and jog over to where Pax and Tonksy are running a few shuttles.

"Pax, I need you for a minute."

He gives me a look but follows me as I walk out of earshot from the rest of the team.

He's been by my side, literally my entire life, but when I turn to face him, I feel nervous as hell. He's my best mate – my brother – and I can't have anything coming between us.

I've just got to lay it on the table and hope he'll understand. Even though I'm not entirely sure I even understand it myself yet.

"I'm sorry, man. You were right. About all of it. I was out of line. I should have talked to you about her."

He nods, his eyes trailing over the ground at my feet.

"And it might drive me insane, but she's your friend, or *whatever*, and if you want me to, I'll stay the hell away from her. I should have asked you first. I should have shown you the same respect you've always shown me."

His gaze flashes to mine and he's quiet for a few seconds, mulling over his reply.

"I'm your brother. Just talk to me, that's all you need to do."

"I know."

He nods, satisfied.

"I fucked up," I tell him.

He nods again.

"Just tell me what you want me to do about her."

"She's the one you really fucked up with, bro," he tells me. "My opinion might not mean fuck all if you've been a piece of shit."

I rub at the back of my neck, unsure how to respond. I still don't even know what to make of that situation. "I... I don't –"

He cuts me off, chuckling. "I know."

"You know *what*?"

He shakes his head, his easy-going, joking nature already restored. "No way, man, you're going to have to figure that out for yourself. I can't solve your girl problems for you."

"*What?*" I reply, dumbfounded.

He laughs again. "Berlin. You're still not getting it."

I don't know why he's finding this so funny, but I am surprised by his laid-back attitude. Last time the two of us talked about the new girl, he all but ripped my head off.

"You wouldn't care if I did... *get it?*"

He smirks, then his expression shifts into something more serious. "It was never about her. Not really. It was about you being an inconsiderate asshole. And if you two have something, then you have something. But

I'm warning you – we have something too, and I dunno exactly what that means, but it is what it is."

I nod as though his warning doesn't confuse the fuck out of me.

I don't know what to say to that.

"Are we good?"

He nods. "Fuck yeah, as long as you've pulled your head out from up your ass, we're good."

"Can we talk about girl bullshit later? We've got a fucking game to win."

He grins, wide and easy, a sparkle in his eye. "Fuck yeah, cap, let's kill these stuck-up pricks."

He holds his knuckles out to me and I give him a fist pump.

He chuckles and claps me on the shoulder.

A classic male apology if I've ever seen one.

Now I can get my head where it needs to be – on the game, and leading the boys to victory.

"You're going to smash it, Cull. I know that too."

I nod, my nerves getting to work. He can tell I'm feeling the pressure. He knows me as well as I know myself.

We walk back towards the rest of the team, and I can't help it – my eyes search the stands, looking for her.

It'll be fucking impossible to find her in the mass of people even if she is here, but that doesn't stop me from trying anyway.

"She'll be here, bro, chill."

He's smirking at me in that 'know it all' way he's got so well locked down.

I don't even bother trying to argue, I just flip him off, shove his shoulder and round up the boys.

It's game time.

SEVENTEEN

Berlin

"I can't *believe* you made me come here." I pout.

Soph rolls her eyes at me – her sass game has really lifted in the past couple of weeks. I like to think she's been learning from the best.

"Oh, yeah, it was a *real* challenge to twist your arm."

Carissa laughs.

It's just the three of us. Laura has a babysitting gig on, and Mel got herself grounded for something trivial. Her mum sounds like a real pain in the ass.

"I'm here to support my dad," I say pointedly.

They both give me a look that says they don't believe a word I'm saying, but it's whatever.

I know they think I'm here for Cullen, and they're

not entirely wrong. Part of me can't wait to see what he can do out there. Apparently, he's got something special, and I like to think that I've seen enough rugby in my time to be able to judge whether or not the talk is true.

I've spent the past however many days, intentionally *not* looking at him, and I'm d-low buzzing at the chance to do the exact opposite.

I *hate* that I'm buzzing.

I hate that I'm *anything*.

I also kinda hate that I've let myself become so transparent to my friends. It's been a while since anyone other than my dad knew me well enough to make correct assumptions.

I haven't even told the girls about him kissing me yet. They'd lose their shit big time if I spilled that secret, and they're already up my ass about it enough.

Not that a guy kissing you, bailing immediately after and then avoiding you for two weeks is anything to get excited about anyway.

Stupid fucking male.

We decide on a spot in the stand and start weaving through the crowds to get there. It seems like the whole school has turned out for this game, along with a shit load of St. Marcus' students and families too.

We go around a group of parents and come face to face with the last people I want to see.

The cheerleaders. They're not on duty tonight – no chanting skanks required for pre-season games apparently.

Liana isn't with them, thankfully, but still, these girls are a pain in my ass, even without queen bitch to show them the ropes.

"Ew," Carissa whispers when she sees them.

"Shhh," Sophia hisses at her.

I can't help but laugh. If she thinks she's still off these girls' radar at this point, then she's seriously delusional. That ship well and truly sailed when they all watched Cullen carry her wasted ass out of Bryson's party, or when she got kissed by Bryson himself after the game of beer pong.

"Well, well, well, if it isn't the trailer trash, come to stink the place up," Becky drawls as we reach them.

The girl has been watching too many chick flicks; her insult game needs some serious work.

"*Rebecca*," I purr, knowing full well – thanks to Pax – that she hates being called by her full name.

I come to a stop in front of her, Sophia flanking me on one side, Carissa on the other.

Becky hands off a sharpie to one of her minions, and I can't help but notice the number nine she's drawn on her hand.

Oh, she didn't.

This is *too* good.

"Did you seriously just write one of the guys' jersey numbers on your hand?" I can barely contain my laughter.

Her face flames bright red. "Piss off, Berlin, just because you don't have a boyfriend on the team."

"Jesus, you're *such* a girl, you even put a little love

heart. There's no way your parents are proud of you." I bite back my laughter. "And newsflash, crazy, you don't have a boyfriend on the team either."

I really don't know if that's true one way or the other but given that Pax went on and *on* about how she'd slept her way through half of the team last year, I'm fully prepared to go out on a limb and say that none of them would be willing to give her an official girlfriend title.

"You're such a bitch." She sneers – clearly unable to come up with anything more original.

I laugh, right in her face as I walk around her. "Have a little dignity, for the love of God. It's embarrassing."

We brush past her and her army of slappers, getting death glares as we go.

I'm still amused when we make it to our spot and sit, Sophia in the middle.

Carissa is grinning like some kind of crazy person – she always loves seeing a bitchy girl get put in her place, and lucky for her, I'm only too happy to oblige. But Soph looks like she's seen a ghost. She's all pale and her eyes are glassy.

"What happened?" I ask her.

She shakes her head but doesn't answer me.

I look at Carissa and she shrugs.

"Soph?" I demand.

"The number on her hand," she mumbles.

"Yeah?" I reply, confused. I didn't know we were

getting offended by numbers these days, but apparently, I'm mistaken.

"That's Bryson's number," she explains.

Oh, bless her sweet little heart. She's jealous. She's so jealous she's about to lose her shit.

I want to laugh, but I'm sensing she's on the verge of tears – I'm such an empath – so I hold it in.

"*Trust me*, Soph, you don't need to worry about some stupid girl writing a number on her hand."

"But that's *his* number. Why would she write his number on her hand if she's not his girlfriend?"

"Because she's a psychopathic bitch?" Carissa offers.

"What she said." I nod in agreement. "The girl is a pain in the ass, and she probably thinks doing something *that* lame will get her on his radar."

"You guys are just trying to make me feel better."

"Oh, yeah, because other people's feelings are always my main focus before I speak," I tease.

She gives me a small smile, but she looks so sad. Like someone just kicked her puppy.

"Seriously, don't even give it another thought. A blind man could see how into you he was at his party."

"So interested that he hasn't spoken to me since?" she replies, brow raised.

The girl makes a good point.

I shrug. "I never said he was smart."

She sighs heavily, and I have to admit, I can sympathise.

I don't know what it is with these stupid rugby

meatheads and their pashing and dashing, but it is not *it*.

I can handle the cold shoulder, but Sophia here is too precious for that shit.

"Fuck them anyway, maybe we should cheer for the opposition."

They both look at me like I've just sworn at a nun.

I hold up my hands in surrender. "I was kidding, *Jesus*. But I'm not cheering for anyone other than Pax. The rest of them are dead to me."

I'm completely full of shit. I get so caught up in the game – in the atmosphere – that I'm bound to be yelling and cheering for every one of them in no time, but it makes me feel better if I can at least pretend I don't care, for a little while.

I watch the boys running drills while Carissa and Sophia go on about some project they're working on.

I'm watching Cullen catch high balls that one of the other guys is kicking for him. He runs to catch the ball, and then kicks it back down field. He's quick, good with his hands, and has one hell of a left boot on him.

I'd rather I didn't want to watch him, but I can't look away.

A shrill whistle blows, and the team stops what they're doing and jog over to the coach and my dad.

I still can't believe he's helping out with the team. Word has got out big time. I've had dudes I don't even know high-fiving me in the hallways, and now that the games are starting, it's bound to spread like wildfire. If the looks and comments the group that are unmistakably the single mums are giving him, he's going to be *very* popular with a range of people within the school community.

Love that for me.

He yells something to the team, and they all jog over to the side of the field and start stripping off their jackets.

Cullen grabs a ball off the ground and walks towards the sideline, the other guys filing in to line up behind him.

He's about to lead the team onto the field for kick off. He looks good. *Damn* he looks good.

They all run out into the centre, the crowd going crazy around us as the 'Black Diamonds' are welcomed like the royalty they think they are.

"Here we go," I breathe.

"ICE! YOU CAME!" I hear Pax's voice over the excited chatter surrounding me.

I look around, but he's scooped me up into his arms and swung me around before I can barely lay eyes on him.

I laugh and shove at his shoulders until he puts me down on the ground in front of him.

"You threatened my life if I missed your game," I remind him.

He chuckles, totally unashamed. "I had to get you here somehow."

He grins at Sophia and Carissa over my shoulder. "Car, you're looking *good*, girl."

"*Don't*," I warn him with my finger pointed as I step away from his ridiculous-sized body.

Carissa gives him a filthy look.

I still can't tell what she really thinks of him – or him of her, for that matter. What little relationship they do have, seems to be pretty love-hate. Like a couple of little kids.

He laughs and turns his attention to Sophia. "And how about you, blondie? No puke tonight?"

Sophia glares at him. "You've made that joke for weeks now and I haven't puked again once."

He chuckles and tries to tousle her hair like she's his baby sister. "No one ever remembers all the times that you didn't, but they *always* remember the one time you did."

She flips him off and honestly, I'm a little proud. She's still a fair way off having the good old Davids' backbone, but she's one step closer at least. Progress is progress.

He's still wearing the classic Pax huge grin. He's clearly buzzed from their win, and rightly so. I didn't even want to like this game, but I was impressed. They were down heading into the last few minutes when Bryson sent a killer pass back to Cullen, who made an epic run down field, Pax hot on his heels. Cullen lured in two defenders and offloaded to Pax at the last second. Try time. It was the play of the game.

"Congrats on the win, Paxikins."

He beams as though the praise has made his year.

The boys are all still in their playing kit, hanging around to talk to their supporters before heading back into the changing rooms.

"Why thank you, ice queen. Were you impressed?" He waggles his brows at me.

He's such a fucking flirt. The guy oozes charm.

"I wasn't disappointed, let's just leave it at that," I say with an amused shake of my head at his obvious digging.

I can see Sophia out the corner of my eye. She's trying to watch Bryson without looking like she's watching Bryson.

She's also failing miserably. Poor bitch.

"What's the deal with your boy ignoring my cousin?" I ask Pax, deciding to cut the crap and get straight to the point.

Sophia gasps and whacks my arm.

More outrage. Put it on my tab.

To be fair, I wouldn't exactly say he's ignoring her; he's watching her, *always*, like right now as she turns bright red and becomes suddenly very interested in her shoes. He's watching her, and completely ignoring everyone trying to talk to him – the tramp with his number on her hand included.

Knew it. Called it. Never had any doubt.

"*What?*" I roll my eyes at her. "You're not fooling anyone anymore, and its only Pax. He's not going to squeal. He knows not to cross me."

Pax gives me a challenging look but doesn't disagree.

"Even your mum thinks you should make a move," I tell Soph with a roll of my eyes.

Me, her, and Aunt Alyssa had a massive girl talk after school the other day, and I filled her in about Soph's crush. Sophia was mortified. Aunt Alyssa was thrilled.

"Don't know what his problem is, blondie, I'd do you in a heartbeat." He winks at her.

"Oh, go play in traffic, you creep," I tell him as I shove his chest.

He chuckles loudly as he backs away.

I catch sight of Cullen out the corner of my eye, and I can't help but turn my head to get a better look – the guy is one tall drink of water.

He's looking between me and Pax, and I don't know what to make of his expression.

I look away quickly. I don't care what I'm meant to make of it.

Nothing like lying to yourself.

Pax is talking to some of the boys now, but he smirks knowingly at me – he didn't miss the interaction, unfortunately for me. He seems all too aware of my inner turmoil.

I scowl at him as he goes back to his conversation.

We're surrounded by people and chatter, but it's impossible to miss the brunette chick making for Pax like a shark that's smelled blood in the water.

I know who she is – her name's Lucy and, unfortunately for me, I overhead a conversation she was having with her friend in the bathroom about a week ago. Apparently, she *really* likes giving head, and sharpened her skill set by sucking off half the soccer team all in one night.

That girl's jaw must have taken an absolute hammering.

Overall, it was a pretty grim conversation to overhear, but I did pick up a couple of tips thanks to her thorough research, so it wasn't all bad for me.

I was right about her target. She sidles up to Pax, her tacky fake nails skimming across his chest.

I can't hear what she's saying to him, but I'd be willing to bet my last dollar that it's got something to do with his dick and her lips.

She may as well be on her knees with her mouth open right now, that's about as subtle as she's being with the moves she's making.

She pushes up onto her tippy toes and whispers something in his ear. A sly grin crosses his face.

Nope.

I'm absolutely not having it.

His standards are about to be lifted, whether he likes it or not.

I cross the small space between us and tap her on the shoulder. She's still whispering into his ear, and I shit you not, I can almost smell the aroma of skank in the air.

"Uh-uh, hoe bag, *not happening*, go find some other jock to fall all over, this one's off limits."

She gapes at me in shock, her eyes wide.

"Ice, what the fuck?" Pax demands, but I can tell he's at least mildly amused by my outburst.

I ignore him, pry her off his limbs and give her a gentle push away from us. "Off you go."

She stumbles slightly, her jaw slack. Could be from shock, could be from all the dick she's had in that zone. It's anyone's guess.

"What just happened?" he asks, a bewildered, yet amused, look on his face.

"You'll thank me when the soccer team all have the clap and you don't, Pax, trust me. That girl is a ginormous slut."

I glance over at her and she's staring, eyes wide as hell. "Run along now, hon, give that jaw a stretch somewhere else."

She scampers off, probably to go tell her friends on me.

Pax pisses himself laughing, confirming that I'd been right on the money with my guess of her promises.

"You're something else, Ice."

"No shit. I would say sorry about cockblocking you, but truly, do better. You'll catch an STD or something."

"I have heard they're going around."

"That's what happens when you bury yourself inside anything with a pulse. Seriously, up your game."

He chuckles. "Meh... what do I care? She's only the standard anyway."

I raise a brow in question, unsure whether or not I

really want to hear the answer. "What does that even mean?" I ask warily.

He shrugs. "You know… she's like the yard stick. A solid five. Anyone better-looking is considered doable, anyone less attractive is… *not*."

"That's disgusting."

He looks totally unashamed. "Yeah, maybe, doesn't make it any less true though."

"Go get changed, you stink." I wave him away with my hand.

"You sound like my mum."

"Whatever gets you in the shower, big guy."

He smirks at me and heads off towards the changing rooms with all the other guys to do as he's told.

Bryson tries to slip past me, but I grab his arm, halting him.

Sophia is going to kill me if she sees me doing this, but I don't care – it's about time Bryson Decker made a real move and stopped tip-toeing around in the background like some type of pussy.

He freezes and looks at me in surprise. The two of us have never really exchanged words. In fact, at this point, I'm not sure I even believe that the guy can speak.

"I'm just letting you know, that if you don't do something about it soon, someone else will. She's not going to be there, single and waiting for you, forever."

His eyes dart to Sophia and then back to me. He looks like he has no idea what to say, and in true

Bryson fashion, he doesn't speak, just nods his head once.

I figure that's probably all I'm going to get out of him, so I nod once in return and release his arm.

The exchange lasted all of about three seconds, but I still wouldn't be surprised if Sophia noticed. She's got that Bryson radar pretty finely tuned.

I wander back over to the girls, being careful not to look in the direction I last saw Cullen.

"What was that all about?" Carissa asks me.

"Huh?" I ask, feigning innocence as her and Sophia stare at me hard.

"You throwing that girl off Pax? Do you like him or something?" Sophia asks.

Oh yeah *that*. Maybe I got away with the Bryson chat after all.

"No," I snap.

They both look at me, confused.

"Well, *yeah*, of course I like him... but not like that. He needs me to protect him, he's clueless."

I can tell they don't believe a word I just said, and I'm about to work on strengthening my argument when I notice both their eyes widen at something behind my head.

What fucking now?

I spin around to see what the big surprise is and come face to face with Cullen's chest.

I take a deep breath, then look up at him, with what I hope is a bored expression on my face.

"Twilight," I quip.

"New girl," he replies, his voice deep and gruff.

I sit my hands on my hips, trying my best to use my attitude to disguise my racing heart. "Can I do something for you?"

"Meet me in the car park in thirty minutes."

It's not a question. It's not a request. It's an order.

"Excuse me?" I demand.

His jaw clenches, his teeth grinding. "I didn't stutter."

I open my mouth to argue, but he steps closer, so close we're physically touching, my chest against his.

He leans his face close to mine and my eyes flutter closed of their own accord. "Do what you're told, new girl," he whispers at my ear.

He moves away, and by the time I remember how to open my eyes, he's gone.

"I don't know if I'm turned on or scared," Carissa murmurs.

Yeah. That makes two of us.

EIGHTEEN

Cullen

The game's over. I led my team to victory. I played like a champ.

I'm literally on top of the world right now, but honest to God, the only thing I care about as I rush through showering and changing, is that *she* better be waiting for me in the carpark.

I don't even know what I'm going to do or say when I get to her, but I know one thing; I can't go much longer without doing *something*.

I've been fighting every urge day in and day out, but after that game and talking to Pax, I've got no fight left in me. I'm ready to give in to whatever this is.

I throw my bag over my shoulder and meet Pax's eyes as I go to turn.

He grins at me. "Can I come watch?"

I don't know what I was expecting him to say, but it wasn't that.

He knows me as well as he knows himself – he knows I'm going to meet up with her. If she's finally learned how to listen, that is.

"Absolutely fucking not."

"Oh, c'mon, bro, sharing is caring." He waggles his brows at me.

"I don't share."

"Yeah, I know, learnt that the hard way with toys as a kid."

I huff out a laugh, and he grins wildly.

"We good?" I ask, more sincere.

He nods. His expression is relaxed, but there's a hardness in his eyes. "We're good. Just don't fuck her around."

I don't know what to say to that. I don't know what to make of any of it, but thirty minutes is up, and I've got places to be.

Bryson tosses me his car keys. "Scratch it and you're dead."

I look at the keys I've just caught, and then to him, in confusion.

"What else are you gonna do? Ride the bus?" he questions me.

It would seem that once again, Bryson is entirely aware of everything that's going on around him.

"Thanks, B. You're the man."

"Does this mean *we* have to ride the bus? Pax whines at him.

I escape the changing rooms before anything more can be said, last thing I need is the team getting wind of me and the new assistant coach's daughter. In fact, the last thing I need is *anyone* getting wind of *anything*.

I push open the doors and the cool evening air hits me across the face.

There are parents, players, and students loitering around, waiting for everyone to come out of the changing rooms and call it a night.

I scan the car park, the darkness making it hard to see. I don't see her, but I look again, still hopeful.

I know she can't stay away either. There's this *energy* between us and it has to explode one way or another.

I'm getting more and more irritated with every second that passes where I don't have eyes on her.

She's not fucking here.

I step forward, still looking, and still coming up empty.

Fuck.

I hear talking behind me and I already know it's going to be my boys. And I know that Pax is going to give me so much shit if I've been stood up.

"What's going on, Romeo? Juliet got a mind of her own?" Pax taunts me.

I turn to glare at him.

Even Bryson looks like he finds this entertaining.

I'm raging on the inside, but I won't let them see it.

"It would appear so."

"You know, I heard them talk about going to the diner after the game," Pax says, nonchalant as hell.

I nod, my mind already made up. "Get in the car."

Pax bounces up and down like a little kid. "Fuck yes."

I stride towards Bry's car, throw my bag in the boot and climb into the driver's seat. I barely wait for the boys to have their doors shut before I'm tearing out of the car park.

Fucking new girl.

Every God damn thing with this girl has to be a battle, and what I hate the most about it is that it only makes me want her more.

"This feels kinda stalky," Bryson says after we've driven in silence for five minutes.

"Don't care."

"Maybe she doesn't like you, bro," Pax says from the back seat. I can hear the fucking taunting in his voice.

"Bullshit."

"That's some serious ego, man. Maybe you should consider the possibility."

I know he's just trying to wind me up, and it's working.

I clench my jaw and refrain from replying.

Prick.

I have to say though, even though he's driving me

insane, I'd take that over his silence any day of the fucking week.

We pull into the diner, and I see Carissa's car in the parking lot.

Bingo.

I'm out of the car and stalking towards the door of the diner before the engine's even stopped.

I don't care if Pax and Bryson are coming in here or not, I'm a man on a mission. I'm not waiting for anyone.

I snap my head back and forth until I spot the three of them sitting at a table down the back. Berlin has her back to me, Carissa and Sophia are facing me, and there's no doubt that they see me coming.

I cross the space in a mere few strides.

I hear Sophia breathe the words "oh shit" just before I reach them.

"You stood me up." I bark the words. My voice is gruff, and I don't bother trying to hide how unimpressed I am.

Berlin freezes for a fraction of a second before slowly turning to face me, her eyes caressing me from head to toe before finally settling on my face.

"Well, hello, golden boy. Imagine seeing you here."

"I imagined seeing you somewhere else."

She gives me a put-on pout. "That's too bad for you, right?"

She drives me insane, I crave this shit from her now. I *need* it. My heart is racing like a fucking junky.

"You can't ever do what you're told, can you?"

She pops a shoulder and stands up, turning that

ridiculously fucking hot body of hers to face me. "Bold of you to assume you're allowed to give me orders."

She rests her hand on the back of the chair next to her and leans into it. The picture of casual calm.

Meanwhile, I'm on the verge of turning into a fire-breathing dragon.

"You ran away from me," I accuse.

"I didn't run away. I had plans with my friends." She gestures behind her. "And you didn't use your manners."

"Fuck the manners."

The corner of her mouth twitches up, like she wants to smile, but she's refusing to let herself give in to it.

She stands tall, her arms crossing at her chest. "Did you want something, Cullen?"

Those sexy lips caress my name in a way I know damn well is intentional. It does fucked up shit to my brain.

"Yeah," I growl as I step forward, cupping the back of her neck in the same moment. "You're damn fucking right I did."

I slam my lips against hers, not caring where we are or who the fuck might see.

I can't even think straight with her smell swirling around me, her sassy words floating in my head, and my dick rock-hard in my jeans.

Consequences be damned, I have to taste her again.

She gasps, just like she did the first time I kissed her, but her surprise is short-lived before she's kissing me back, our mouths duelling for control, because even now, she can't give it to me. She has to fight back.

She sinks into me, and I wrap my other arm around her middle, tugging her even closer.

I don't know when her hands weaved into my hair, but they're there now, tugging at the strands.

The moment is interrupted by loud cheering and a blast of a wolf whistle. I guess the boys decided to follow me in after all.

This is why I don't do all that PDA shit, but this time it's different – *she's* different. She's breaking all my rules.

We break apart, breathing heavy, our hold on one another not loosening.

"Get a fucking room, mate." Pax's voice comes from behind me.

Berlin peaks up at me, her cheeks flushed and eyes wide.

She's so fucking irresistible.

"Seriously, it's embarrassing." Pax speaks again, but this time it sounds like he's talking around a mouthful.

Berlin looks first, her fingers unknotting from my hair as she does.

I look down at the table and sure enough, Pax has made himself at home, sitting next to Carissa, stuffing his face with fries, his usual laid-back smile plastered across his face.

"Oi, fuck off, those are mine," Berlin tells him as she moves to pull away from me.

I tighten my grip. She looks up at me again and I

smirk, loving the way I can feel her heart rate accelerate from my touch.

I let her go and she wobbles, just a tiny bit, before reaching across the table, taking her now half-eaten food back from Pax, and then sitting down in her chair. Pax scowls at her and tries to snag Carissa's milkshake.

I take that as my cue to sit down next to Berlin.

"There's six chairs, bro," I say, my comment directed at Bryson, who I'm sure is lingering behind me. "Better sit the fuck down."

He steps into view and pulls out the only remaining chair, in-between me and Sophia.

He's watching the blonde like he's never seen anything like her.

Carissa, Pax, and Sophia are all staring at me and Berlin.

"What?" I demand.

Sophia blushes and averts her gaze.

I smirk. I'm going to have some fun messing with that little thing.

"Oh, so you're just a thing now then?" Carissa asks, her finger pointing back and forth between Berlin and me.

I don't answer.

"No," Berlin replies.

I raise a brow and turn to look at her. I don't know what the fuck is going on here, but her denying there's something winds me the fuck up.

"What?" She frowns, reading my expression far

more easily than I'd like. "You think you can kiss me once and then I'm yours?"

"Twice," I correct her.

"Oh, well *excuuuuse* me," she sasses me, "I stand corrected. And does this one come with a complimentary two weeks of ghosting too?"

Pax laughs loudly, then steals some of Sophia's food. She slaps his hand. I'm kind of impressed.

"Yeah, Cull, are you going to shit the bed again or what?"

I flip him off but don't say a word.

"And now he goes mute too. What *is* it with you boys?" Carissa asks, looking like she's completely done with us and our shit.

I don't know what to say. I don't know what the fuck is going on. This isn't like me. I'm always in control. I don't make my shit public. I don't do any of this.

I *need* to take the power back before things really turn sideways.

I angle myself in my seat so I'm facing Berlin. I indicate with my finger that I want her to lean in closer, and for once in her fucking life, she actually does what she's told.

"I could make you mine right now if I wanted to," I whisper harshly into her ear.

She laughs. Fucking laughs at me.

This bitch.

"Did you just laugh at me?"

Her smile falters, but only for a second.

She lifts a shoulder.

I bring my lips to her ear. "You're going to regret that, new girl." I graze the lobe of her ear with my teeth, and she shudders.

I smirk to myself as I stand up and walk away.

Berlin Davids has no idea who she's playing with.

NINETEEN

Berlin

"You're so screwed." Carissa laughs as we watch Cullen stride away from the table, never once looking back.

"I respectfully disagree."

"She's right, Ice, you're fucked," Pax says around a mouthful of food that isn't his.

"I *less* respectfully disagree with *you*," I tell him before I snatch back the plate of food I now realise is mine. *Again*.

"Sharing is caring," he grumbles.

"All you're sharing with me is a headache."

He grins at me.

"Don't you need to go after your buddy?" I ask,

trying my best to sound casual about the fact that Cullen has just totally messed with my head.

Pax looks unfazed, but Bryson seems a little more concerned.

I hear an engine revving from the car park and then I understand why. The golden boy is behind the wheel of Bryson's boujee-as-fuck car. I'd be nervous about that too if I were him.

"We're outta here," Bryson states as he stands, his eyes never leaving Soph.

She's looking up at him like a deer in headlights. Poor stunned bitch. I can appreciate that's probably a bit rich coming from me right now, but I'm pretty sure I held my own at least a little more than she is.

"Sophia." He says her name, and it's both commanding and soft at the same time.

I don't know how the dude does it – gets away with saying so little, but it comes out sounding like so much.

"Bryson," she replies, and fuck me, I want to give her a high-five. She might look like a stunned mullet, but her voice did not shake. At all.

Yes girl.

Pax looks like this entire encounter has made his day. He gets out of his seat, the chair making a loud clatter as it moves. He kisses the top of Carissa's head. "Later, babe."

She looks at him, a mixture of shock and distaste.

"I felt like they were leaving us out," he says by way of explanation. "Don't worry, babe, you'll come around to the idea," he tells her as he rounds the table, following Bryson. He stops and kisses my cheek – something he's been doing for about a fortnight now and I've stopped arguing about.

"Keep your brother on a tighter leash next time," I call after him.

"I think he'd like it better if you were the one holding the reins, Ice," he calls back.

I huff out a laugh. Not bad.

And then they're gone. *Finally*. And I can actually breathe again properly.

Fuck, those three are like some type of chaotic whirlwind.

"So, where do we start with unpacking all *that?*" I ask after a few moments of silence.

I know where I need to start – with Cullen fucking Carrington, before my head explodes.

"Cullen," they both say in unison.

Thank God.

I've got a million thoughts going through my head, and they're about to start hearing them.

"I don't know what the hell is going on. He ignores me for *weeks* and then shows up here with nothing other than the fucking *audacity?*" I blurt out, done playing it cool.

Carissa sniggers.

"Well, he also brought that body with him," Sophia adds, swooning.

She's not wrong. It is one *hell* of a body, but it's not going to get him off the hook, not this time.

"He just kissed me, in front of *all* these people," I state.

"Oh, honey, we saw," Carissa reminds me.

"What are you going to do?" Soph asks me.

"I don't even know," I mutter.

I have got less than zero idea what to do here.

"I still think Pax has a thing for you too, just to complicate the situation further."

I groan. Maybe she's right. I honestly don't know what to think anymore.

"Is there a possibility that there *is* something more there with Pax?" Carissa questions.

I rub my temples. "Every nerve ending in my *entire* body wants Cullen." It feels weird to finally admit that out loud, but that's what we're dealing with here. "But I'm drawn to Pax in a way I can't explain. He's like my best friend, and I don't want anything to change that."

"What if he told you that you had to choose?"

"I honestly don't know. I'd advise him not to back me into that particular corner. I love Pax, I really do, and in another life... *maybe*... but in this life, there's Cullen. I'm a hormone-fuelled teenager and *he's* here, and hell... I *want* him."

They're both looking at me like they can sympathise.

"What about Bryson?" Sophia asks me warily.

I roll my eyes. "Don't worry, I'm not after your man. Two rugby meatheads are enough to be running circles around my life. Plus, the guy barely speaks. He's cute, but I honestly don't get the obsession."

"I know." She sighs, seemingly satisfied that I'm not after her crush.

She's crazy. I've got enough on my plate.

There's part of me that can't help but think this is nothing but a giant 'fuck you' on Cullen's behalf.

He's had it in for me from the moment we met – I'm sure he'd love nothing more than to see me go down in flames... but then he just kissed me in front of a restaurant full of people. Nothing about this makes sense anymore.

I'd just finished admitting to the girls about the kiss we shared at the stream when he turned up here, guns firing on all cylinders, and they got a live showing of the topic at hand.

I didn't for a second think he'd hunt me down like that after I pulled a no-show in the carpark. Apparently, I had no idea of the lengths he'd be willing to go to, to get his way.

"Liana is going to lose her shit when she hears about this," Sophia mutters.

"Urgh." Carissa scowls.

I don't give two fucks about Liana, but I also have been enjoying the peace and quiet from her shit for the past few weeks. It's nice not to hear her screeching voice in the hallways or wonder if I'm going to find the crotch taken out of my PE uniform.

"That's Cullen's problem."

Carissa laughs. "Honey, he just necked with you in front of half her friends. This is going to be your problem too."

I groan again. She's right – I'd forgotten that half the cheer squad is on the other side of the room.

"Play stupid games, win stupid prizes," Sophia says with a shrug.

I'm pretty sure Cullen is going to be the stupidest game I've ever played.

CULLEN: **We need to work on the photos today.**

It's Saturday morning and I'm still in my pyjamas. I haven't even had my morning coffee – so I'm in no way equipped to deal with Cullen just yet. Especially when he's still giving me orders.

He didn't text me last night after the diner, and I hated how many times I checked my phone, just in case his name appeared on the screen.

I ended up turning it off and going to sleep – there was no way in hell I was turning into one of *those* girls.

That 'treat 'em mean, keep 'em keen' shit is not the life for me.

I pour coffee into my favourite cup and sit down in the sun streaming into the kitchen.

I get about fifteen minutes of peace before Dad rolls in.

I heard him get home around midnight last night, and I'm dying to know what had his attention so late.

"Well, well, well, look what the cat dragged in. Big night, old man?"

He chuckles as he fills his own cup with coffee, leans his hip against the kitchen bench and looks at me, his eyes dancing with amusement.

Oh yeah, he's definitely happy about *something*.

"You know, if you're going to be out late, you should really text or call. I was worried."

He laughs. "Oh yeah, I bet you were really distraught. What'd you think of the game?"

"Don't change the subject."

"There's no subject to change, B."

"Oh, but I beg to differ. Where were you until the wee small hours?"

He raises a brow, a smirk gracing his lips.

"Did those single mums catch up with you?" I pry.

He chuckles. "Maybe."

"The blonde in the leather pants, if I had to guess."

He laughs louder. "You know your old man well."

"I don't know whether I'm proud or disgusted."

"I could probably provide you with some content that'd sway you towards disgusted, if you're interested."

I grimace. "Jesus, Dad, keep it in your pants."

He's full-on laughing at my grossed-out expression. "I'm joking, kiddo, chill out."

"I bet you're not though."

"I had dinner with a woman. It was fine. Very PG, nothing that'll scar you for life."

My phone chimes and I glance down at it.

Cullen: New girl. I'm picking you up in twenty.

I groan.

"Problem?"

"Nothing I can't handle," I mutter.

"What is it with you and 'handling' all these problems? You sound like some kind of Mafia boss."

"If the slipper fits," I tell him as I scoop up my phone, down the last of my coffee and head towards my room.

"That wouldn't have anything to do with the school's star fullback, would it?"

I freeze in my tracks.

I could dance around it a little bit, deny any and all involvement, but this is a small town. People talk. And besides, me and my dad have always had a reasonably firm, no-beating-around-the-bush policy.

I decide to take the head-on approach.

"What do you know, old man?" I ask, spinning back around.

"Depends on what you're about to tell me."

I narrow my eyes at him. "Don't play me like that."

He laughs but offers nothing more.

"We're partners on a project at school, and he's not real good at dealing with females who have a mind of their own," I explain.

He smirks at me over the rim of his mug. "Well, good luck to Cullen, then."

"Precisely."

He knows full well there's more, and *I* know full well that he already knows the goss, so we both agree with nothing more than a look, to leave it at that for now.

"Good chat." I wave at him over my shoulder as I make my escape. I have to get ready if Cullen is going to show up on my doorstep.

I consider texting him back and telling him to fuck off, but I'm well aware that tactic is not going to work with him. The diner incident proved that.

If he wants something to happen, chances are, it's going to happen. Unfortunately for me.

Best I can do at this point is push back a little.

I tap out a reply while the shower warms up.

Berlin: I'll be ready in thirty.

I'm about to climb into the shower, but his reply comes in quickly.

Cullen: Got to fight me on every fucking thing.

I laugh to myself. The poor boy has no idea.

I shower quickly but take my time picking out something decent to wear and doing my hair and makeup.

I'm fairly confident that I've gone well over the time given, but I don't give a shit. If the guy is going to start throwing out orders at a moment's notice, then he better get used to waiting for me to fulfil them.

There's no way I'm going to be caught dead on camera looking like I just rolled out of bed.

I finally make my way down the stairs. I glance at my phone, half expecting to find a bunch of texts reminding me that I'm late, but surprisingly, there's not even one message.

I hear the click of a shutter in the otherwise quiet house.

Cullen is standing off to the side of the staircase, camera at his face. Just the sight of him sends my heart into a gallop.

"How'd you get in here?"

The shutter clicks again as I continue my descent.

"This isn't prom, get out of it," I grumble.

He chuckles and lowers the camera, revealing that handsome face of his. God fucking dammit, he's a work of art.

Sculpted to perfection.

I doubt you ever get used to a face like that.

"Your dad let me in."

"How good of him, and where is he now?"

"He took off for a run about five minutes ago."

Unbelievable. I'll be having words with the old man over this. He can't just be letting teenage heart throbs into the house willy-fucking-nilly. I swear, the man needs a lobotomy sometimes. Only *my* father would leave the captain of the school rugby team alone in a house with his teenage daughter.

It's really no wonder he got my mum pregnant so young.

"How long have you been here?" I ask as I make it

to the bottom of the staircase and head towards my camera equipment on the hall table.

"About twenty minutes."

I groan. "So, you've had a chance to have a real good chat with my dad then?"

He smirks. "He's the assistant coach of my team, new girl, it's not like we've never spoken."

I swing my bag onto my shoulder and finally make my way towards him – the danger zone.

"So, you're telling me you only talked ball?"

"Nope, he grilled my ass about dating his daughter."

My step falters. "You're not dating his daughter."

He just smirks.

"You don't even like me, golden boy."

He doesn't bother replying, the prick. Instead, he just lets his eyes trail over me in a way that is becoming stupidly familiar.

"We should go," I say warily.

He gestures with his hand for me to go ahead.

I roll my eyes as I walk past him, intentionally brushing against him as I do.

I'm almost past him, and I honestly think I've gotten away with it when his hand lands on my arm and tugs me back.

I've got my back flat against a wall, his arms caging me in before I even register what the hell just happened.

I hold my breath as he runs his nose along my jaw,

up to my ear. "Did you think you'd get away with teasing me like that?"

"Only be disappointed if I did," I say on an exhale.

He chuckles, and the vibration of his body against mine makes my stomach flip.

"Just when I think I know what you're going to do next, you surprise me."

I can't tell if he thinks that's a good thing or a bad thing, but the thought is lost when he presses his lips to the sensitive skin below my ear lobe.

Tingles race up and down my spine and my head turns without my permission, allowing him easier access to my neck.

He takes full advantage of that, kissing, sucking and nibbling gently.

It feels so good, I'm getting lightheaded.

Just when I think I can't take any more of this gentle torture, he wraps his arm around my middle, pulling me to him before shoving me back against the wall again with a thud. His other hand grips just under my jaw, lightly grasping my throat.

A moan escapes me as his lips slant over mine, completely owning me.

I want to challenge him, but I can't. Not this time. He's taken control and my traitorous body is all too willing to let him have it. All I can do is hang on for the ride.

His hand slides lower, from my throat to my boobs, leaving a trail of fire.

I gasp as he goes lower again, over my belly and down to the band of my skirt.

He pauses, and I buck my hips into his hand, encouraging him to carry on.

He doesn't need to be told twice, he slides his hand beneath the bottom of my skirt and cups me through my underwear, his big palm like a warm blanket.

"Fuck, Berlin, I want to feel you so bad," he rasps as he pulls away from the kiss.

I can't believe I'm letting this boy feel me up in my father's hallway, but that's exactly what's going down, and I'm in no state to stop it.

"Do it," I pant, desperate for more.

He growls, deep in his throat before shoving my underwear aside. He rubs me up and down before sinking a finger deep inside me.

I cry out, desperate for more contact.

"I got you, baby."

He hoists me up with his other arm, pining me between his body and the wall. I wrap my legs around his waist, and he slips another finger inside me. Our camera equipment is long forgotten, on the floor at our feet.

"Oh, *fuck* yes," I moan, grinding myself shame-lessly on his hand.

"Jesus Christ, you're so fucking hot." His voice is rough, like he's on the verge of losing control too. "Show me how good it feels."

His warm breath at my ear, the filthy words he's

muttering and his fingers working their magic send me crashing over the edge out of nowhere.

"*Cullen.*" I gasp as I come on his fingers, riding out every last shake.

"Just like that," he murmurs.

Fuck, it feels so good, I'm an absolute goner.

Like, so good I legit see stars and my ears are ringing. I feel like I'm made of jelly. It's a little out of control.

He slips his fingers out of me when I finally still, and I watch in shock as he sucks them clean.

Jesus Christ, this boy is going to be the death of me.

TWENTY

Cullen

I just finger-fucked the assistant coach's daughter about five feet from a door he could have walked in at any minute.

That was a dangerous game, and everything about it makes me want to do it again.

She's cast some kind of spell over me, and I can't get enough.

I'm in way over my head with this chick.

I should run a mile, but I can't make myself do it.

Even just sitting here in the front seat of the car – she's pure fucking sin.

We pull into my driveway; I forgot the tripod for my camera, and I need it for the shots I have planned today, so I'm going to have to risk a trip home to get it.

I borrowed Mum's car today, and with a bit of luck she'll still be sleeping off her shift from last night. Ma talked about going to the farmers' market, so I was hopeful she wouldn't be here, but given that her car is still parked up, I think I might be shit out of luck.

"You wanna wait here?" I tell Berlin.

She looks at me like that's the stupidest question she's ever heard. "Yeah, I don't think meeting your mother is on my to-do list today."

I couldn't agree more.

About time we agreed on something.

I swing the door open and fling it shut behind me.

I make it about five steps before I see Pax coming out the front door, a sly smile on his stupid mug.

"Nah uh, Romeo, you're not getting away that easy. Ma wants to meet this one."

The prick looks so pleased with himself.

I should have just managed without the god damn tripod. I knew this was a bad idea.

Short of running back to the car right now and driving away, I don't think I'm going to get out of this unscathed.

"Ice! Get your ass in here, Ma wants to meet you," he yells to Berlin.

I sigh deeply.

He's such a pain in my ass.

Berlin reluctantly opens her door. "What are you yelling at me for?"

Pax grins wide and jogs over to retrieve her from the car. "C'mon, you have to meet Ma."

She looks like she'd rather stick pins in her eyes, but she lets him drag her out of the front seat.

He leads her past me, right to the house, with her glaring at me over her shoulder the whole time.

To his credit, he seems to be able to control her better than I can; she isn't even fighting him. She's swearing at him, but she hasn't tried to smack him one or anything.

I'm impressed.

I huff out a laugh at the look on her face. She's as concerned about this meet and greet as I am. Somehow that makes me feel better about it.

I've never really brought a girl home to meet Ma or Mum. You bring a girl home, and they get all kinds of stupid ideas in their heads about living happily ever after or whatever other bullshit subscriptions I'm not currently offering.

I've had the odd one turn up unannounced and uninvited – Liana style – but that doesn't count. It's not the same as walking into fire willingly.

Fuck it all.

Maybe I'll get away with it on a technicality. She's being brought in by Pax, as his friend. I might get to slide under the radar.

Fucking dreaming.

I kick off my shoes at the door and groan as I hear not only Ma's voice, but Mum's too.

Cool. Cool. Cool.

What a big old family affair this is turning out to be.

I hustle down to my room to find my tripod. With a bit of luck, we'll be able to make a hasty exit after the small talk has been made.

I find what I need and reluctantly head into the kitchen. I tip-toe into the lion's den, hoping for the best but expecting the worst.

Pax is sitting on the bench, not a care in the world, Berlin is standing next to him, her hip resting against the kitchen as she talks to Mum, who's making everyone a cup of tea, by the looks of things.

Jesus Christ.

"Morning, darling," she says when she spots me.

"Morning, Mum," I reply, moving to give her the kiss on the cheek I know she's expecting. "Did you have a good shift?"

She smiles brightly at me. "Very uneventful, thankfully. Cup of tea?"

Uneventful is good in the life of a nurse. I hate to think about the shit my mum has seen.

I shake my head. "Me and Berlin have a lot of work to get done. We kinda need to get going."

"Nonsense. It's only early, you've got all day," Ma pipes up from the other side of the kitchen.

"You didn't tell me she was so pretty," Mum whispers to me.

I'm pretty sure I didn't tell her fucking *anything* about Berlin, but if I had to guess, I'd say my brother did the honours on my behalf. He's a real good cunt like that.

He gives me a smug smirk.

Prick.

I'll remember this and pay back will be sweet.

I dart a glance at Berlin. She's looking back at me, surprisingly amused and at ease, standing here in my house.

Mum steps away and gets out another mug – for my cup of tea if I had to guess.

This morning is going to hell, *real* fucking quickly. I don't even like tea.

Between fingering Berlin in the middle of her house after a heart to heart with her dad, and now drinking tea with my mothers, it'd be safe to say this day isn't turning out the way I planned.

Ma ushers us to the dining table and starts grilling Berlin about what subjects she's taking at school, if she plays sports... the whole nine yards. I'd find it funny if it wasn't my parents that were interrogating her.

She takes it like a champ though, and it's pretty clear to me that she's charming the shit out of the women who raised me.

Pax is seated next to Berlin, and when I finally give in and join the three of them at the table, I take the seat on the other side of her.

Maybe that will stop me from wringing his neck.

Mum sets down a cup in front of each of us.

"Thank you." Berlin smiles warmly at her.

I don't know who the fuck this well-mannered, polite girl is, but it's not the same one who sasses the shit out of me every opportunity she gets.

What a dangerous creature.

"And you're new to town I hear?" Mum asks her.

She nods after she's sipped her tea. "Yeah, I grew up in Australia, but my dad is from here and he wanted to move back... so here we are."

"Remember, I told you the other day that her dad is the new assistant coach," Pax reminds my mum.

"Oh, yes, I remember now." She turns to Ma. "We went to school with him. I forgot to tell you about it."

"Oh really?" Ma questions. "Who's your dad?" she asks before taking a sip of her drink.

"Cole Davids," Berlin replies.

"Oh *wow*. I haven't heard that name in *years*. I had *such* a crush on your dad when I was about sixteen." Ma swoons.

"Really?" Berlin laughs, her eyes alight.

"*Really*. He was the most popular boy in school."

"Geeze, Ma, chill, I know he's the man, but have some composure," Pax jokes.

"You really had a crush on my dad?" Berlin asks, her tone excited.

She's probably never had the chance to talk about what her dad was like before she was born.

"I did too." My mum laughs. "I think half the girls in our year did. Your dad was a good-looking guy back in the day. I'm pretty sure I remember scribbling his name on my notebook once or twice. I think he even took me out to a movie once."

"*Everyone* thought he was gorgeous," Ma agrees.

"He's still a stone-cold fox," Pax chimes in.

I scowl at him. "You're a weird dude, eh."

This whole thing is weird. Mum and Ma start talking about shit from their 'hay day'. Berlin is listening animatedly, but I need to get the fuck out of here before this can get any cosier.

Next thing they'll be setting up one of my mothers with her father – shit is already crazy enough around here.

"New girl, we gotta go, need the right light," I lie.

She looks up at me, those big dark eyes seeing right through my bullshit. Surprisingly though, she doesn't call me on it.

She smirks, stands, and picks up her mug without argument.

"Thank you both so much for the tea, it was so nice to meet you, but he's right, we better get to it."

It takes us a solid ten minutes to get away from the women of the house and another five to pry Berlin away from Pax.

It's a fucking circus, and I'm so bewildered by it all that I'm not even close to being on my game.

Note to self: don't forget the fucking tripod ever *again.*

We finally make it to the car and pull out into the street, and to safety.

I can feel Berlin watching me, but there's no way in hell I'm willing to make eye contact with her right now.

"So, that was... interesting," she says, amusement thick in her voice.

"Don't even start with me, new girl."

She laughs. "Your mum *loves* me. So does Pax's."

I groan. She's started with me. Because *of course* she fucking has.

"Probably just happy Pax has finally made a friend."

I see her shake her head out the corner of my eye. "If that helps you sleep at night, big guy."

WE'VE BEEN TAKING photos for hours, but I'm still not done. I could look at that face all day.

I haven't kissed her again, but I've thought about it at least a hundred times.

She's like the sweetest drug I've ever tasted and I'm just an addict chasing his next hit.

She's got her lens pointed at me and she's clicking away virtually non-stop.

All the silence while we work isn't good for my head. I'm overthinking *hard*. I've seen Pax and Berlin interact together – I know they're close, but every now and then I can't help but think it might be more. Seeing them together at home, so natural and easy, it was weird.

"Head a little to the left," she murmurs. I turn my head, my mind still racing.

"What's the deal with you and Pax?" I blurt the question out of nowhere.

She freezes. "What?" she asks, her face hidden behind her camera.

"You and my brother, what's the story?"

We're both sitting on a blanket, I'm leaning against a tree and she's sitting in front of me with her legs twisted beneath her.

She sits her camera down and looks right at me. "We're friends."

"Is that all you are?"

"Shouldn't you be asking *him* these questions?" She fidgets with the hem of her skirt.

"I have," I reply coolly.

"And what did he say?"

I smirk at her. We both know I'm not going to tell her the answer to that.

She rolls her eyes at me and shrugs. "We're friends. Sometimes I feel like he knows me better than anyone else at this school does."

I don't like that. I want to be the one to know her best, but the reality is, I don't know shit all about her – not yet.

I mull over her answer.

"I don't know what you want me to say, Cullen. If you've got a problem with something Pax said, you'll have to take it up with him."

"He said you *have something*... I know you guys have a bond; everyone can see that."

"We do... he understands me in a way most people don't. I don't know what to tell you, we're close. He's important to me."

She's not telling me anything I don't already know, but it still twists like a knife in my gut, nonetheless. At least she's being honest, most people aren't honest with me – they tell me what they think I want to hear instead of telling me the truth.

"Why are you asking me this anyway?" She asks the question in a rush, like it's a demand, like she's sick of my shit. Sick of beating around the bush.

I look at her, hard – she's so fucking stunning. "I need to know, before..."

"Before *what*, Cullen?"

"Before it's too late," I growl. "Before you're mine and we can't take it back."

Her dark eyes widen in surprise. "You think you're going to make me another girl on your list of cheer hoes?"

She's so far from it, it's laughable. She's nothing like those girls. She's nothing like *any* other girl.

The two things are like night and day.

I lean forwards and press her shoulders backwards until she's laying on her back on the blanket. I hover above her, holding my weight off her body.

"You could never be just some cheer hoe, Berlin."

She looks up at me, a smirk on her face. "I could be a cheer hoe if I wanted to be."

Of course she'd even argue *that* with me.

This *fucking* girl.

She laughs softly when she sees my reaction.

"You don't even like me, Cull. I don't know if I like you either."

I know what she means. She's the bitchy new girl I'd like to see eat shit hard if it'd simmer her attitude down, and I'm the cocky prick jock who's sworn to make her life hell.

Somewhere along the way we've managed to get lost in translation.

Maybe, just fucking maybe it's because those bullshit fronts are only what we let everyone see, and in reality, there's a big wide = world outside of high school and its stupid social rules. She's a hell of a lot more than some sassy chick who rocks the boat every chance she gets, and there's more to me than throwing a ball.

I brush a stray strand of hair from her face and tuck it behind her ear.

"I'm going to be honest with you, new girl, I had every fucking intention of putting you in your place around here, but every time I get a chance, I wind up thinking that your place is right here, beside me."

That's probably the sappiest shit I've ever said in my entire life, and I'm nervous as hell for how it's going to go down.

I've never cared this much about a girl before. I've never had so much riding on it. This feels like a championship final game, and she's the trophy I want to win by the last whistle.

"*Cullen*," she whispers. She seems as surprised by my confession as I am.

"You tell anyone I said that and I'll –"

She cuts me off with a laugh and then she's kissing me, dragging me down on top of her.

We're a mess of lips and hands, we're both desperate to touch more of each other.

I'm hard as a fucking rock from her grinding herself on me, and when I feel her slip her hand between us and rub my length through my shorts, I nearly lose my mind.

She pulls on the waistband and slides her hand inside. Her fingers are so warm and soft and when they grip my dick, every nerve ending in my body stands up and takes notice.

"Oh, fuck," I groan as she grips me tighter.

I push back onto my knees a fraction so I can see. "Take me out. I want to watch," I tell her.

She looks around, side to side, checking we're still alone out here in the wooded park area. Honestly, I completely forgot we were in public, but I don't give a fuck either. I wouldn't stop for anything right now.

She tugs on my shorts, freeing me from my boxer briefs. Slowly, she starts working my length, sliding her hand up and down, and *fuck me*, I don't think anything has ever felt like this before.

She licks her lips as she watches her hand fucking me, and I swear to God, I nearly blow my load.

Everything she does turns me on.

I've literally got my dick out in a public park and I've never been so fucking turned on. She's next level sexy.

I'm *dying* to touch her. I reach for her skirt and lift it up, exposing her black lacy underwear. I didn't give it the appreciation it deserved earlier, and I'm too close to the edge to do it now either.

Next time, I'll take my time.

I drag the lace to the side and expose her to me. I hear her moan as I run my thumb over her clit and her hand speeds up, working me harder.

I'm so close to the edge, but I have to take her with me.

"I want to taste you." I growl the words at her.

Her hand stops moving, and she looks up at me with lust-filled eyes.

I take the opportunity to replace her hand with my own, and as I sink down to taste her pussy, I fist my dick, hard and fast.

She cries out and arches her back off the ground as I make short work of bringing her right to the brink with me.

"Come all over my face," I tell her as I slide a finger into her, hooking it to find the spot that drove her crazy earlier.

"Oh, fuck, I'm coming." She screams – the sound echoing out into the park.

I suck her clit hard, and she bucks again.

So fucking hot.

Her moans of pleasure push me over the edge, and I come hard, all over the blanket and her thigh.

We're both breathing hard, coming down from a high.

I hear noises of a kid laughing and playing. Sounds like it's coming from the playground on the other side of the trees.

We meet each other's eyes and crack up laughing at the state of us.

We're bringing a whole new meaning to the term 'horny teenagers'.

I tuck myself back in and tug her skirt down to cover her. Don't know what the fuck we're going to do about this blanket though.

TWENTY-ONE

Berlin

"You did *what?*" Mel shrieks.

"Shhhhhhh," Sophia shushes her, glancing around. The girl is forever concerned about making a scene.

I roll my eyes. "You heard. I didn't stutter."

If you're going to let a guy give you head in the middle of a public park, you pretty much just have to own it.

The five of us are grouped around mine and Sophia's lockers and I'm filling Mel, Carissa and Laura in on what went down over the weekend.

"Please tell me that you got photos of that," Carissa jokes, fanning her face.

"Oh, yeah, nothing like a bit of underage porn for a school project." Laura laughs.

Sophia looks horrified... or turned on, I can't really tell.

"Then what happened?"

"Well, the blanket was... *dirty*... after that, so we packed up and he took me home."

Sophia grimaces, Laura smirks.

"Have you talked to him since?" Carissa asks me.

"Yeah, we've messaged a bit."

It's only kind of a white lie. We *have* talked, but it's more than a bit. We were up texting until two in the morning on Saturday night until I fell asleep, and then it picked up again Sunday morning when we woke up.

I've been glued to my phone for the past thirty-six hours.

It's official, I'm one of *those* girls.

We have so much more in common than I ever could have thought – just the fact that both of us have lost a parent that we didn't, or didn't really, know is uncanny, but there're so many other things... our taste in movies, food we like and dislike, even the fact that we both like our shower scalding hot.

"So, are you exclusive now? Are you going public or what?" Mel demands, looking like she's all kinds of flustered with the direction my love life has gone in, even though every single one of them apparently 'called it' from the start.

"I don't know," I say with a roll of my eyes. "Who even cares?"

"I think I can speak for everyone when I say that we *all* do," Carissa replies.

I open my locker and pull out the books I need for my next class. I'm just shutting it when I hear a chorus of gasps around me.

I've barely even turned around and he's pushing me against my locker, kissing me so hard I can't breathe.

He pulls back and murmurs against my lips, "Morning, new girl. One day is too long."

I'm breathless.

"Well, I guess that answers that question," I hear Laura say dryly.

It certainly has answered the question about us going public; as if the diner wasn't public enough.

"Morning," I manage to reply.

He kisses me once more, a sweet, soft kiss, then pulls away, and just like that, he's leaving again. Walking off down the hall, all swagger and sexiness. People move out of his way, parting like the fucking red sea. It's ridiculous. I don't even know if he realises how aware everybody in this place is of him.

Just like the day I met him, he really needs taking down a peg or two.

"Hey, golden boy!" I yell after him.

He looks back at me over his shoulder.

I flip him the middle finger, a wide grin on my face.

He chuckles and returns the gesture.

I notice for the first time that Pax is next to him, and we exchange a look. He's smiling, but I don't know if it quite reaches his eyes.

I make a mental note to talk to him about it later.

I don't know what the fuck is going on with me and

Cullen, but one thing I do know for sure is that I don't want it to mess up my friendship with Pax.

"Okay, but that was hot as *fuck*." Carissa swoons.

"Tell me about it, if the guy fucks like he kisses, then I'm going to be in *so* much trouble."

"Berlin Davids, that language is *not* acceptable," Mr Perkins, an English teacher, scolds me as he's passing.

"Sorry, Mr. P," I reply. "It's all the hormones. I tried to get my dad to send me to an all-girls school, I really did."

The girls are all sniggering behind their hands or folders.

Mr. P looks at me like I'm a filthy little whore, but thankfully he doesn't stop and write me up for detention. Today must be my lucky day. I don't know how I would have explained that one to the old man.

"Okay but seriously, can we get back to the fact that *that* guy gave you head on a picnic blanket in the park? Like what the actual fuck, how does that even happen?" Mel wants details apparently. Doesn't surprise me, she's such a nerd.

Lucky she's cute as shit.

I shrug. "One thing just led to another."

Her eyes widen. "Yeah, I can totally relate... not."

I huff out a laugh. "Look, I'm not saying it was ideal, but sometimes the moment gets away on you, and we were alone. It's not like we did it on one of the tables in the kids playground with an audience."

"Can't say I'm familiar with the concept of a moment getting away on you," Sophia grumbles.

"Have to have a moment in the first place," Mel agrees.

"Hold up." I gesture for them to come in close, and I lower my voice. "Are you guys all virgins or what?" I ask.

Sophia goes bright red. That's a yes. Unsurprisingly. I'd already figured that one out. She's a total babe, but she may as well have a giant 'v' tattooed on her forehead.

Mel nods. "Girl, I've barely been kissed, let alone dicked down."

I can't help but laugh at her choice of words.

"What about you two?" I turn to Laura and Carissa.

"Carissa's the hoe of the group," Mel pipes up.

I raise a brow at Carissa.

"Two guys, okay? I've slept with *two* guys. I'm hardly a hoe."

This is surprising to me. I'm more than a little proud.

We all look to Laura.

"I've done everything but... *it.*"

Well, turns out they're not all as innocent as originally anticipated. Go team.

"What about you?" Carissa nudges me with her elbow, our huddle still tight.

"Just one guy back in Australia. My boyfriend of a couple of years. I've messed around with another couple of guys, but only second and third base kinda shit."

"I'm not going to lie, I thought it'd be more of a list," Sophia tells me, her surprise obvious.

"Well thanks," I reply sarcastically. "Are you trying to say I look like a whore?"

"Little bit," she jokes.

"Maybe it's time you caught up."

She sighs. "I think you need a male who's willing first."

I roll my eyes. "Oh, *please*. Half the guys in this school would kill to go on a date with a pretty little thing like you, let alone get into your pants."

She opens her mouth, no doubt to argue, but I cut her off when a light bulb flickers in my brain.

"I'm a *genius*."

"Why?" she demands. She's already wary, and in this case, her wariness is well placed. I'm absolutely up to no good.

"*Any* guy would trip over themselves... so that's what we're going to do. If Bryson can't pull the trigger, we'll show him that someone else will."

She groans. "I *knew* it was going to be something stupid. Absolutely not. Not happening."

"Incoming," Laura hisses, interrupting my scheming.

I glance over my shoulder and see Liana strutting down the hallway, flanked by two bitchy-looking cheerleaders on either side of her.

The look she gives me would send a weaker woman

to her knees. As it is, I'm pretty sure Soph sways on her feet from the second-hand venom in the air.

None of them say a word as they pass us, but the matching death glares make it pretty obvious that the cat is out of the bag about me and Cullen hooking up, and once again, I'm enemy number one.

No surprises there.

"Oh god, oh god, oh god," Sophia chants in a whisper.

"Relax," I demand.

"She's going to drug us again. Oh god, she's literally going to kill you this time."

I ignore my cousin, she's gone manic.

"I told Mum you'd be the death of me," she carries on.

I have to laugh at that comment. Aunt Alyssa is probably happy to see her little girl finally having some type of fun.

"Whatever." I shrug, unfazed by the bitch brigade and their stare down tactic. "Let's get back to the plan of making Bryson jealous."

I MAKE it to my drawing class with only one minute to spare. Talking Sophia into immature teenage bullshit was proving to be more difficult than I anticipated.

I'm sure that half her problem is that she thinks none of the males around here would be interested in her, but I already know she's wrong. She might be naive to the looks she gets, but I'm not. Especially these past few weeks. She's finally taken some advice on clothes, accessories, and her hair. It's nice not to see her hiding behind a braid anymore.

She was starting to look like she was super into horses or something.

Pax is already in his seat, the space next to him empty and waiting for me. He looks up when I approach, and that carefree smile widens.

Maybe I imagined something being off earlier.

"Ice!" he says enthusiastically.

"Paxikins!" I return.

"You're late."

I slide into my seat and rush to get my stuff ready for class. I'm hoping it's an hour of free drawing to work on our sketches – it's the only time we really get to talk while we work, and I feel like I haven't talked to Pax one on one in forever.

"Technically I'm right on time."

"What's new?" he asks, after we're thankfully told to continue working on our projects.

"Just been convincing Soph that the best way to get Bryson moving is to make him jealous."

"Turning toxic. I like it." He nods thoughtfully.

I laugh. "Yeeeaaah, it's probably a bit lame, but I'm sick of his bullshit. We all know he likes her so maybe he just needs a little motivation."

"I'm all for it." He smirks. "I'll even volunteer my services if you want."

"That's a negative, cowboy."

"You never let me have any fun." He pouts.

"And you certainly *won't* be having any with my cousin, I can tell you that for free."

"You know, we all managed just fine before you arrived here," he says, taunting me with his grin.

"Pffft." I roll my eyes. "You didn't even know who Sophia was until I got here."

"You know it's hurtful that you think that."

"It's the truth and we both know it."

He pauses for a moment, probably weighing up if he wants to keep up the ruse or get on with the conversation.

"Yeah, you're right, no clue who she was. Didn't even notice how obsessed Bry was with her until now too, if I'm being honest."

"It shocks me to my core that *you* were unaware about things going on around you," I say sarcastically. "Self-absorbed much?"

He chuckles and nudges my elbow. "So, you and Cull, huh? Bout time he finally got around to shooting his shot."

I fidget with the pencil in my hands. "Yeah... I don't know what to tell you about that, but it's something alright."

"Keeping your enthusiasm at bay... good call. Can't have the guy getting more of an ego."

I laugh. "It's not that, it's just, like... I don't know. It just happened and there's something there, but we almost hate each other a little bit, you know? I don't even really know him."

He chuckles. "I hate to break it to you, Ice, but I think that's how it works."

I lightly smack his shoulder. "You know what I mean."

"All I'm hearing is hot, angry sex." He waggles his brows at me.

"Why don't you say that a bit louder, I think a few people down the back missed it," I hiss.

He sucks in a big breath, like he's going to repeat it, even louder – and he'll do it too. But I'm quick enough to clap a hand over his mouth and stop him.

"You need a leash. And a muzzle." I scowl at him.

"Bit rich coming from the spiciest cat in town."

Mrs. Richie passes by our table, so we both work away in silence for a few minutes.

I don't really know how to go about asking Pax if we're cool, since the whole Cullen thing started, and I've never really been great with tact, so I decide to just go for it.

"Are we good, Pax?"

He stops drawing and frowns at me.

"You know... with me and Cullen being *whatever*... are you and me good?"

"Why *wouldn't* we be good?"

I refrain from rolling my eyes at his totally noncommittal, digging for more information, answer.

If he's not willing to put his balls on the line, then I will.

"I don't know. I guess because we're close, and I don't know if you were hoping for more or what..." I can feel myself blush. "But now this has happened, and I just don't want to lose our friendship. Don't let it go to your head, but you're kind of one of the few people around here that I actually like."

It all comes out in a rush, but he seems to have caught it all.

"You're kind of highly strung when you're nervous."

"Shut up."

He laughs. "We're good, Ice. I like you, more than I like anyone else in this hole, and I want you to do whatever the fuck you wanna do. If that's my brother, then have at it. Just so you know, I've warned him that if he messes with you, he messes with me. You're not going to be the next skanky bitch on the list."

"That's what *I* said."

That's also what I was afraid of. When Cullen and I go up in flames, *when* not *if*, because let's face it, we're two very flammable objects, and sooner or later this thing is going to ignite – I don't want to come in between the two of them. I don't think there's any going back on this connection I share with Pax – it feels like we've known each other our whole lives, but him and Cullen have *actually* known each other their whole lives, and I'm not going to be the thing that gets in the way of that.

"You two will not fight over me or about me, under *any* circumstances," I warn him.

"Too late," he mutters under his breath. "But it's all good, Ice, he's been told. I'm not saying you have to stay together forever and get married or some shit, but he can treat you with respect, even if it ends. He's not a moron. If the prick can make straight A's, he can figure out how to treat a girl right."

The sentiment warms my cold, black heart. No one other than my dad has ever stood up for me like that, especially not to someone so important to them.

Straight A's... dayum.

"I kind of forget that he's not all tits and ass and no substance," I joke, attempting to lighten the mood before I do something lame, like shed a tear.

He laughs, loud enough to earn us a look from the teacher. "The guy is medium-level intelligence, at least, Ice. Give the kid a break."

We laugh quietly together, and it feels just like things did before I hooked up with the golden boy.

"Smart and talented. He's actually a real prick... there's not a lot of guys who can play rugby like a legend and then when they get injured, get on the sideline and take a bunch of photos that are worthy of making a shrine in the gym with."

Wait, what?

"It's lucky he's an ugly fucker," he jokes, "or it'd all really be going to his head."

Cullen took those pictures...

I can't believe he didn't tell me they were his.

Pax is totally oblivious to my revelation.

"You two and your situationship should be safe... the only thing we ever really fight about is my lack of dedication to my sporting ability," he says after a few moments.

I watch him out of the corner of my eye. I can't help but think he wants to get something off his chest.

"Cullen's words?" I prompt.

He nods. "He takes footy so seriously, you know? And that's cool and good for him, but I dunno... I've never really been motivated to fully commit to it being a life choice, I guess."

Something tells me I need to tread carefully here. I'm fairly confident I'm about to become privy to one of Pax's secrets. For someone who's always talking, he never actually says too much. It's a skill he's mastered, so if he's trying to open up, then I need to listen.

"You don't want to play rugby for a living?"

He mulls over his answer for a moment before answering. "I don't know. I know I could be good enough, but I always sell myself short. Get drunk when I shouldn't or don't show up to training two days before a big game... I hardly ever get out for my runs. I don't know... sometimes I feel like I'm self-sabotaging."

"So, don't do that then? If you're sick of letting yourself down, then don't."

He shrugs his shoulders. "Yeah, I know. Something has always been missing. I don't know how to explain it. Ever since I was young, I've loved the game, but it's not the same... other kids had their dads there for the dads vs kids game, and me and Cull just hung out at the back. It's like it's tainted the sport for me."

The direction of the conversation catches me off

guard. It's not what I was expecting him to say at all.

"And I know it's not just me; Cull has the same deal. No dad around to do guy shit with, but I think I always took it harder than he did."

"You don't know your dad at all?" I question.

He shakes his head. "Never met him. Everyone says he was a teacher at Ma and Mum's school, *and* that he was married. Maybe that's true, because Ma hasn't even told Cullen's mum who he is. She said *one day*, she'll explain. Maybe that's why I struggle more than Cull – it fucking sucks his dad's dead, but at least he knows."

"That's hard. She must have a good reason for not telling you – as hard as it might be for you, maybe it's for the best."

"Yeah, I think about that all the time. I'm sure she has a really good reason. It's just hard. I wonder what he's like, what he did with his life, if he ever played... I just wish I knew and I could talk to him about my future."

"Those women love you, Pax, they'll support you, no matter what, you know that, right? Just because your dad isn't around, doesn't mean you don't have support."

"I know," he replies quickly, "they're the best. It's just something a boy talks about with his dad, ya know? But my dad's probably a flake. Makes me wonder if I'll ever be able to fully commit to anything. Maybe it's in my DNA."

It might not make sense to a lot of people, but I can relate. Like when I got my period, or my first boyfriend, or when I wanted advice on what I might want to do one day – I needed my mum, and she wasn't there.

I've second-guessed a lot of things in my life purely because she's not around.

She made her choices and those choices led to her not being there to support me or even know me. I can only assume Pax's dad made some questionable choices of his own.

"It's not in your DNA," I tell him.

"You don't know that."

"You're right. I *don't* know that, but I do know that the only person who can decide what you want to do with your life, or whether or not you flake out on shit you love, is *you*. Not your MIA dad, not your Ma, or Cullen. It's on you, Pax. You determine what you become. You wanna be the useless prick who doesn't commit to anything and fucks around, then that's on you, pal."

"Shit, Ice, you read that on some motivation website this morning or something?" He laughs.

Harsh, but it worked though. I got him laughing.

I roll my eyes and grin at him. "Shut up, loser. You came to me for advice, remember? Don't hate on me for giving it to you."

"You're right. I know you're right. I'm just making excuses."

I shrug a shoulder at him. "It's your call how long you want to keep doing that for."

"This is why I like you, Ice, you tell it like it is."

That I do.

TWENTY-TWO

Cullen

Just the fucking sight of her has my pulse racing.

She's laughing with Pax as they walk out of their drawing class. She's less guarded when it's just the two of them. She's always so composed when she knows someone is watching, and even though I've managed to get a fair few genuine reactions out of her now, I want her to drop her guard completely with me too.

I guess shit like that has to be earned. She doesn't trust me yet and it's probably smart of her. I don't know if it would be wise of her to trust a guy like me.

She looks around, her eyes skimming past me, before the realisation hits and she snaps back, her eyes cutting to mine.

I'm leaning against the wall opposite their door,

waiting for her.

"Aw, you came to pick me up from class. That's so sweet," Pax coos, absolutely rinsing me.

"Go fuck yourself," I tell him without even bothering to look at him.

"And what are *you* doing here?" Berlin asks me, her hands resting on her hips as she comes to a stop in front of me.

"Waiting on you."

She arches a brow. "Waiting on me for *what?*"

I answer with a look that wouldn't take a genius to decipher.

She licks her lips.

"You look hungry, bro." Pax chuckles.

He's not wrong. I *am* hungry, but not for food. I'm hungry for something so much sweeter.

Berlin is looking right back at me with that same hunger in her eyes. The sooner we get out of here, the better.

"Beat it," I tell Pax with a grin.

"I'll remember this when I get a girlfriend one day," he replies.

He leans in, kisses Berlin's cheek and jogs off after some of the guys from the team who have just walked past, leaving us alone outside the classroom.

"No training tonight?" she questions.

"Not tonight," I say with a shake of my head.

She tips her head to the side, eyeing me curiously. "And you thought you'd just come by and steal me away from my important plans?"

"You don't have important plans," I reply gruffly as I snag her hand and pull her closer to me, her chest hitting mine.

"And how would you know?" She looks up at me, all sass as she bats her lashes.

"Forced your cousin to tell me."

That gets a huge grin out of her. "Oh, I would have paid to see that conversation go down. She would have completely shit herself."

I chuckle and intertwine our fingers behind her back. "Yip."

"Let me guess, blushed bright red and stuttered?"

"Pretty much."

"And then sold me out." She pouts.

"Barely even hesitated," I reply proudly.

She rolls her eyes. "I really need to work on her backbone."

I've got her hands behind her back, and I can't help but notice that she's completely at my mercy.

I dip my head and brush my lips against hers, ever so softly before pulling back.

Her eyelids have closed as I look down at her.

"Tease," she whispers.

I chuckle.

"Do you want to get out of here?"

Her lids flutter open, and she looks up at me with those beautiful dark eyes. I don't know how the fuck I thought she wasn't my type. At this point she's the literal definition of my type.

"Are you actually asking my permission for once?"

"Maybe."

"That's a shame, I kind of like it when you boss me around."

I shake my head at her. Little fucking fruit loop.

"There's no pleasing you, is there?"

She smirks up at me. "I think we both know that's not true."

I like where her head's at. My dick likes it too.

"I think we need to leave before I get suspended for doing bad things to you right here and now." My mouth is at her ear, and I can see the goosebumps covering her skin.

"Promises, promises," she mutters.

Fuck I love it when she challenges me. It only makes me want to make her submit more.

She's like a wild untameable cat.

"Lead the way, golden boy."

I growl deep in my throat. I'd much rather spin her around and pin her against the wall right here and now, but I'm pretty sure Coach would be pissed if I got caught hooking up with his assistant coach's daughter – on school grounds.

I release one of her hands but keep hold of the other so we can walk hand in hand.

Who the fuck even am I?

Holding hands like some kind of sap.

We've gone public with this shit now anyway; I may as well do the fucking thing thoroughly.

We stroll hand and hand through the school, taking our sweet time. I ignore all the sideways looks and whispers we cause, and Berlin does the same. Our hands swing between us as we talk.

We're talking about nothing, but I'm hanging off her every word.

There's just something about this girl. I can't seem to get enough. She's so different to everyone else around this place. She's addictive as fuck, and not just her banging body, but the shit that comes out of her mouth has me hooked too.

She's funny. And real kind of funny isn't that common.

She's talking about her old school in Australia and the friends she left behind, and I know damn fucking well I could just listen to her talk for hours.

I've got it bad.

I've got no choice but to accept that fact. I've got it bad for this girl. I'm in way over my head and I'm help-less to stop it. It is what it is.

I hate it as much as I love it.

We leave the school grounds and we're just walking down the street. I don't know where we're going, and I don't even care as long as she's here and she's talking.

I want to know fucking *everything* about her.

"I think it's your turn to tell me something about you. I'm rambling."

I tug her closer, let go of her hand and sling my arm around her shoulders. She looks up at me with a satis-fied smile on her face.

"My favourite colour is blue," I reply, giving her the most generic piece of information I can think of.

"Huh," she muses. "I'd have guessed black."

"Like my soul?"

"You said it, not me."

"Smartass."

"Because you're the king of *Black* Diamonds," she explains.

I smirk. *The King of Black Diamonds*. That's a new one, but I could think of worse things to be called.

"Mine is pink."

Seems a bit cute for someone so sassy.

"Did your mum say anything about me after the other day?" she asks.

"She thought you were alright."

I hate to admit it, but my mother was a *big* fan of Berlin Davids. She has not shut up about her since.

Words like 'sweet' have been getting thrown around – so clearly my mother is a hell of a lot naiver than she realises, because the only thing sweet about this girl is the way she tastes.

She smirks up at me. "Mothers love me."

"Well lucky for you, I've got two of them."

I point out a bench seat in a quiet little rest area, just off the side of the footpath.

I sit down on the bench, sprawling out, and she crosses her legs, sitting facing me.

"I don't know if I should be scared or excited when you say things like that." Her tone is vulnerable, and for once I think that maybe I might be seeing the version of herself that she keeps so deeply buried beneath attitude and wit.

"Things like what?" I ask, taking her hand and bringing it into my lap.

"Just things that imply I'm going to be around for more than five minutes. I don't want to sound like a bitch, but I know that's not really your style."

"Are you implying I'm not the commitment type?"

She rolls her eyes. "I'm implying the only thing you've ever really committed to is a team of boys throwing a ball around."

It's a fair call.

"Maybe you've changed me."

"I don't believe in that."

That gets my interest.

"You don't think people can change?"

"I didn't say that. People *can* change... but only if they really want to. I don't think people change for someone else. They change for themselves. They change because they want something – sometimes that's a person. I'm not saying it's a bad thing, but we're all selfish creatures by nature."

She makes a good point. Here I am, falling for this girl hook, line, and sinker... willing to change my ways, because *I* want *her*. Because I'm not willing to give her up.

"Maybe I want to change because of you."

Her features soften and I think I might even see a hint of pink on her cheeks.

"Well, I'll reserve my judgement until I see that for myself."

She's a smart girl, but I mean it. I'm not giving her up.

"I want you to be my girlfriend."

She smirks at me, then shakes her head. "No."

"What do you mean, *no?*" I demand.

She laughs lightly. "No. It's the opposite of yes, which I'm sure you're familiar with hearing, golden boy."

"Why the fuck not?"

"Take a girl on a date before you expect her to be your girlfriend, Cullen."

Should have seen that coming.

"Let me take you on a date, Friday night."

"Friday is my birthday."

Even better.

"Good. I'm taking you out for your birthday."

"And what if I already have plans?"

"Cancel them," I say. My tone leaves no room for argument, and shockingly, she doesn't even try. Instead, her teeth sink into that sexy bottom lip of hers and she nods.

"Okay."

"CULLEN?" I hear Mum call from the kitchen as I'm about to walk out the door for school.

It's pissing with rain, and Bry is in the driveway waiting in his car for me.

I don't know what the fuck has gotten into Pax, but

apparently, he had Ma drop him off at the gym on her way to work at six this morning, so he could get a run in on the treadmill before school.

Shit is getting fucking weirder around here by the minute.

"Yeah, Mum?"

She appears in the doorway in front of me.

"Bry's waiting out front," I tell her.

She nods, and I already know she's got something she wants to say.

Ever since I got home late last night with a goofy grin plastered across my face, I've been waiting for her to say something.

Pax had informed her that I was with Berlin – God damn snitch – and I know our mums... they've pretty much always got something to say about everything.

"I know, I won't keep you long." She shifts her weight from one foot to the other.

"Just say it, Mum." I grin at her.

I hate it when she gets nervous. It makes me nervous. I'd rather she just came out with it.

"I just wanted to make sure that you're being careful."

Oh Jesus.

I groan. "We've had this talk. Years ago, Mum."

She shakes her head, smiling. "This is not the safe sex talk, Cull."

"Then what is it?"

"This is the first love talk."

I open my mouth to make it clear that she's got the wrong end of the stick, but she cuts me off.

"We don't need to get into it right now, but I know young love when I see it, and I also know my son, so all I'm saying, is be careful – with your heart... and with hers. Okay?"

I don't really know what the fuck to do with that, but thankfully for me, Bry toots the horn again, giving me the hurry up.

"I gotta go," I stutter.

I'm pretty sure my expression is giving a clear picture of how glad I am about that fact. I feel like a deer in headlights. She's managed to catch me totally off guard.

She laughs. "Off you go then, it's not like I don't know where you live."

Yeah, cool. Reeeaaaal cool.

I shrug my bag higher on my shoulder and escape while I still can.

I don't know what the worst part of that conversation was – having it with my mother – or the fact that she might have been right on the money.

I get into the car, drenched from the few metres I had to run, and we head off in the direction of school.

For once, I'm grateful for Bry's silence.

I've got enough thoughts running through my head to last me all fucking day.

I'm *so* fucked.

I don't know *how* this happened.

I don't know *when* it happened.

I can't be in love with Berlin Davids – I just fucking *can't.*

I shove it all down deep where I can't even reach it. I'll do what I do best and deal with it another time. Bury it under rugby and working out until I'm ready to face facts.

Me and Bry barely exchange anything more than a few grunts and clipped sentences, and I dunno what's on his mind, but he's even quieter than usual. I don't even ask – I've got enough of my own issues without diving into his. It's every man for himself right now.

We go our separate ways, and I jog to my locker to get my shit for maths class. It's probably one of my least favourite classes.

I grab my books, shove them in my bag and head for class.

I'm looking down at my phone, reading a message from Pax, so I don't notice her right away.

She's leaning against the wall, one leg bent, exposing her thigh in her short-ass skirt.

I can't help but look; I'm a straight male after all.

"Can we talk?" she asks, her tone seductive as I approach.

Why today?

Jesus Christ, apparently, it's the day for females to come after me. First Mum and now Liana.

I must have a flashing neon sign over my head, telling every female in a five-mile radius that I've turned soft, and they should tell me their opinion.

"Do we have to?" I deadpan.

"It's just a conversation, Cullen," she snaps, before quickly regaining her composure and giving me a sickly-sweet smile. "I can ask again another time, if you'd prefer something more... *public*."

It sounds like a threat.

I don't know what the fuck she wants to say to me, but I know one thing for certain, it's *not* going to happen with an audience.

I glance up and down the hallway, checking to see if anyone is watching us, before grabbing her elbow and leading her around the corner and into an alcove.

"What do you want, Liana?" I cross my arms firmly across my chest.

"You don't have to give me the attitude, I'm not trying to cause trouble."

I know I don't have to, but it's on the house.

And *bullshit* that she's not looking for trouble. Liana is *always* trying to cause trouble. She thrives on that shit, and she does it well. The girl gets away with murder in this school.

I don't reply, just raise an eyebrow at her.

"So, you're dating Berlin now then?"

She's trying to lay on the charm real thick, but I'm not falling for it. I can see the way her eye twitches when she says Berlin's name, I can see the tightness in her shoulders. She's not fooling me. She's wild.

I know she didn't come after me to state the obvious either.

"What's it to you?"

"We only broke up like five minutes ago."

We didn't *break up* and it wasn't five minutes ago either, but it seems like Liana is all about twisting facts in her favour.

I feel my nostrils flare. I can't be fucked with this shit, but I've had it coming for weeks – I'm not dumb enough to think this was never going to happen. I don't know why it's taken her this long, but I still have less than no time for it.

"Make no mistake, Li, you were *never* my girlfriend."

She looks hurt, but to her credit, she stands strong.

"Maybe not, but you kept me around longer than anyone else. There has to be a reason for that."

I know what the reason was. So does she, but she wants to believe she's wrong.

Well, bad fucking luck.

"I kept you around because you were a decent fuck, Liana, and because you suck dick like a champ. *That's* why I kept you around, nothing more, understood?"

Her expression morphs into a sneer.

I'll admit, it was fucking harsh, but I couldn't care less about it at this point. Liana is a grade A bitch, and spending time with Berlin has only made me see that more. On the outside, the two girls have their similarities – they're both confident to the point of being arrogant, outspoken and beautiful – but Berlin has a soft side, she really cares about people and things. Liana is rotten on the inside. There isn't a person she wouldn't shit all over to get a leg up in this world.

"Fuck you, Cullen. I've moved on anyway."

I huff out a laugh. "Lucky guy, does he know you're still chasing me?"

"I am *not* chasing you."

"Then what the fuck are we doing here, Li? What do you want?"

She looks like she's about to explode. I can tell she desperately wants to play it cool, but the word *desperate* is key here.

"You're going to regret making me look like a fool."

Her words are like ice, but what she doesn't seem to be getting is that I already do regret it. I regret ever laying a finger on her.

"Consider it done," I ground out the words.

I turn around and stride away from her.

"And tell your little girlfriend to watch her back," she calls after me.

I freeze, and I actually hear her inhale sharply in surprise from behind me.

She's done it now.

I'm vibrating with anger.

She can threaten me all she likes, but she so much as touches a hair on Berlin's head and she's done. I'll end her life as she knows it.

"I'd be *very* careful about what you do next, Liana." I don't even bother to turn and face her when I speak.

I know she's listening.

What she does with my warning is up to her. I've got far more important shit to worry about.

TWENTY-THREE

Berlin

"But she was snooping around your locker." Sophia's eyes are wide as saucers as she hurriedly tells me about how she's just come across Liana hanging around the hallway near our lockers.

I shrug my shoulders. "She's probably just mad the cleaners wiped off that stupid writing she did."

"What if she puts drugs or something in there and then tells the teachers?"

"She won't."

"She *drugged* us, B, she totally would."

"They put up cameras, Soph, seriously, *chill*. After the drawing on my locker and the cut-up uniform, they put cameras in that hallway. Have you seriously not noticed?"

She's ready to keep coming at me in her panicked state, but my words must get through to her, because she just opens her mouth and then snaps it shut again.

"Oh," she finally mutters.

Maybe if she didn't spend so much time with her nose stuck in a fucking book – she might actually notice what goes on around her.

I've got a pretty solid suspicion that my dad had something to do with the installation of those cameras, but I can neither confirm nor deny my theory given how tight-lipped he's been on school matters lately.

I'm pretty happy with the outcome either way, because Soph's right – I'm starting to think that Liana doesn't have any boundaries, and I don't really feel like getting expelled for something I didn't do.

"*Oh,* is right. Liana's crazy, but I'm not worried about my locker. That'd be too easy. She was probably just trying to intimidate you."

"Well, it worked," Sophia mutters.

No shit.

I can't exactly blame her for being on edge, Liana went too far at Bry's party and Soph is scared.

It makes me think that maybe we *should* go to the police with the video and the drug test results. Maybe I'm being stupid by trying to get more before we take her down.

I want to talk to Cullen about it, but after I saw him and Liana having a hushed conversation tucked down a deserted hallway this morning, I'm starting to wonder how much I can actually trust him.

It's fucked with my head.

I felt like I saw the real Cullen yesterday. Not the bullshit version he presents to the world, but the real guy that's under the surface. But after seeing him and Liana only a foot away from one another, talking in whispers, I can't be so sure.

I think it would be smart of me to tread carefully and not jump to conclusions but keep my cards a little closer to my chest.

Talking to Pax about it seems like a better option, and one I decide I'm going to go with, tonight.

The team has training after school, but Pax has detention for swearing too much, so hopefully I'll be able to catch him after that, while Cullen is still at practice.

I park that thought to think about later. Right now, I need to fill the girls in on the scheme I've had unfolding behind the scenes for the past week.

"I need to show you guys something," I say quietly as Carissa and Laura arrive at our usual lunch spot.

They all look at me curiously, but along with Sophia and Mel, shuffle in closer.

"I've been talking to Liana online."

"What? *Why?*"

"Why the fuck would you talk to that bitch?"

"Whaaaaaat?"

"Ew."

The responses all come at once and I can't help but laugh.

"Oh, shut up, do you think I'm an idiot?"

"I'm starting to have my concerns," Sophia mutters.

I take a glance around and when I'm satisfied that the third formers that just walked past us are far enough away that they can't hear, I lean in closer.

"I'm not technically talking to her, but *Jaxon* is."

"Who the fuck is Jaxon?" Carissa whispers.

"He's a guy I made up." I bite back a laugh.

I watch as one by one; they figure out what I've done – that I'm catfishing her.

"You are a straight-up badass." Carissa beams.

"Holy shit, I'm going to wind up on a TV show," Sophia says dramatically.

"That would be epic, but I doubt it," Mel says.

"Oh my god, tell us what she's been saying. And how did you start talking to her? I have so many questions."

I smirk. I have to admit, I'm a little proud of myself. I know it's morally questionable, but fuck it, save me a seat on the bus ride to hell.

Sometimes you have to fight fire with fire.

"So, I set up an Instagram for Jaxon Wright, and I text a guy I knew from back in Aussie who I know hates social media and has no profiles, and asked him if I could use his pics to fuck with a bitch who was giving me grief."

"And he said yes?" Carissa asks, shocked.

I pop a shoulder. "Yeah, he's a good guy and he's kinda in love with me, so it didn't take much convincing."

"I want to be you when I grow up," Laura tells me.

"So, I added a bunch of pics, made a heap of fake accounts and followed him from them to get the ball rolling and then the genuine follows started coming in. He's got about fifteen hundred people following him and I only started this a week ago."

I grab my phone and pull up the account before showing the girls my handiwork.

"*Dayum.*"

"That is one *hot* guy."

"I know, right? So anyway, Liana's profile is public, because of course it is, so all I did was follow her and wait for her to follow back – which obviously she did. Then I just waited for her to post a story about some mundane aspect of her life and boom... slid into those DMs."

"You scare me," Mel comments.

I nod in acceptance. I scare myself sometimes.

"I told her that I live like twenty minutes away, recently moved here for work after I left school, and she ate that shit up. She's been telling me all about her asshole ex and how he's parading his new slutty girlfriend all over school."

"Oh, this is too good." Carissa's grin is bigger than I've ever seen it.

"I'm going to suggest playing some pranks soon, see if I can get her to own up to doing any of the shit we know she's already done to me. It can't hurt to have that in writing, but even if she acts the innocent little blonde and doesn't say shit, I have to admit, it's *so* much fun to fuck with her."

"You're slightly unhinged," Sophia says, but I can tell that even she thinks this is funny. And if miss goodie two shoes thinks it's funny, then you know it's deserved.

All bets were off the moment she drugged me.

"Oh god, she's not sending you nudes, is she?" Laura asks, grimacing. "I mean, don't get me wrong, she's a beautiful girl, but I still wouldn't want to see her coochie."

Carissa starts sniggering and then we're all full-on laughing together.

"Oh god." I wipe the tears from under my eyes. "*Coochie*. Are you eighty?"

"Well, I wasn't about to call it a *vagina*."

We all look at one another and lose it laughing again.

It hits me then; this is what it's like to have real friends. People who actually give a fuck about you and who you give a fuck about in return. People you can be yourself with.

I have to admit. It's kind of nice.

"Okay, but seriously?" Laura prompts as the laughter dies off again.

"No nudes," I tell her. "A couple of cheerleading outfit selfies, but she's playing it coy."

"And then home boy just hooks you up with pics to send back to her?"

I raise a brow at Mel. "Have you ever used the phrase 'home boy' in your life?"

"Not once."

She's adorable.

"But yeah, Taj sends me a few pics a day and I just use whatever I want."

"Of course his name is Taj," Carissa says. "I bet he surfs too."

"He sure does."

He's your quintessential Aussie surfer dude. Tanned, blond, and ripped.

Good luck to Liana.

"And I may have come up with another little method of payback to get involved in while we wait for this other one to marinate." I smirk.

"I don't even think I want to ask," Soph says with a defeated sigh.

I grin wickedly. I was inspired by something Liana once said to me.

"I think we should remind her there's a not-so-fresh fish in town."

"YOUR MA SEEMS KINDA NERVY TODAY."

"She's been a bit weird lately. I don't think she can figure you out."

"*Me?* What do you mean?" My voice rises an octave. "What's it got to do with me?"

He chuckles. "I don't think she knows whether you're with me or Cull." He waggles his brows at me. "Or *both.*"

My jaw drops. "You don't think she thinks..."

"That we're double teaming you? Yeah, I think she just might."

I grab the pillow off his bed and throw it at his head. "That was a visual I didn't need."

"You and me both." He laughs as he flops down onto his back.

"Does she not like me?"

He throws the pillow back at me. "Don't be stupid. She thinks you're great. But things have been different since you've been around, I guess, and she probably doesn't know what to make of it all."

"Different how?"

He shrugs. "I've never seen Cull like this. He's smitten as fuck with you."

It's embarrassing how much that warms my heart.

As much as it pains me to admit something so stupidly girly, I'm smitten too. He's stubborn, cocky, abrupt and demanding, but all that only makes his sweet side so much sweeter. Nothing about our relationship – because I guess that's what the fuck it is now – is simple, but I've never been one to do things the easy way, anyway.

"Wipe that look off your face, right now," he warns me.

"*What* look?"

"That stupid dreamy look girls get. Trust me, I know it, I've seen hundreds of girls look at me like that."

I shake my head in amusement. "Nice work staying humble, pal."

He grins at me, but there's something in his eyes

again that makes me think he's still not quite one hundred percent accepting of me and his brother.

I can't help but wonder sometimes if I would have got together with Pax, if Cullen weren't in the picture. Ironically, it's kind of a *Twilight* situation. Pax is my Jacob.

He's like my best friend. Him and I, we'd make sense. But me and Cullen... it's just something different.

It's also something I need to be wary of – especially after I saw him and Liana and their secret conversation today.

That's why I'm here right now, getting Pax while he's away from the golden boy. He's probably the only person that can help me figure this out.

He's the only person I trust outside of the girls, but he's also the person I worry about the most, because if he thinks for a second that Cullen might be going to hurt me – or when he finds out what Liana did – he's going to flip a lid, but I have to tell him.

"I saw Cullen and Liana talking today."

"What? Where?"

"In a little hallway in the maths block."

He narrows his eyes at me. I take it as my cue to give him more information.

"They were huddled together in a little alcove. I wasn't stalking him or anything. I dropped my pen when I was walking to class, and it rolled in that direction. I never would have even looked that way otherwise."

"Did he look pissed off?"

"I don't know, his back was to me mostly, but they were standing close and talking quietly."

He looks like he doesn't like the sound of it any more than I do.

"She was probably feeding him some bullshit to try and get him to take her back since no one else is willing to go near her now."

That reminds me, I need to message her later from my catfish account – see if I can gauge where her head is at.

"I wouldn't even put it past that crazy bitch to pull a fake pregnancy or something. I'm telling you, she's fucking mental," he carries on.

"Seriously? Do people actually do that around here?"

"*Seriously.* Her older sister did it to a guy in the team about two years ago."

Jesus Christ. Clearly crazy runs strong in that gene pool.

"I've never really understood the theory of it – they use a fake baby to trap a dude, but that plan's gonna go tits up when there's no kid at the end of it, right?" he questions.

"I'm not sure it's a plan based too heavily on logic, Pax."

"True." He shrugs. "The guy married her anyway. They still don't have a kid… He wasn't the sharpest tool in the shed."

"This is why you should always wrap your dick. Let this be a lesson to you."

He salutes me. "You're not worried about Cull talking to her, are you?"

"I don't know. A little, I guess. I want to trust him, but I sure as fuck don't trust her."

"Good call. I think she's harmless enough, but you can never be too careful with a girl like that. I don't want her near him either, but that's because she's a head case, not because I think Cull would do anything."

She's certainly *not* harmless, and if I'm going to get Pax's help on this, it's time I told him *everything*.

"I need to tell you something." The tone in my voice changes and he doesn't miss it.

He sits up a little straighter, his eyes hyper focused on me. "I'm not going to like it, am I?"

"Nope." I shake my head. "But you have to be chill and believe me when I say I've got it handled."

He gives me a look that tells me he's absolutely *not* going to be chill.

I tell him everything. About the drug tests, the video, about how we haven't gone to the police. I even tell him about me being 'Jaxon'.

I expected him to laugh about that part – I was hopeful it might have lightened the mood – but I think he's gone way past laughing. He's radiating anger. I can actually see his hands shaking. He's furious.

"Have you told Cullen?"

I shake my head. "I was going to, but after seeing

him talking to her today, I can't. I don't know who to trust anymore."

"You can trust me," he says, his voice unwavering.

"I know." I nod my head.

I feel my phone vibrate in my pocket and I pull it out, grateful for the distraction from Pax's intensity.

The minute I read the words on the screen, I wish I hadn't.

Liana: Man, I've had the WORST day. My stupid ex keeps trying to get back with me, it's so tragic. How has your day been? x

I can feel tears welling in my eyes, which is so massively unlike me, I almost don't recognise it for what it is. I'm not stupid. I know she's not exactly known for telling the truth, but I also know there's a chance she is, and that breaks my heart.

I'm going against my better judgement with this boy, and I hate that I've given him the power to hurt me. He's steam rolled every wall I've put up to protect myself.

I stare at the screen, willing the moisture in my eyes to go away.

Pax holds his hand out for my phone, and I give it to him.

He reads the message and I hear him growl. "She's a lying piece of shit, Ice, and she's going to fucking pay for doing this shit to you. I swear to God, if it's the last thing I do, I'll make her sorry."

He pulls me into a hug. His massive frame wraps

around me like a warm blanket. It's not until he's holding me that I realise how much I need it.

I know I do it to myself – I make out like I'm unshakable, that nothing fazes me or gets me down, but truthfully, I barely know myself after a few weeks here. I have friends – real friends who know me so well in such a short time. I've got Cullen, and Pax.

I have things it would hurt to lose, and I don't know how to manage the feelings that go with that.

"We'll figure it out," he murmurs against the top of my head. "I promise. And don't write Cull off, okay? I know he's not exactly known for being loyal, but he is to you."

He's right. I need to give Cullen the benefit of the doubt.

"I put a fish in her air vent." I sniff.

He pulls back to study my face.

"You put *what, where?*"

"A stinky bait fish, in the air vent of her fancy car," I say through the few tears that managed to escape.

He stares at me blankly for a few moments before pissing himself laughing and pulling me back in for another hug.

"Just when I think I have you all figured out." He chuckles.

TWENTY-FOUR

Cullen

Berlin laughs her head off at me as I climb through the second-storey window into her bedroom. It was no small feat, I tell you what. That trellis was not built to hold someone my size, but thank fuck there's a tree growing close enough that I could make it work without breaking my neck, or her house.

"You could have just come in the front door. My dad thinks the sun shines out of you," she says with a roll of her eyes.

I chuckle as I pull the window shut behind me. "Most girls would be happy that their dad liked their boyfriend."

She raises a brow at me. "Boyfriend? And who gave you that title?"

I wrap my arms around her middle and lift her up to kiss her.

She wiggles to get free at first – stubborn little fucking thing – but she quickly gives in, her legs wrapping around my waist and her arms holding on tight to my neck as I kiss her into submission.

I pull away and she groans, wanting more.

"Tell me you're my girlfriend," I growl.

"No."

I nip at her neck. "Give in, just one fucking time." It's meant to sound like an order, but it comes out almost begging.

She runs her hands through my hair, her nails skimming my scalp. I'm still holding her in my arms, in the middle of her bedroom.

"But you don't *do* girlfriends," she says, a smug smirk playing on her lips.

"I do now."

"I don't think I'm worthy of the privilege," she sasses me. Using the same line she did the first time we met.

I growl. "Do what you're told for once."

"I told you to take me out on a date first."

"You're a pain in my ass, new girl."

She laughs at me, so I kiss her again, turning us towards her bed. I sit on the edge, her still in my lap.

"Be my girlfriend." I'm looking right into those big dark eyes of hers now.

I can see her resolve wavering. I'll take her on the

date. Fuck, I'll take her on a hundred dates – none of that needs to stop her from being mine – right now.

"Ask me nicely," she whispers.

I have to laugh at that. Points for fucking consistency. She wants me to play her games... I can play. I'll do whatever it takes.

"Berlin Davids, will you be my girlfriend?"

"Manners."

"Jesus fucking Christ, can't you just –"

"Yes," she cuts me off, laughing.

"I swear to God, if you're messing with me..."

She sinks her teeth into her bottom lip and runs her hands through my hair. "I guess I'm just another girl that can't say no to you now."

I chuckle. "Guess so."

She lightly smacks my shoulder and rolls her eyes.

"Only difference is you're the only girl I'm saying yes to."

I can't say for sure, but I think that might melt the ice queen, just a little fucking bit.

We kiss again, soft and sweet this time.

I don't even know who the fuck I am anymore. I don't do soft and sweet. I don't do girlfriends. I don't do any of this shit, but everything changed when I met her.

"What are you doing in my bedroom, golden boy?" she asks as she nuzzles into my neck, kissing the skin below my ear.

"Losing precious sleeping hours," I groan.

I know damn well I should be at home catching

some much-needed rest, but I can't stay away from her. She's got me hooked.

She looks pretty happy with my answer.

"You should go home and get some sleep."

"I was thinking I'd get some sleep right here..."

"You inviting yourself for a sleepover, big guy?"

"Maybe."

She looks a little bit torn. I bet I know where her head's at. We haven't fucked yet; we've come pretty damn close though, but that's not why I'm here anyway.

First time I've ever snuck in a chick's window, and it's not just been about getting my dick wet.

I watch her battle with herself internally.

"You'll have to sneak out before Dad gets up, since you didn't come through the front door like a normal person."

"Too easy."

The trellis might have a different opinion, but fuck it.

She fidgets in my lap.

"Let's go to bed," I tell her.

She nods. I can't be sure, because she's always so hard to read, but I think she might be nervous.

I cup her face in my hands. "I just want to sleep. I don't want to rush things. Not with you, Berlin."

I can definitely tell she liked that answer.

I'm getting better at this shit. I've never particularly gone out of my way to try and make someone else happy, but it's addictive. It's like a never-ending challenge. A kick where the goalposts just keep moving.

She stands up, and I smack her ass for good measure. She's got on these little satin pyjama shorts that'd make a much tougher man than me crumble.

She's so fucking sexy and she's not even trying.

She giggles as she ducks out of my reach to turn out the lights.

I kick off my shoes and jeans, followed by my hoodie and t-shirt, and slide into her bed. The room goes dark, and I hear the patter of her feet as she crosses the space.

She slips under the covers next to me, and I grab her and pull her body as close to mine as it can get.

She's so soft and warm and she smells so good.

"How was training tonight?" she whispers into the quiet room.

"It was good," I reply, relaxing further into her, my eyes already getting heavy. "Tough though. Coach made us each carry a tackle bag the length of the field and back in between drills."

"That shit's Old Testament."

"Coach is Old Testament."

She's got her back to my front and when I run my fingers up her bare thigh, she squirms, her ass grinding against my dick.

That is not going to help my resolve to take things slowly with her.

A moan escapes me, and she realises what she's doing.

"I'd say sorry, buuuut I'm not all that sorry," she teases.

"You better go to sleep before I change my mind about taking things slow."

I don't know who the fuck I'm kidding, I'm basically half asleep.

She yawns and I feel her body relax even more in my arms.

"Promises, promises," is the last thing I hear.

***

"YOU REALLY CARE ABOUT HER, don't you?"

My hammer pauses mid-swing. I look over to where Cole has been putting the finishing touches on the door.

It's obvious he's referring to his daughter.

Sounds like it's also obvious that I *do* really care about her.

I didn't think it was possible to care about something outside of rugby and my family, the way I care about her.

We might have only known each other a couple of months, but we've spent countless hours talking, messaging, and hanging out.

I know things about that girl she doesn't know about herself.

I know a crease appears in her forehead when she tries to lie. I know she acts so tough to hide how she really feels. I know she wishes things had been different with her mum... I know she's fiercely loyal once she eventually lets someone in.

And more importantly, I know what she does to me. She makes me more human somehow.

"Yeah." I nod at him. "I care about her a hell of a lot."

I wouldn't be here, working on a last-minute surprise for her birthday while Pax gets all the glory of taking her out for dinner otherwise.

I hope she likes what we've done here – I know she's been hanging out to get back in the dark room.

He nods his head as though he expected my answer.

Cole is a seriously good dude. He's accepted mine – and Pax's place in his daughter's life without question, and with a surprising amount of trust, given we're two stereotypical, testosterone-fuelled males.

I've never had a dad around, but I can't imagine that they'd all be as cool as Cole is.

He's been an absolute legend to every single one of us on the team, but me especially. He was a fullback, same as I am now, and his knowledge has been invaluable to me. He's taken the time to go over and over things with me – make me a better player, and not only a better player, but a better leader. I can't fucking wait to see what he can teach me by the end of the season.

All round, Cole Davids is a real good dude. If my dad were alive – I'd have wished for him to be just like Cole. I think half the guys on the team would replace their dads with him if they could.

"You know what? I think she really likes you. I've never seen her like this, and when it comes to my daughter, I've just about seen it all. That girl is *a lot*."

I chuckle. "She's sure as fuck got a lot of personality."

"No one's ever going to accuse her of being boring," he agrees.

He's looking at me with something that feels a lot like approval. It's not like I was expecting him to answer the door with a gun in hand when he found out I was dating his daughter, but I also didn't expect this.

If someone had told me six months ago that I'd be spending my afternoon fitting out a corner of the garage for my girlfriend's birthday, with her dad – I'd have told them they'd lost their mind. But here we are.

"She's a good kid, Cullen. Be gentle with her. I know she puts up a front of being tough, but I think when it really comes down to it, she needs someone she can be soft with."

The old me would have buckled under the responsibility of that statement, but that isn't me now – taking care of Berlin and making sure she's safe... nothing has ever felt more natural to me. She might not need it, but I'll be there waiting regardless.

I know I'm only eighteen, I've got my whole life ahead of me, but I can't imagine it without her. I still want to play rugby, I want to travel the world and do all the things I've been planning for years, but now I don't want to do them alone.

"Thanks, Cole." And it's not just for his approval,

it's for all of it. His support, the way he's welcomed me, for helping me build this fucking dark room.

He clears his throat. "Well, that's enough of that shit."

I chuckle. "Agreed."

We go back to working in silence.

Thankfully, once the walls are up and the light is all blacked out, I only need to set up all the shit Berlin already has stored down here. I'm on the home straight.

There are tables, developer chemicals and baths, an enlarger and everything else you need. She's got a plug-in red light that I'll set up for her too.

It's not much of a gift, since all this shit is actually hers already, but I'm hoping it'll be one of those 'it's the thought that counts' presents.

I've got a couple more tricks up my sleeve too, but they're sure as fuck not things I want or need her father to help me with.

I plan on making my girl's birthday one to remember.

TWENTY-FIVE

Berlin

Eighteen years old. I still remember being fifteen and thinking this day was *never* going to come. I couldn't wait to be old enough to drink and smoke... and go out to nightclubs. I can vote – not that I know fuck all about politics, but the fact that I can is exciting.

I skip down the stairs to the kitchen where I can hear my dad rustling around.

It's hard to believe I'm the age now, that he was when he and my mum got pregnant. There is no way in hell I'd have any idea what to do with a baby.

He was nineteen when I was born, and I honestly don't know how the fuck he did it – alone.

"Moorrrrrning," I call out in a sing-song voice as I come up behind him.

He turns and grins at me so wide it looks like his face is going to break.

"My baby is all grown up," he gushes as he pulls me in for a huge bear hug. "Happy birthday, B."

"Thanks, Dad," I choke out. He's squeezing me so tight I can barely breathe.

He finally lets me go and hands me a cup of coffee he's already poured for me.

I take it gratefully. I like birthdays as much as the next guy, but they can get a little bit tiring. Especially now that I have friends and a boyfriend and shit.

Who even am I?

I take a sip and sigh. The old man makes the best coffee.

"You're making me feel old here, B."

I glance at him. He's just sitting there looking at me, and if I'm not mistaken, his eyes are a bit glassy.

"You getting emotional in your old age?"

"I think I just might be."

"If you launch into a sentimental speech, I'm leaving."

"Leave now and you won't get your present."

I've been wondering for the past month what my dad could possibly have gotten me for my birthday. I kind of already have everything. I wouldn't say I'm ridiculously spoiled, but Dad isn't short on cash and he's a generous kind of guy, so I don't ever really go without.

I told him a hundred times that I didn't need anything, but I know he's ignored me – he always does.

Gift-giving is his love language and no amount of arguing with him is going to change that.

"We can't have that, can we?"

He chuckles. I'm willing to bet at this point that he's gone overboard. I only hope he didn't choose me jewellery. His intentions are good, but his taste in jewellery is bad.

He opens a drawer and pulls out a small, wrapped box. One that looks like it would quite comfortably fit some god-awful necklace.

I try not to laugh at myself. I *had* to go and put that out there into the universe.

"Happy birthday, my darling," he says as he hands it to me.

I hug him again. I don't care if it's the ugliest necklace I've ever seen, he's the best father a girl could ask for.

"I'm so proud of you, B. We've been through a lot, you and me, but we made it. You're officially an adult, and I think I did a pretty good job, if I do say so myself."

"Yeah, I think I turned out okay."

"So far anyway." He chuckles.

He finally lets me go and nods at me to open my gift.

I rip off the paper and lift the lid on the plain, black box.

He didn't...

Sitting inside the box is a car key.

"Are you serious?"

I flip it over and almost go into cardiac arrest when I see the words 'Range Rover' written down the side.

I've wanted a Range Rover ever since I paid enough attention to know what one was.

"I figured that was what you'd want, since you pretty much froth at the mouth every time we see one."

Okay, so I'm willing to admit that maybe I *am* a little spoiled.

"You got me a *Range Rover?*"

He nods. "Picked it up from the dealership last night. It's sitting in the driveway."

I run to the nearest window and sure enough, there's a shiny, pearly white Range Rover sitting in the drive.

"Holy shit!"

"I know. I'm the man."

On this occasion, I couldn't agree more.

I run to the front door and throw it open, not giving a single fuck that I'm wearing pyjamas and no bra.

It beeps as I hit unlock, and I climb into the front seat like an excited little kid.

It smells like new car in here and when I power up the dashboard, I see that that's because it *is* a new car. My outrageous father has literally bought me a brand-new fucking car.

It's so excessive and I couldn't love it more.

I look back at the house and see Dad standing in the doorway, watching me, a huge smile on his face.

I jump out and run back towards the house, throwing myself into another hug.

"You're insane but I love it so much, *thank you.*"

"You're welcome. You better not drive it like a psycho, that thing was expensive as hell."

I'm well aware what one of these things retails for, and it's out of control.

"No shit. I can't believe you spent that much money on a car. I promise I won't drive it like I stole it."

I got my driver's licence back in Australia. I wouldn't say I'm a *bad* driver, but I definitely get road rage in traffic. I haven't even driven once since we moved here, but I can't imagine traffic is going to be too much of an issue around this sleepy little city at least.

"I got white because all the snotty little bratty girls in movies drive white SUVs."

I can't help but laugh at that. "Hey, if the slipper fits, right?"

"Start calling you *Cinderella.*"

"Better yet, I'll call the car that."

He raises a brow at me. "You're going to call your car *Cinderella?*"

"Cindy for short."

He shakes his head in amusement. "Whatever you say, kiddo."

"I better go get ready for school."

"Yeah, you can drive yourself now. I won't have to taxi your ass around anymore."

I'm totally going to text Soph and tell her I'm picking her up.

I let out an excited noise that is uncharacteristically

girly for me, and take off inside, up the stairs to get ready.

CULLEN WRAPS his arms around my middle from behind me, his chin resting on my shoulder.

It makes me smile. He's always touching me, moving closer to me.

I come across as being pretty tough, but nothing melts me like someone showing me affection.

"Have you had a good day?" he murmurs in my ear, sending shivers down my spine.

We're back at my house, and I've just discovered that my dad's second birthday gift was him giving me and Cullen the house for the evening.

Cullen insisted that he give me his gift here, after school, and then we're having our highly anticipated first date.

"I've had a great day," I tell him honestly.

I can't ever remember a birthday that my cup was this full. I've had some great birthdays over the years with Dad, but this one takes the cake, and not just because of the Range Rover.

Pax surprised me with a drawing he'd done – of me. It's absolutely incredible, and I had no idea he was doing it. It's so personal, so intimate. In some ways I feel bad that he spent so much time and effort on something just for me. I was slightly concerned about how Cullen would feel about it, but he just spent a long time looking at it, then told me it needed to be framed before giving Pax a fist bump and telling him it was epic.

Soph gave me a delicate gold heart on a chain, Carissa gave me a framed photo of the five of us and baked me a cake, and Mel and Laura got me a voucher to get my nails done at this cute little local place we saw on Instagram.

I've honestly never felt so special in my life. Everyone put so much thought into making today great for me.

I run my finger over Pax's drawing on the bench in front of me with all my other treasures.

I can't believe he did this for me.

He might be an amazing rugby player, but I hope he never gives this up. He's got a gift.

"He's pretty talented, right?"

I nod my head in agreement, my gaze trailing over my own features on the sheet of paper.

"One day when he's famous, I'll be able to say I've got an original Pax Benson."

He chuckles. "And I'll be able to say I gave him a wedgie when he was ten."

I laugh at that. I can just imagine it.

"Are you ready to see what I got you?"

He kisses my neck, and I can safely say that I'd rather stay here doing this than pretty much anything else; gift be damned.

I tip my head to allow him easier access, and a

moan escapes me when he moves higher to the sensitive skin just below my ear.

He chuckles, obviously pleased with my reaction – wanker.

Too soon he pulls away, and before I even get a chance to turn around, he's covering my eyes with some kind of fabric.

"Seriously, a blind fold?"

He ties it behind my head. "Don't even think about arguing."

I've already more than thought about it, but part of me kind of likes being at his mercy.

When he's satisfied that it's fixed in place well enough, he grips my arms and steers me wherever it is he's taking me.

We walk down the hallway, and then he pauses to open a door, into what I *think* could be the garage, but I can't really be sure – my sense of direction has always been questionable at best.

He directs me into the room, and now I'm sure it's the garage, the flooring in here is different.

"Are you ready?" His voice is raspy at my ear.

"I think so?" It comes out like a question, because honestly, I'm confused about what the hell we're doing in here.

I hear him laugh as he unties the blind fold.

I blink a couple of times before my eyes adjust and it clicks exactly what I'm looking at.

"No way."

I take a step forwards, and then spin back to stare at him in shock.

It's my dark room. The corner of the shed that I'd been eyeing up to have my dark room fitted out in, now has exactly that.

"You did this?"

He shrugs. "Your dad helped me, but yeah..."

I go inside the open door and see that he's completely fitted out the whole space with all my stuff.

He's thought of everything, right down to the carpet on the floor to make it more comfortable.

"How did you pull this off? I breathe.

I have no idea where he found the time, or how he managed to do this right under my nose.

"I'm resourceful." He smirks. He's following me around, watching me take it all in. "Plus, your dad loves me."

I ignore his last comment, because we both know it's true.

"You built the walls and everything?"

He nods. "Did most of it last night."

"Holy shit. Put *that* on your CV."

His lips curl up into a heart-stopping smile.

I can't believe he did all this, just for me.

A series of photos hanging up, catch my eye.

I approach them, unsure what they could possibly be, but dying to find out.

My breath gets caught in my throat when I figure out exactly what I'm looking at.

They're all of me, and they're *beautiful*.

I had no idea he took a single one of these photos. There's one of me sketching while I sit in our lunch spot, waiting for the girls. There's another of me at my locker, one of me reapplying lip gloss in a quiet hallway, but the one that stands out the most is of me walking to class, it's from my first week here – I know, because my bag doesn't have my school ID clipped to it yet.

He took this beautiful photo when he hated me.

"I don't understand."

He comes up close behind me and reaches out to hold the image between his fingers.

"I was taking photos of some birds in the trees, and then I saw you... you might have been a pain in my ass, new girl, but I know a good shot when I see one. So, I took it, and I'm glad I did."

"You're a closet romantic, Cullen Carrington."

"You tell anyone that and I'll deny it."

I smirk. "I'm going to tell *everyone*."

He shakes his head, a mixture of amusement and frustration if I had to guess.

"Do you like it?" he asks as he pulls me into his arms.

Do I like it? What a fucking stupid question... I *more* than like it.

"I *love* it. Thank you. I seriously feel like the luckiest girl in the world," I reply as I stretch up to wrap my arms around his neck.

It's not like me to be so vulnerable or honest, but I can't deny that being with him is changing my outlook on everything. I'm struggling to keep my guard up at all.

"I'll admit, it wasn't all selfless. I've been hanging out to get back into a dark room."

"Well, you're welcome here with me anytime, golden boy."

"Like to hope so, given I built you the fucking thing," he replies playfully.

He leans down and kisses me. It's so sweet it gives me butterflies. I've never felt like this before – I can't even explain what he makes me feel.

He presses his lips to mine again once more, soft and sweet.

"I've fallen for you so hard; I don't even know myself, new girl. You've got me all messed up."

His words settle in my chest, warming me from the inside.

I feel exactly the same way. I don't know how it happened, but I do. He's got me so deep under his spell.

There are so many things, *so* many factors that could be at play here, but for now – until it's proven that I should do otherwise, I decide to tune them out and just be here with him.

My happy place.

TWENTY-SIX

Cullen

"Close your eyes again."

"*No*, no more surprises, this is already too much."

"It's not another present, it's time for our date."

"But I don't want to leave this room yet." She pouts.

I chuckle. I'm over the fucking moon that she loves it. And her desire to stay put, plays out well for me, since that's exactly what we're doing.

"What if I told you that you didn't have to?"

She looks up at me with those dark eyes that could bring me to my knees, and smiles. "I guess that'd be okay then."

Her lids flutter shut, and I gently slip out from her hold.

"Stay there. Don't look."

"Yes, Sir." She salutes me.

I turn her around and slap her ass, just for good measure, before darting out into the garage to retrieve the bag I stashed in here straight after school.

I bring it back into the dark room.

"Keep them shut."

"Yeah, yeah," she replies.

I lay out the blanket and all the pillows and cushions, then the platter of snacks and the bottle of wine.

Last thing I have to do is plug in the galaxy projector.

I take one final look, decide that it'll do, and walk back over to her.

I reach out and gently hold her arms. "Okay, open."

She opens those gorgeous eyes and looks around, up at the stars on the ceiling before seeing the set-up on the floor.

I've never really seen a woman melt before, but that's what she does. She looks like her eyes are welling up.

She looks around again, awe written all over her face.

"This is so freaking cute, Cullen. I can't even deal."

"Well, you're going to have to deal because you owe me a date."

"Oh, *I* owe *you* a date, do I?" she questions, brow raised, attitude in full swing.

"I think it's the least you could do for your boyfriend."

She rolls her eyes at me dramatically, but I can tell she's fucking loving it.

The fact that I can tell that about her, just by looking at her reaction, makes me proud as hell. I know this girl. I really fucking know her. Little, minor shit that other people probably wouldn't even notice – I see it. Not only do I see it, but I'm borderline obsessed with it.

With her.

"Why are you looking at me like that?"

So many possible answers, but I go with the one that's screaming at me the loudest.

The one that's probably the most honest shit to ever come out of my mouth.

"Because I love you."

I know it for sure, all of a sudden... I just know. Seeing her standing here in front of me, the stars from the projector dancing across her face... I'm in love.

First time for everything.

Head over heels for a girl I swore was nothing but a thorn in my side – is *still* a fucking thorn in my side... but I love her anyway.

She throws herself at me, and our mouths meet almost in a frenzy.

I lift her up in the air and her legs wrap tight around my waist as her hands cling onto the back of my neck.

Her breath is heavy, and I'm pretty conscious of the fact that we're totally alone for once.

My dick is hard as a fucking rock, and the way she's

rubbing herself against me isn't helping the shred of self-control I have left.

"Jesus Christ, Berlin." I growl as she sinks her teeth into my bottom lip.

I hadn't planned on this being that kind of date, but I'm about thirty seconds away from stripping her bare and fucking her brains out.

"*Cullen.*"

That one word is all it takes. I hear it *all* in the way she says my name.

She's on the ground on her back, my body over hers before I can even think about the best way to do it.

Her fingers are clawing at my shirt, trying to pull it off me.

I push back to my knees, looking down at her and her sexy fucking body as I strip it over my head and throw it away.

Her eyes are all over my body, looking at every inch of me.

"Fuck it turns me on when you look at me like that."

She makes a moaning noise in response that makes my dick jump in my jeans.

She's so sexy.

"You're like a work of art."

I can't take any more of this. I need to see her... touch her... taste her.

Her top is gone in a flash and she's tugging on the button of my jeans.

Those come off and get thrown across the room with her school skirt close behind it.

She's laying beneath me in nothing but her underwear, and fuck me, I've never wanted someone so badly.

"Do you have a condom?" she asks.

I always carry one in my wallet, which is in the pants I just sent across the room.

I grab it, and she watches me as I roll it on.

"Jesus Christ," she moans.

I reach for her underwear and slide it down her legs. I dip my face to taste her, but she grabs a handful of my hair and tugs on it.

"I want to come with you inside me."

Fuck, that makes me even harder. I can't argue with that.

My girl knows what she wants.

I kiss her neck instead and slip a finger, and then two, inside her, working them slowly in and out.

"You're so fucking wet for me, baby."

She reaches down and grips my dick in her hand. "And you're so fucking hard for me."

I've never wanted to bury myself in someone like I do right now.

She's pushing me to the brink of my self-control already. I want to take my time, enjoy every inch of her for as long as I can, but the way she's grinding herself against me has me close to blowing.

"Fuck, Berlin, you keep doing that, and this isn't going to last long."

"That only makes me want to do it more." She moans as I push deeper inside her.

"Always pushing the limits, aren't you, new girl?" I say, my voice husky as I watch her climb towards coming. I slow down intentionally, dragging it out while I still can.

"Stop toying with me," she begs. "I want you."

Fuck, I'm helpless against giving this girl what she wants.

I slide my fingers out and fall forwards, hovering over her. She reaches between us again and guides me towards her pussy.

She lines me up, and I push inside, slowly at first and then all at once when I feel her push back against me.

Noises of satisfaction come out of both of us as I bury myself, balls-deep inside her.

She tips her head back, her tits pressing into my chest.

She's so fucking hot and she feels un-fucking-real.

I'm going to behave like such a virgin right now; I'll be done in thirty seconds.

She lifts her hips, wanting me to move. That spurs me into action, and I move, fast, hard and relentlessly.

She clings onto me, her moans filling my ears as I thrust in and out of her, like I'm desperate for release.

She gives back as good as she gets, bringing her hips up to meet me, seeking every last bit of contact she can get.

"You're going to make me come." She chokes out the words.

I'm close now too. She's getting louder and louder, and I'm right there with her.

"Oh my god," she whimpers, "that's it."

I steal a glance at her face as she falls over the edge. She's looking up at me, her lips parted, and she's so fucking hot, it sends me over the edge with her.

I come so violently it makes my head spin.

"Fuuuuuck," I groan as I ride out what has got to be the longest orgasm of my life.

I can't take any more, I give it one last thrust and then stop, wrecked.

My head falls forward to rest on her shoulder. All the energy feels like it's been sucked out of me.

"Holy shit," I mutter.

"Mmmm hmmm."

I look at her gorgeous face. "That was intense."

"Happy birthday to me." She smirks.

TWENTY-SEVEN

Cullen

Just when everything was perfect – it starts to fall apart, and all from a few simple words. Words I never wanted to hear even a fucking whisper of until I was thirty. At least.

I think I might be pregnant.

I stare at the words on the screen of my phone for the hundredth time, and I can feel my whole world tipping on its axis.

I've got a pretty good idea that Berlin saw Liana's name on the screen of my phone yesterday too, and then there's the fact that I acted like a fucking dodgy cunt and bailed on the rest of our afternoon, which did nothing to make me look any less guilty.

Dickhead move.

I still haven't replied to Li, and surprisingly, she hasn't contacted me again, but I'd be willing to bet the team's championship record on the fact that she'll find a way to speak to me at school today.

Liana *doesn't do* being ignored, so this peaceful silence is probably about to come to a screaming end.

I just want to see Berlin and make sure that her and I are good – if I can pretend long enough. There's something about that girl that makes me want to spill my guts and tell her every secret I've ever had.

We had the best weekend together. After her birthday on Friday night we spent the rest of the weekend just hanging out together and with our friends. I even managed to drag her to the gym with me – all she did was drool and watch me lift weights, but it still made my day. It sounds lame as fuck, but it was a perfect weekend.

I can't tell her about this Li bullshit, not until I know what I'm dealing with. Liana is as crazy as a bag of cats, and we all know the rumours that went around about her sister and the way she apparently trapped her dipshit boyfriend with a fake pregnancy.

Liana has probably been getting tips out of her even crazier sister's diary or something. I fucking hope that's what it is. That I can deal with. But maybe she's for real. I can't deny there's a chance. We used protection, but that's not fool proof.

A potentially pregnant ex-girlfriend... Kill me now before my mother does.

I shove my phone into my pocket and it's only then

that I notice the halls have filled up around me. Fuck knows how long I've been standing here against her locker, contemplating my own death.

Berlin.

It's like I can feel when she's near. I look towards the door right as she walks through it.

She looks around, over to where my locker is, and I think I see a look of disappointment on her face when she doesn't see me standing there. It's short-lived though when she spots me waiting on her.

She skips over to me, a coy smile on her lips, and fuck, I feel ten pounds lighter already, just from looking at her. She looks like seeing me has made her day, and it makes me wonder if I was wrong about her seeing the notification with Liana's name on it after all. She doesn't look like she's suspicious.

The girl is so hard to read sometimes, I can't be sure. I've gotten better at it, but every now and then she still throws me a curve ball and I find myself at a total loss.

"Golden boy," she says as she reaches me.

"New girl," I reply before grabbing her and pulling her flush against me and kissing her hard.

I hear her gasp at the unexpected PDA, but she doesn't fight me on it. In fact, she melts into it, soaking up everything I have to give.

"Mr. Carrington, Miss. Davids!" I hear a teacher yell at us.

Fucking buzz kill. Although this time I can't really blame them; I've got her pressed up against her locker now, and her hands are knotted in my hair. It's not exactly screaming appropriate behaviour – like I give a fuck.

"Break it up!" the teacher calls again.

I pull away and smirk down at Berlin, whose breathing is ragged.

"We should go to class," she whispers.

"Before we give that teacher a heart attack."

She grins at me wickedly.

I take her hand in mine and we walk in a content silence to photography.

I've still got a little bit of work to do on my boards, but I'm pretty sure Berlin is ready to hand hers in.

Her shit is pretty good – the girl has got talent.

We get into class and make small talk as we work away on our projects. This is exactly what I needed. Her near me without the worry of saying something I shouldn't. It's not until I think about it, that I realise Liana has been totally pushed out of my mind and replaced by thoughts of Berlin.

This fucking girl.

She does crazy shit to me.

"I think I'm done," she announces before stepping back and looking at her project.

"I might be biased, but that's a good-looking set of photos." I grin.

She rolls her eyes and I chuckle.

"I'll carry it over to the arts centre for you."

"I'm perfectly capable of carrying it myself."

"I don't give a shit. I'm doing it anyway."

"My knight in shining armour. What ever would I do without you?" She bats her lashes at me dramatically.

All that fucking attitude. Makes me want to bend her over the desk and fuck it out of her.

She's watching me closely, and my expression must be telling how I really feel.

"You can't look at me like that in here."

"I'll look at you however I like, new girl."

"Check you out, acting like you run the cutter," she teases, a playful glint in those sexy, dark eyes.

"Look at you, acting like you can say no to me."

"Careful, big guy, I'll have to knock you down a few pegs."

"I've got a peg I wouldn't mind knocking into you."

She starts pissing herself laughing, and fuck, that sound is the best one I've ever heard. I don't know when I turned into a whipped cunt, but I don't give a shit – she's the best thing in my life.

I smirk at her as I scoop up her work and start carrying it out the door, leaving her with nothing to do except follow behind me.

She bitches and moans on the walk – some crap about being a strong independent female that I ignore – all the way into the arts and drama centre. I let her find her name and watch as she takes the boards from me with a look that's a cross between a sickly-sweet smile and a glare.

I can't help but laugh at her – it's cute that she thinks she is intimidating me.

"Alright, alright, I'm fine now. I think my tiny little girl muscles can handle it from here," she says with a wave of her hand – dismissing me from my duties as boyfriend of the year. "You can run on back to class now."

She starts messing around with the already perfect arrangement. This is her first art submission at Westlake, and I'm pretty sure I'm sensing some nerves.

I'm about to leave and let her do her thing but decide my girl could use one last comment from me.

I come up behind her, wrap my arms around her middle and rest my chin on her shoulder.

"It's amazing, B. I know I've been a real prick, but I'm so glad we got to work on this together." I kiss her neck. "I love you."

"I love you too," she murmurs, leaning into my touch.

I kiss her again, one quick peck, and slip away – leaving her to critique her already perfect display.

I'm in my own world, so it takes me longer than it should to see the demon waiting for me up ahead, but when I do, every muscle in my body tenses.

I fucking called it.

I knew there was no way she could go an entire day without seeking me out.

"What do you want?" I growl.

"*Cullen*," she says, fake hurt in her tone.

I keep walking, with no intention of stopping.

"I think we need to talk about the fact we might be having a baby," she calls after me. "Don't you?"

I stop dead in my tracks. "Keep your fucking voice down," I demand.

I'm shaking with anger.

I spin around, checking that no one is around to hear this bitch and then drag her around the corner so we can talk without being seen.

"Ow, Cullen, you're hurting my arm."

I let go of her bicep and she stumbles a little.

She rubs at her arm. Dramatic bitch. I barely touched her. I really need to watch myself around this cuckoo bird though; next thing she'll slap me with an assault charge and my rugby career will be over before it even starts.

"Can you not yell about that shit for everyone to hear?"

"Well, you didn't message me back. You're trying to ignore me. I had to do something."

"Yeah, because as far as I'm concerned, Li, you're full of fucking shit. And even if you were knocked up, there's nothing to say it's mine. We haven't been together for ages."

"I haven't slept with anyone since you," she says, her bottom lip quivering.

I don't fucking buy what she's selling. Not one little bit.

I don't buy this pregnancy shit. I don't buy her not having fucked another dude. I don't buy any of it.

"Just keep this shit to yourself until we straighten this out."

"What's the matter, Cull? Don't want your little

girlfriend finding out?" She asks the question with so much hate in her tone – her fake mask slipping.

"Leave her the fuck out of this."

"And why should I?"

"Because even if she wasn't in the picture, I'd *never* consider touching you again. Not for all the money in the world."

"You know she put a fish in my car, right? That's the level of maturity you're dealing with."

"That's a pretty rich comment coming from the girl who graffitied school property and cut up her uniform."

She goes to reply but catches herself.

She snaps her bullshit act back in place, and her eyes well with fake tears. "I'm just scared. I don't know what to do."

Fuck me. The state of the drama coming out of this bitch.

"Have you even taken a test?"

She shakes her head.

Of course she fucking hasn't. This thing is smelling more like bullshit by the second.

"I didn't want anyone to see me buying one. I don't know what to do."

"Go to the fucking doctor or something, I don't know, Liana. Google it."

"Will you go with me? I could really use your support."

I see what she's trying to do here. She's looking for excuses for us to spend time together. I don't fucking think so.

"I've got a better idea. I'll meet you here at four, I'll bring the test myself, and you can take it while I wait."

"*What?* At school? *Today?* I don't think that's a good idea. I should come over to your house and we can do it there," she says, scrambling.

"Absolutely fucking not," I snap. "I will meet you, right here, and you'll piss on a stick and then show it to me. Got it? I'm not playing your bullshit games, Li. If this is for real and I got you pregnant, then I'll take responsibility for that. But if you're fucking with me – trying to mess with people like your spinner of a sister did, then you picked the wrong guy."

"I'm not fucking with you. I missed my last period and I feel sick all the time."

She starts trying to tell me all this shit that I honestly just couldn't care less about.

There's no way she's knocked up. She can't be. Life wouldn't be that cruel.

"You'll meet me here at four, and I swear to fucking God, Li, you even try and pull any shit on me, and I'll make your life a living hell. Do you understand?"

I watch as the colour drains out of her face.

"Do. You. Understand. Me?"

She nods.

Good.

I'm done with her. I don't even look at her again before walking away.

TWENTY-EIGHT

Berlin

"It might have been nothing, B, they were just talking –
it doesn't mean there's anything going on." Soph tries to
reassure me, but we both know she's wasting her time.

It's been too many times now. It's not just a one-off
incident anymore.

I should have known that *something* was bound to
kill my mood before long. I've been floating around on
cloud nine, like some kind of smug fool. I should know
better than this. I *do* know better than this.

Idiot.

I swore I was *never* going to become one of *those*
girls, and not only did I become one, at this point I may
as well be the captain of the mothership. Tattoo it
across my forehead – I'm there, bells and all.

He's got me giggling and blushing, texting all night and looking at stupid pictures of us together with butterflies going crazy in my stupid stomach.

Stupid. Stupid. Stupid.

I'm so fucking stupid.

I *knew* I smelt a rat. I just fucking knew it, but I did that bullshit us girls always seem to do, and I talked myself out of it. I made excuses, crafted myself a scarf out of red flags like I'm a champion sewer or some shit.

"Uh oh, the red mist has taken over." Carissa grimaces.

Fuck the red mist, I'm already raging.

"It's probably not nothing, though, is it?" I finally snap. "Liana has been banging on and on to *Jaxon* about her ex wanting her back. I've caught them talking once and now you guys have seen them again. I think it's time I opened my eyes and accepted that this whole thing was probably just some big 'fuck you' prank on the new girl."

"That's not –" Sophia tries to argue with me, but I cut her off.

"I saw a notification on his phone while he was driving my car yesterday. It was a chat in Snapchat. From her."

Carissa grimaces.

Exactly. Nothing good happens on Snapchat.

"And I couldn't see what it said, because it was a fucking Snapchat. Which we all know is where dodgy people communicate dodgy shit. And then he read it, didn't say a word, and started acting all weird."

"That's not great, but she could just be acting all crazy at him."

"Whatever. It's not like I didn't half expect this anyway," I reply, my defensive wall climbing higher by the second.

"Maybe it's not what it looks like." Carissa shrugs meekly. Even she knows that's a piss-poor argument.

"Or maybe it's *exactly* what it looks like."

If I've learnt one thing in my eighteen years, it's that if something looks like a duck and quacks like a duck, nine times out of ten, it's a fucking duck.

"We all see how he looks at you, B – he adores you."

I thought that too – the boy looks at me like the sun shines out of me.

"Or maybe he's a really good actor," I argue.

"Maybe it's all Liana being full of crap and doing what she does best; trying to stir shit."

"Maybe it is." I nod. "But maybe it isn't – and I need to be prepared. Expect the worst and hope for the best and all that."

I can tell by the looks on the girls' faces that they're worried about me, but I'm fine. My ego is potentially a little hurt, but I'm okay.

This is what I get for putting myself out there.

"I have to go," I mutter, "my photography project is due at the end of the day, and I want to make a couple of little changes to it."

I already took my boards into the arts centre, and if it stays as is, then it won't kill me, but there's one little change I wouldn't mind making, since I've got the time.

It's the last thing I feel like doing... staring at pictures of Cullen's devastatingly handsome face all afternoon while I wallow in self-pity, but that's the way the cookie crumbles.

I walk away before they can say another word to me. I appreciate their support, I really do – but I just want to be alone right now. I prefer to suffer in silence.

My phone vibrates as I cross the school in the drizzling rain to get to the art department. If I can get away with it, I'll hide out here for last period and then slip into the photography suite straight after school to fix that one image that's been needlessly bugging me.

I look at my phone screen when I get under the cover of the art block, and see it's Liana again – she's been messaging 'Jaxon' all fucking day, and honestly, I'm sick of it. At this point I'm not even sure what her game is – if I'm right and she's got something going with Cullen behind my back, then I don't know why she's still talking to some other guy. It's crossed my mind that maybe she knows it's me... but that would mean that Pax betrayed my trust, and while I know that it's going to completely break me if Cullen turns out to be the bad guy, it'll totally destroy me if Pax is in on it too.

My brain isn't prepared to deal with that possibility just yet, so instead of worrying about it, I turn my phone off and rush inside.

That one image is pissing me off. I know I'm being pedantic, but I still want to try a different edit.

So much for being finished early.

We're meant to have everything done by the end of the school day, but I'm pretty sure I can convince my painting teacher to let me in there to make a quick swap if I need to – she's a massive hippy and, luckily for me, has a very loose interpretation of the concept of rules.

I slide under the radar hiding out in an empty painting class for last period – it's a hell of a lot better than English would have been – and then slip into the photography studio to try and fix this issue I'm having on one of the computers.

There's only one other student in here, Jeremy – he's in my class, but he's wearing headphones, so I don't even bother saying hey.

I slip into my chair and spend about fifteen minutes watching a YouTube tutorial, trying to figure out how to get the finished product that I want, and when I'm satisfied, I login to our photography class database, select my folder and put in my password.

My eyes narrow as I stare at the empty screen in front of me.

There's *nothing* there.

I frown as I click the back button, double click the folder with my name and type in my password again.

A feeling of dread tingles up my spine when I find it's still empty.

I click back again and repeat the same process three

more times, each time getting more panicked than the last.

I don't know what the fuck is going on. I push my chair back – I'm going to go and ask Jeremy if he can login to his folder, but as I approach him from behind, I can see he's browsing through his – and it's full of images of Keke – his partner for the project. I don't know what he's doing in here either; I've seen his finished project, but I don't have time for curiosity right now. The final bell is long gone by now.

Fuck.

I swerve him, not wanting to make conversation or a scene until I figure out what the fuck is going on.

Maybe it's the computer.

I go back to the computer I was working on – seriously confused and unsure what to do next.

I strum my nails on the desk, thinking.

I've never tried to access Cullen's folder, but I've seen him put in his password a hundred times; I'm pretty sure it's his jersey number and his last name.

I glance around to make sure that Jeremy isn't paying any attention to me, and when I'm sure he isn't, I click on Cullen's folder and type in the password.

It opens up, showing me hundreds of images of my own face.

This is not good.

Something is up, and I've got a bad feeling about it.

I don't know what the hell is going on, but I know one thing – those files were all there earlier today, and now they're gone.

I logout of the computer and try the one next to it, just in case it's some kind of glitch, but I don't have that kind of luck.

My stuff is gone.

I throw my backpack over my shoulder and rush out of the room, heading for the arts and drama centre in the next block, where all our work is being held.

I get there just in time to find Mrs. Oakley – my painting teacher, locking the door.

Maybe I do have some luck after all.

I handed in my painting piece for the show two days early, so I know I'm in the good books with her too.

I barely even have to ask her if it's okay to go in, she's waving me in and telling me to shut the door behind me when I leave, without even so much as a question of why I need to get back in while pretty much all the other students have left for the day.

Bless her heart, the old bat is far too trusting.

I wait for the door to close behind me before I wander into the room, heading for the spot I set my boards up this morning. All the gaps are filled now – everyone submitted their work before the last bell.

I walk towards the corner, to the table that was marked out with my name, and I know before I even round the end of the line of tables, that I'm going to find something bad.

It's like when you're watching a thriller on TV and you want to scream at the idiot on the screen to turn around and run away. Just like that.

I pause for a second, take a deep breath, and round the corner.

My boards are angled away from me now – not how I left them.

Three more steps.

One.

Two.

Three.

"Holy fuck," I breathe.

All my hard work. All my photos. *Everything*. It's ruined.

Not only is it ruined, but half of it has been replaced with offensive words and pictures of me that have been defaced.

I take a step back in absolute shock.

My heart is racing and tears run down my face.

I don't even need to ask myself who did this, because I've only met one human in my whole life who would do something so vile.

I can't even stand to look at it anymore.

I do a full lap of the room. I need to check my other work, but everything else looks perfect.

I'm back in front of my ruined work now.

It's making me feel like I need to throw up.

I back away, then turn and run back to the door I came in.

I hear it slam behind me as I sprint down the empty hallway and into the nearest girls' bathroom.

I throw myself into a stall, lock the door behind me and sink to the dirty floor to cry into my knees.

I EXHALE DEEPLY and feel my head clear enough for me to think straight for a minute.

I've had a good cry now – a bathroom cry is only rivalled by a solid shower cry – there's nothing quite like it, but I can't sit here on this grotty-ass floor feeling sorry for myself anymore.

I have to get up and remember why I'm a bad bitch.

I've got to fix this, so when I see Liana tomorrow, no doubt with a smug smile on her bitchy little face, I'll be able to wipe it off instantly.

She may have destroyed hours and hours of my hard work, but I can't let her beat me.

I still don't know how the fuck she did it – maybe she sucked off one of the nerds from the tech classes to hack into the school server or something... I don't know. It doesn't even matter anymore.

She thinks she's won – and right now, she has. If I keep sitting here on the floor like emo barbie, then she's going to win again tomorrow when the whole school sees that shit show she's produced in place of my work.

That's all the motivation I need.

I pick myself up off the bathroom floor and grab some toilet paper to clean up what I'm sure is a mess of eye makeup.

I sort myself out in the mirror and stand up tall and proud. I've got an idea, and I *have* to make it work.

I slip out of the bathroom and into the still-empty

hallway. I move quickly and out the open door into the cool air.

"*Cullen.*"

I hear her obnoxious voice saying his name and I freeze, my heart pounding.

"Cullen," she says again.

I can't see her. I can't see him. I don't know whether I should stay or run.

"Is it done?" he asks.

Is what done...

"Yeah, I just did it. Like you said."

"*And?*" he demands.

"And you were right. Nothing to worry about."

"Show me."

There's some rustling and then a long pause.

"Did anyone see you?"

"No, Jesus, Cullen, I'm not an idiot."

"Good. I'll destroy the evidence."

"Okay."

I've heard enough.

Honestly, I think I've heard too much.

They planned this together.

I feel so physically sick, I think I could vomit, but I know myself – self-preservation is about to kick in and take over. I'll bury my feelings way down deep where I can't feel them at all, and deal with this later – right now though, I have to fix this.

I *can't* let them win. The preppy cheerleader and captain of the rugby team don't get to win – not this time.

I slip back in the door I came out of and run for the staff room, my plan getting clearer by the minute.

I find Ms. Ainsley in a corner, her head in her laptop.

Ms. A is cool, but I'm hoping today that she's feeling extra cool, because I'm going to need her to be seriously chill if I'm going to have a shot in hell at pulling this off.

She was a teenage girl once – I'll just have to try and appeal to that version of her.

She looks up in surprise at seeing me standing in front of her.

"Berlin, is everything alright?"

I shake my head. "Um, no I don't think it is."

She sits and listens to my whole story – I don't name any names, or voice any of my suspicions... there's no point, and there's even less time. That can be handled another day.

It's close to five now. All the boards are set up ready to go for first thing tomorrow morning. I'm on borrowed time at best.

"Oh my goodness, and you're sure it's ruined?"

Not only is it ruined, but it's straight up offensive.

Poor innocent Ms. A – she's about to see some things.

"It might just be easier if I can show you."

She quickly shuts her computer and follows me out, down into the arts centre and to the door of the room the boards are all in. I wait as she unlocks it and I lead her to where my destroyed work is sitting.

She gasps when she sees it.

It's a fair reaction – all my photos have either been drawn on, ripped or replaced by graffitied ones of me. The most obvious feature is the words 'DUMB SLUT' in bright red lettering across the top, with a defaced picture of me below it. I now recognise that picture as one Cullen took down by the river the first time we kissed – something I was too shocked to notice the first time I saw this mess. I feel tears welling in my eyes at the reminder that he was in on this with her, but I blink them back – I don't have time for a menty-b right now – I'll cry when it's done.

"*Holy shit.*"

I have to laugh at that. Ms. Ainsley is as straight as they come, I'd be willing to bet that 'shit' is a real bad word for her.

"Yeah... So, it's obviously ruined."

"Do you know if anyone else's has been touched?" She's still staring at the boards, eyes wide as saucers.

I shake my head. They're all perfect. I checked every single one. Cullen's was the hardest to look at. It's not like he hadn't shown me all the photos he'd taken of me, but seeing it all together was confronting. If I didn't know better, I'd say it was put together with love. "I think this might have been directed at me personally..."

"Who would do that?"

"That's not really important right now... I just want to fix it."

"Oh, honey, don't worry, I'll grant you an extension,

all the time you need. We'll get to the bottom of this. Whoever did this won't get away with it."

That's what I thought she'd say, but *fuck* that. I don't want to give that little bitch and that lying jock the satisfaction of me pulling a no show tomorrow. I'm a Davids. We thrive under pressure.

"I can't let whoever did this win."

"Sweetie, I promise I'll do everything I can to make sure that doesn't happen. You just take all the time you need."

"I was kinda thinking I'd rather pull an all-nighter and get it done. This is teenage warfare, Ms. A, I have to prove a point now."

She frowns at me. "But you said that all your files were gone..."

"They are." I nod.

"I don't understand what you plan to submit then." She looks like she's got tears welling in her eyes. Poor woman, she's too emotional for this kind of drama.

That's the one thing I *do* know, though. There's one thing those pieces of shit didn't count on, and I intend to use that to my advantage.

I smirk at her. "Well, I got a pretty cool birthday present this year, and I think it's time I put it to good use. But I need your help..."

TWENTY-NINE

Cullen

"Have you heard from Berlin today?" I ask Pax as we walk to our lockers.

He shakes his head. "Nah, haven't talked to her since drawing class yesterday. Why?"

The frown that has been etched into my forehead since yesterday deepens. "She didn't reply to my message and her phone is going straight to voicemail."

"How long?" he asks, a look of concern on his face instantly.

It might still rub me up the wrong way sometimes, but I can't deny that he cares about her as much as I do.

"Haven't heard from her since about lunchtime."

I wanted to ask him the minute he walked in the door last night, but I didn't. The last thing I needed was him telling me that he'd just been on the phone with her while she was ignoring me, but it's gone on too long now. I need to know she's alright.

"What the fuck?" he demands. "Ice is glued to that phone half the time. Maybe it broke."

"Her dad has my number, it's not like she couldn't have called me if her phone got fucked up. She can login to Facebook on her laptop..."

"Did you do something?" He narrows his eyes at me.

"I didn't do fucking anything," I reply. It's not like I can blame him for assuming that, but it still pisses me off.

"I'll see if I can find her this morning." He takes his phone out of his pocket, taps at the screen and then holds it up to his ear before pulling it away again.

Voicemail.

I don't know why, but I've got a bad fucking feeling. We talk *every* night. Yesterday was a fucked-up day in so many ways, but I thought me and Berlin were solid... but now I'm pretty sure she's giving me the silent treatment, and I don't know why. I'm actually scared to find out.

My brain can't handle one more ounce of bullshit right now. It's just a never-ending stream at the minute and I'm sick of it.

Thank fuck it's the last week of term. The drama in this place is getting out of hand.

All hell is breaking loose with the Tonksy-Bryson-Sophia love triangle that is apparently a thing now.

Word on the street is that Tonksy took Sophia out on a date last night and Bryson isn't happy about it. He hasn't said fuck all, but there was this murderous look in his eye that concerns me greatly.

I don't know what the fuck he thought was going to happen. The guy needed to make a move and now it might be too late. She wasn't going to wait around for him forever. But I haven't got the energy to be worrying about that shit – not my monkey, not my circus.

I need a break. I don't want to do anything these holidays other than workout, see my girl, and keep my life as drama-free as possible.

"We have to go to the arts centre now, right?" Pax asks me.

I nod. All the students in our entire year have been invited to view the photography, painting, sculpture and drawing projects today as part of the exhibit.

I can't deny that I'm pumped about what I submitted. I might be biased, but I think they're the best photos I've ever taken.

I think me and Berlin will both get a high grade.

I plan to tape mine to the ceiling above my bed when I get it back. My girl is so fucking gorgeous. I don't think I'll ever get tired of looking at her.

Bryson appears next to me, startling me.

"You good?" I ask him.

He nods, but Tonksy walks past us with a few guys from the team, and I don't miss the way Bry's nostrils flare.

The poor prick looks like he's about to lose it – well,

as much as Bryson could ever lose it.

"We'll talk about it later," I tell him.

He nods again.

I think we both know I mean that Pax and I will talk to him, and he'll respond when it's absolutely necessary, or when he's one hundred percent sure of what he's got to say. As per.

I tip my head in the direction of the arts centre and head that way, Bry and Pax falling into step with me.

It's a shit kind of day; dark, wet, and cold. It's doing sweet fuck all to help me feel better about whatever the hell is going on. Even the weather feels like impending doom.

I can't help but notice Liana and her girls lingering around the entry when me and the boys approach. I can't quite put my finger on what it is with her lately, but it feels like *something* is going on. I can't help but feel like there's something I'm missing.

She's got that cocky bitch attitude about her again today by the looks, like she did before I cut her off. It's radiating off her as she gives me a smug smile.

I don't even let my gaze linger, instead sweeping past her like she's not even there.

Dreams are free.

I knew that her innocent bullshit act would come to an end sometime, but I don't know why now. I don't know what the fuck she thinks she's got to be smug about. I called her bluff on the pregnancy test – the jig is up.

I search the room, hoping to find Berlin, but there's

no sign of her.

Pax is doing the same, but he's coming up as empty as I am.

Fuck.

"There's the girls," Pax grunts, and before I can even reply, he's making a beeline towards them.

I follow him, but Bry doesn't. Sophia is with them, so that's hardly a surprise. *Pussy.*

"Yo, where's Ice at?" he asks the girls as we reach them.

Sophia frowns and looks from Pax to me.

"Aren't you two pretty much joined at the hip?" she asks me, an edge of suspicion to her tone.

"She's not replying to me."

Carissa arches a brow. "What'd you do, hot shot?"

"Fucked if I know," I reply, the words coming out in a rush.

"Well, she told me to meet her here this morning and she said she was going to be pulling an all-nighter. That was yesterday, late afternoon... haven't heard from her since."

That makes no sense. She submitted her work before I did. It's done and dusted. There's nothing for her to spend all night working on.

I don't even bother replying, I just turn and move at pace towards where I watched her set up her boards yesterday, but I can't see them.

I look from board to board, and if it weren't for the fact that all the images are of me, I probably would have missed it completely.

"What the fuck?" I mutter under my breath.

These aren't pictures I've ever seen, and they're not digital either. These have been developed in a dark room, from negatives – the old-school way.

I didn't even know she'd taken these photos.

There's some of me at training, me playing rugby. There are images of me at lunch and before and after school. There's even one of me asleep.

They're *incredible*.

"Not what you were expecting, huh?"

The relief I feel from hearing her voice behind me is short-lived when I turn around and see the cold, hard look in her eyes.

She looks like she's broken, hurt, and exhausted.

I want to hug her, but the look on her face makes me stay put.

"Hey," I breathe. "Are you okay? Why'd you change your work?"

Pax and the girls find us then, and they all look as confused as I feel.

"You alright, B?" Sophia asks as she touches Berlin's arm.

Berlin nods once, a sharp, jerky bob of her head.

"I think you already know the answer to that," she says, staring at me hard.

Me?

I quite literally don't know anything about anything. I couldn't have less idea about what the fuck is happening right now.

I run my hand through my hair as I look between

the group. "Honestly, I don't even know what is going on at all." I exhale heavily. "What the fuck am I missing?"

Berlin arches a brow at me. "You want to know why I changed my work?"

I nod.

"How about I give you a refresher." She's all sass and attitude, but the edge of venom in her tone isn't something I've ever heard before. She's fucking wild and it's *barely* restrained.

I just have no idea about what.

She pulls her phone out of her jacket pocket and taps on the screen before turning and showing me the image she's just pulled up.

It takes me a minute to figure out what the hell I'm looking at, but when I do, my blood runs cold.

She wouldn't...

But even as the thought enters my head, I already know she *would*. I've clearly underestimated just how fucking insane Liana is, and what lengths she'd go to, to get her 'revenge' on Berlin.

"Fucking hell," I growl. "Why didn't you tell me? I could have helped you," I ramble. "Jesus Christ, B, are you okay?"

The words leave my mouth in the same moment that my mind makes the connection. Her words, her attitude... all of it... she thinks *I* had something to do with this.

She's showing the girls now and there's a chorus of

gasps. It's obvious this is the first they're hearing about this too.

Pax is the last to be shown and I can see the rage rising inside him.

I don't know if she thinks he was in on this sick bullshit too or if I'm the only one she doesn't trust.

I notice Liana and her minions out the corner of my eye. It's clear as day they've come for the show, but they're going to be disappointed. My girl has one-upped them yet again.

This whole interaction has been quiet as hell, but it may as well have been a full-on screaming match for the way it's hit me. I feel like every person in the room is staring, when in reality, no one has a clue what's going on.

"Berlin, I –"

She cuts me off by holding up one finger and taking a slow step towards me.

"Don't you stand there and lie to me."

"I'm not, I –"

"They were *your* photos, Cullen."

I open my mouth to deny it, but she's right. Some of those were mine.

How the fuck did Liana get my photos?

"I always was just a complication to you, right?"

No.

"Well, your life just got a lot less complicated, Twilight. We're done."

It's eerily quiet, but it cuts me to my very core.

She turns and leaves and I'm so shocked, I let her.

"WHAT THE FUCK, BRO?" Pax demands. He looks torn between staying here and talking to me, or going after Berlin like all her friends did. "Did you –"

"Of course I fucking didn't," I snap as I push past him, heading straight for Liana.

She looks smug, but I see the moment her eyes leave me and wander over to where she's expecting to find what is undoubtedly her handy work. Her eyes widen in surprise.

Yeah, that's right, bitch. Not today.

Her and her friends are all exchanging frantic, confused glances. Obviously this one was a team effort.

"What's the matter, Li?"

She slides her cool, bitchy face back into place. "I don't know what you're talking about."

"You look like you've got something you want to say."

I feel Pax come up and stand at my side.

"No... it's just." She looks over at Berlin's boards and frowns. "That's not what that little girlfriend of yours has been working on," she mutters.

"Sounds like you know something about it."

She smirks at me, catching herself before she says anything more. "I don't know what you're talking about." Her voice is sickly sweet.

I take a step towards her, my fists balled at my sides. I'm so angry, it's radiating from me. I'd never, ever hit a woman, but I can't deny that I want someone to. Maybe someone needs to knock some sense into this bitch.

She cowers back as my tall frame shadows her.

"You lose, Liana. Time to stop playing the game. It's over."

My voice is a harsh, deep growl.

She just looks up at me, meek and pathetic.

I can't even stand looking at the bitch for a second longer. I push past her and almost run out of the arts centre after Berlin.

I don't know where the fuck she went, but I have to find her.

It's pissing down out here now, but I don't care.

I see what looks like a group of the five of them, huddled under a shelter.

"Berlin!" I yell.

They all turn around to look.

I blink through the pelting rain, walking closer.

Berlin comes out from where they're hiding and crosses the path to meet me. She stops short, her arms crossed tightly across her chest.

I want to hug her so bad, pull her into my arms and promise her that I had nothing to do with this, and that I'll help her get Liana stopped, whatever it takes. But I think if I tried to touch her right now, she'd probably scratch my eyes out.

"What do you want, Cullen?"

"I want to talk to you; I want you to listen to me tell you that I didn't help her do that to your work."

"I don't believe anything you say anymore." She's trying to act tough, but her lip quivers when she speaks.

I try to reach for her, but she rocks backwards. *"Don't."*

Fuck that cuts me deep. Deeper than I thought another person could ever have the power to cut me.

"Ice, he wouldn't do that. He loves you."

His voice startles me. I didn't know Pax had followed me out here, but I should have assumed as much. He cares about her as much as I do in his own way. He cares about both of us.

"I don't want to hear it. I don't want to hear *any* of it. You could have told me, but I guess this has been the plan all along."

Fuck. She's hurt. She's so hurt right now.

"I didn't fucking know, Berlin. I didn't know, *I swear."*

"Alright then. Let's say that's true."

Those words should bring me some comfort, but the tone she's spitting them in, ensures they sure as hell don't.

"Let's say you didn't have anything to do with this particular incident... fine. But you've been keeping *something* from me, haven't you?"

Fuck.

I should have just told her everything from the start, but like a little bitch, I backed out and now I'm paying the price.

"Just remember, Cullen, you have no idea what I

already know – honesty is the best policy here, if you're even capable of that."

"What's she talking about?" Pax cuts in.

I ignore him.

"There's nothing that changes anything about us, new girl, I promise."

She looks at me like she's so disappointed in me. I don't blame her; I'm disappointed in me too.

"Alright then, guess we'll do this the hard way." She stiffens her spine and stands up a little taller. "Have you, or have you not, been talking to her behind my back?"

"I haven't been *talking* to her, I've *talked* to her," I admit.

"I'm not hearing the difference you so obviously think is there, Cullen. It's the same fucking thing," she almost yells. She's soaking wet, the rain has plastered her hair to her forehead and her makeup is starting to run.

It occurs to me that I should be cold, but I'm too numb to feel anything.

"No, it's not, Berlin, *Jesus*. I know what you think is going on here and you're wrong. You couldn't be more wrong."

"I *heard you*, Cullen. I heard you and her whispering about whether or not she'd done it yet. You asked her for evidence. This is all right after I find my work destroyed. I heard you with my own ears. Are you going to stand there and tell me I didn't hear that?"

Shit. Shit. Shit. Shit.

"What the fuck is going on here?" Pax demands. "One of you better tell me or so help me God, I'm going to lose my shit big time."

I pay no attention to him. I've got enough to deal with right now. All I care about is the girl in front of me and making sure that she knows she's the most important thing to me... because that's exactly what she's become – I care about other shit a hell of a lot, but not as much as I care about her. Not anymore.

"I know this sounds like a line, but it's not what it looks like."

Fuck I sound pathetic.

"Are you, or are you not keeping a secret from me that involves *her*?"

I exhale heavily. "Yes, but –"

"But *nothing*, Cullen. You don't want to tell me something, that's fine. That's your choice, okay? But it's my choice not to trust you anymore. It's my choice to walk away."

I can literally feel my heart breaking. I know I can just tell her everything right now, but the problem is that even if she believes me, she doesn't trust me anymore. I should have told her the minute I got that text. I should have let her help me handle this mess. *I should have trusted her.*

She turns on her heel and starts to make her way back to her friends.

I already know it's not going to make a difference now, but the words pour out of me regardless.

"She told me she was pregnant, okay. She lied. I

made her take a test. That's what you overheard me talking to her about. I gave her a test and made her take it while I waited outside the door. She had no more tricks up her sleeve."

Her step falters and she just stands there with her back to me, in the pouring rain.

We're both wet to the skin by this point anyway, so who even cares anymore.

"Berlin!"

She turns around, so, so slowly. "Your ex-girlfriend tried to trap you with a fake pregnancy, and you didn't think to tell me? The girl who has tried to make my life hell from the moment I arrived here, and you didn't think to talk to *me* about it?"

"I didn't know what to say, okay? I was fucking *freaking out*. I didn't know what to believe. I was scared to tell you. I've never had anything worth losing. I knew she was probably full of crap. I know her sister pulled that shit. I'm not an idiot, but what if she really *was* pregnant? Then what the fuck would I do? I didn't know how to tell you." I'm full-on rambling, but I can't stop.

I can feel Pax standing slightly behind me. He hasn't said a word, but he's here, in a silent show of solidarity.

"Keeping secrets with *her* was more important to you than being honest with *me*, and that right there tells me everything I need to know."

She walks away, and there's nothing I can do but let her go.

THIRTY

Berlin

"I think you're maybe being a little too hard on him. It's not really his fault that his ex is a crazy bitch."

Sophia really has gotten brave. Two months ago, she'd have never told me her opinion like that. I'd be proud if I wasn't so emotionally ruined.

We've piled into my car, still in the school carpark, dripping wet – while we re-group and think about what we're meant to do from here. The last thing I want to do is go back into that school and risk running into Cullen, or Liana, but I'm well aware it's only first period, and I can't expect the girls to ditch the day. I've spent the past fifteen minutes getting them up to speed on the last twenty-four hours and the chaos that has been my life.

"He might not have been the one to physically destroy my work, but he still had a hand in it."

"Did he though? I dunno, B. He looked genuinely shocked," Carissa says quietly.

She's right. He really did look shocked when he saw those pictures on my phone. But maybe he's just a good actor. I'm tired of trying to see everything as half full. Sometimes it really is half empty.

I don't even know what to think anymore.

"I know he's fucked up, Berlin, and I'm not saying you have to give him another chance or anything like that, but I think we all just need to take a minute and think about this logically."

I feel tears welling in my eyes.

I sure as hell could use a minute.

I've been on a mission ever since I found my work in a mess and overheard Cullen and Liana talking. I've barely stopped for thirty seconds. I'm mentally and physically exhausted, because on top of all this emo relationship bullshit, I had to produce eight weeks' worth of work in about fourteen hours, and I haven't had a wink of sleep.

I'm tired, emotional, and hurt. It's not a particularly fun combo.

"I'm so tired," I say, my voice cracking. "I'm sad, and exhausted, and I don't even know what the fuck is the right thing anymore. I don't know who I can trust."

I'm full-on crying now, something I haven't done in front of people, probably since I was a toddler.

"Oh, B," Sophia says. She's sitting in the front

passenger seat and pulls me into an awkward hug over the centre console.

I feel the other three pile on in from the back, all of them draping a hand or arm over me in a show of support.

"You can trust us," Carissa murmurs.

I know I can, and I already do, I realise. But outside of these four and my dad, I'm not so sure. This whole thing has even made me sceptical of Pax, which I hate.

I hate not being able to trust my instincts. I hate doubting myself.

I pull back and they all reluctantly let me go. I laugh as I brush the tears off my face. Nothing kills me more than showing emotions in front of other people, so this really is the cherry on top of a shit sundae for me.

"You know, I was wondering if you'd ever crack. You're the toughest bitch out, it's nice to know you're human after all," Mel says with a laugh.

"You tell anyone and you're going to be in so much shit."

"Yeah, yeah, you'll fuck my dad and make me your stepdaughter," she says with an exaggerated roll of her eyes.

That gets a solid laugh out of me. It's that whole if you don't laugh, you'll cry thing – and so we're all hysterically laughing after a few seconds. I feel a little better already.

"So, what do you want to do, B?"

I shrug. "I dunno. You guys should just go back in for second period. You don't need to miss class because of me – no one will even know we missed the viewing of the exhibition."

"And what are you going to do?"

I flip down my sun visor and look at the state of myself in the small mirror. It's not pretty.

"There's no way I'm going back in there looking like this. I'm soaked. I should probably just call it a day. I'd literally kill for a nap right now."

"I really wish we'd got to see Liana's face when she realised her bitchy plan didn't work."

Just knowing how much she'll be fuming on the inside is satisfying enough for me, but my mind is going crazy, wondering if her and Cullen are talking right now.

He really did seem so genuine, but I'm not going to just take his word for it. Even if I'm wrong, and this was nothing to do with him, he's still been sneaking around behind my back and lying to me – he's not innocent here.

Either way, I'm steering clear of this whole mess until I get some sleep and figure some shit out.

"I still can't believe she did that to your photos. And how did she get into the computer database? She's such a fucking slime ball."

I don't have a clue how she managed to pull that off, but she did. Even Cullen didn't have my password, so it wasn't from him. The girl is resourceful, I'll give her that much.

"She's nothing if not thorough, right?" I reply.

"It's lucky you're such a creepy little stalker and

had all those other pictures from your private collection up your sleeve," Sophia says.

Cheeky bitch.

I flip her off and close my eyes as I lean my head back against the head rest.

It's also incredibly lucky that I had my own in-home dark room to process the images after my digital files were lost. I'm doing my best not to think about the fact that Cullen did that for me – it doesn't fit the narrative of him being the bad guy – so for now at least, I need to push it to the back of my mind.

"I really need to learn to save all my shit to a USB or something," I grumble. It would have taken me only half as long last night if I'd made backups of my files.

Lesson learnt.

"Oh my god, duck!" Sophia hisses as she plasters herself to her seat and slinks down.

I copy her, not having a clue why but doing it anyway.

Carissa, Mel, and Laura all hit the deck too.

"Why are we hiding?" I whisper yell at her.

"Liana and Becky are coming this way."

I peek up out the window and see that she's right – they look like they're heading for Liana's car, a few rows back from mine. They'll pass right by us in a second.

"Why do we need to hide from them?" Carissa whispers.

The girl asks a good question.

I have no idea why I'm hiding. I haven't done fuck

all to this bitch – if anything, she should be hiding from me.

In fact… maybe it's time that *was* the situation after all.

Before I can even think through what I'm doing, my car door is open and I'm out, following the demon herself.

The rain has chilled out, and it's only lightly spitting now; not that it would matter at this point, every inch of me is saturated.

Liana's back is to me, and she's got no idea that I'm behind her. Her and Becky are walking close together, talking. I can't tell if they're celebrating or commiserating.

I spot a wet, dirty shirt or something that someone has dropped in a puddle of muddy water on the ground, and before I can even think it through, I've picked it up and hurled it through the air towards Liana.

I hear a gasp behind me. The girls have obviously followed me, but I don't look around to check. My focus is purely on the filthy ball of wetness as it finds its target with a large splat on the back of her blonde hair.

Liana shrieks. So does Becky, who's managed to catch more than a bit of the splash.

"Oh, good lord," I hear Sophia whisper.

Liana spins around, a shocked expression on her bitchy little face.

I wave at her.

A look of total fury takes over from the shock.

Bring it, bitch.

I think I might have actually lost the plot a little at this point. I've always been ballsy, but this is possibly a bit much, she looks like a giant bird shat directly on her head. I'm finding it pretty hard to feel even one ounce of remorse for my rash actions though. As far as I'm concerned, she deserves a lot worse.

After all the shit she's done, with no consequences so far, a bit of mud in her hair shouldn't be too big of a deal. And I can hardly get in trouble for it after everything she's done to me.

I can hear the phrase *two wrongs don't make a right* in my head, but I don't care anymore. Sometimes you have to fight fire with fire, or in this case, mud.

She stalks back towards me, and I don't know what I'm expecting, but it's definitely not a blood-curdling scream as she claws at the back of her filth-coated hair.

"I've never hated someone as much in my whole fucking life as I hate you!" she screams in my face.

I smirk. "Tell me how you really feel why don't you."

She squeals again and I almost laugh. Here I was thinking I'd lost it, but this bitch is over here screaming like a banshee.

She takes another step closer, so she's right up against me, but I'm not having it. I shove her off me, hard. So hard, she falls backwards onto her ass and into a puddle with a thud.

"Fuck off, bitch." I sneer as I look down at her.

Becky, who must have still been wiping mud off her

face until now, runs over and tries to pull her stupid friend up.

"Berlin, what the *fuck* do you think you're doing?" I hear from behind me.

I exhale heavily. *Just* the person I want to be here for this moment.

<hr>

"OH SHIT," one of the girls mumbles.

My father in the mix. This is *exactly* what I need. *Not.*

"Girls, get to class," he commands.

"But –" Sophia says.

"*Nope.*" He cuts her off. "Class. *Now.*"

I can tell by his voice that he's right behind me.

Liana is out of the puddle now, thanks to her little skank friend.

"You saw what she did to me, right? That's assault," Liana snaps.

"You wouldn't be Liana, by any chance?" he asks.

I risk a peek out the corner of my eye as he comes to a stop next to me.

She pops her hip. "Yeah I am, and I'll be telling the principal about this."

"Interesting," he drawls. "I've just spent the past half an hour reviewing surveillance footage from the arts and drama centre from yesterday..."

Her face visibly pales.

"Was actually just on the way to see the principal myself, can I walk you there?" he offers.

Fuck I love my dad. I don't doubt for a second that I'm in *massive* shit here, and I'm sure he'll find a way to teach me a lesson, but he is *handling* Liana right now, and I am *so* here for it.

She looks like she's about to go full panic stations, but then she straightens her spine and turns her stuck-up little nose into the air.

"I'm not going *anywhere* looking like this."

I don't know whether it just occurred to her that my dad isn't actually a teacher here, or whether she just figured she'd give leaving a go and see what happens, but she turns around and walks away, her sidekick following after her like a pet dog.

We stand there, watching until they both get in Liana's car and drive away.

"Uncle Cole, can I –" Sophia starts.

"Not now, Soph, can you girls just get your bags and go to class please. Or go home. Or go *wherever*. I'm not your teacher, I don't care if you blow off school. I just need to talk my daughter. *Alone*."

I finally turn around and watch as the girls all shoot me sheepish looks before scuttling away to grab their stuff from my car and rushing off back into the school.

Then it's just me and my dad.

"There aren't any cameras in the art and drama centre," I tell him.

"I know that." He nods.

Sly son of a bitch.

I shiver. Apparently, it gets pretty cold when you're outdoors, drenched, in the middle of winter. Who would have thought.

"I'll see you at home. Get warmed up and then we'll talk."

I don't bother answering, it was an order – he's not looking for feedback.

I sigh heavily as he stands there, waiting for me to leave.

I get into my car and drive home in total silence other than the blasting of the heater. I'm too tired for this shit. When I'm tired, I get emotional. Actually, I don't need to 'get' emotional, I'm already fucking there.

I go inside, shower, and put on my pyjamas and dressing gown. I'm not even going to pretend that I'm not going straight to bed after this talk.

I'm making myself a cup of tea and ignoring the texts I've been getting from Pax, when my dad comes through the front door.

"Coffee?" I ask him.

He nods. "Make it a strong one."

I do as instructed, hand him his cup, then sit down at the table opposite him.

He rubs at his temples. Poor guy is clearly stressed. Must run in the family.

"I'm going to need you to fill in some gaps for me."

I figured as much.

"Where do you want me to start?"

"Start by telling me why blondie hates you enough to destroy weeks' worth of your work."

"You talked to my teacher?"

"She called me into school this morning and told me what happened. I don't know why you didn't tell me yourself last night, B."

I shrug. "I was in a panic. I didn't have time for *this*." I gesture between him and I. "I was going to tell you; I just had a lot to do last night."

"Have you slept at all?"

I shake my head. "Not a wink."

He groans. "God help us all."

I huff out a laugh. The man knows me well.

I nod, thinking about what to tell him and where to start.

"Liana hates me because she's Cullen's ex-girlfriend."

"*And?*" he asks, clearly not getting what that means.

"And this is high school, old man, bitches be crazy. Dating someone means that their ex automatically wants you dead. I don't make the rules."

A hint of a smile twitches at the corners of his mouth, but he fights it off. What a battler.

"She's hated me since the day I arrived. I *might* have ruffled a few feathers when I first started."

"Couldn't possibly imagine," he mutters. "She's the same one who cut up your uniform?"

I pop a shoulder. "Yeah, her and her minions. But I don't have any proof. Not yet anyway."

He sighs. "That 'yet' fills me with dread."

That's entirely fair.

I'm probably not going to mention the whole catfish thing to him – no sense really jamming myself under the bus I've already thoroughly thrown myself under, and besides, I haven't actually done anything with that yet. It's still sitting there waiting for its moment to shine.

"I haven't done anything to this girl, but she just doesn't quit."

He raises his brows at me.

"Okay *fine*, I gave her attitude, and I might have put a fish in her car one time... but other than pushing her in that puddle, I haven't done fuck all."

His eyes widen for a second, then they close as he shakes his head, taking a minute to really soak it in.

"Yeah, so, you're grounded."

Urgh.

"Oh, come on, don't act like you were an angel as a teenager."

"I was nothing of the sort, but you're still grounded. I know high school can be hard. You've moved here in the middle of the year and this girl is clearly a little bitch, but I raised you better than resorting to violence."

I knew I went too far when I pushed her. Cole Davids might have been on the field during many a match brawl, but he's never once thrown a punch. He lost a mate from a coward's punch once and he's never fully recovered.

"For how long?"

"I wouldn't ask me that question right now, B. I'll be likely to say for the rest of your life."

I groan. I'm not surprised. He's a parent, he's got to do what he's got to do, but it still sucks. I haven't done to her half of what she's done to me, and I'm still the one being punished.

"Fine." I pout.

"I am really sorry she destroyed your work, B. I know you worked really hard on that, and I'm going to make sure they sort this shit out because it's getting seriously out of hand."

He's got no idea just how out of hand it really is.

"Have you told Cullen?"

I feel my eyes well with tears at the mere mention of his name.

"Oh *shit*, not the waterworks," he mutters before getting to his feet and coming around to my side of the table to hug me. "B, is everything okay?"

I shake my head.

Fuck me, I thought I was all cried out, but having my dad here hugging me like I'm a little girl again sets me off.

"Me and Cullen..." I say through hiccups and tears. "I don't know what happened."

"If he did something to hurt you, I'll wring his God damn neck."

I sniff and laugh at the same time. "I don't know what to believe anymore."

He nods, and I think he understands that he's not

going to get one more ounce of sense out of me without me getting some serious sleep first.

He always was a smart man.

"Bed," he says as he lets me go. He leans back down and kisses the top of my head. "Turn your phone off, get some sleep and we'll talk some more and figure it all out when you're not teetering on the edge of an absolute meltdown."

If only it were that simple.

THIRTY-ONE

Cullen

"Still nothing?" Pax asks me.

I shake my head. I don't even bother asking him if he's heard from her or not – I overhead them on the phone last night and I know I'll lose my shit if I talk about it with him.

"What are you writing?"

I cover the page with my hand. There's not a lot of things I keep from Pax, but I don't need him knowing my business on this one. This letter is the most personal shit I've ever put into writing.

"It's a letter for Berlin. I figure if she's not going to talk to me then maybe she'll read this instead."

"It's only been a few days, bro – she'll come around."

"Exactly. It's been *days*, and I haven't had a single word from her."

"Have some patience. She's a smart girl, but she's hurting."

It makes me angry to have to listen to him talking about her. It pisses me off that they seem to still be on okay terms, but she won't even speak to me. She won't let me tell my side of the story. But Pax, it seems, she doesn't have any issue believing he wasn't part of this shit.

"*Chill out*," he groans.

It's only then that I notice I'm gripping the pen so hard it's bending.

"She's fucked off with me too, if that makes you feel any better. She doesn't know who to trust anymore, and I don't blame her."

He looks like he's debating whether or not to tell me something.

We meet eyes and exchange a look.

"Fuck." He drags his hand over his face. "I'm not meant to say anything... but she hasn't told you everything, Cull. Liana has been coming after her hard."

I drop the pen. "What the fuck do you mean, she hasn't told me everything?"

He grimaces. "She knew you'd lose your shit if you knew everything that went on, and she didn't trust you back then."

"Oh, but she trusted you, did she?" I say, getting to my feet.

I know my anger is misplaced, but I can't stop myself from getting wound up.

"Don't be a cunt. I know you're having an emotional crisis or whatever, but you can't blame me or Ice for her not trusting you. You were a prick to her from day one. And then when you finally started giving her the real treatment, your leech of an ex took over with the bullshit, and you started being a dodgy cunt having secret conversations and keeping shit from everyone. I don't know what you expect, man... play stupid games, win stupid prizes."

He picked up that phrase from Berlin, she's got us all copying her ridiculous one liners.

He's right. I fucking know he is.

"What'd Li do to her?"

He eyes me warily. I can tell he doesn't want to tell me, which means it's bad – it's real fucking bad.

"You remember the night of Bry's party, and Ice and Sophia were real smashed all of a sudden?"

"Yeah..."

"Well, it turns out Liana might have slipped some ket in their drink."

I swear I almost black out on the spot.

She drugged them? What in the actual fuck?

"You better be joking."

"Do you think I'd joke about that shit? One of the girl's sister works in a lab or something and she tested them for drugs. Berlin and Sophia had ketamine in their systems."

"And how does Liana fit into it?" I growl. I need all the information and I needed it weeks ago.

"They tracked down some videos of the beer pong game. It's not the best footage but you can make out Liana in the background. It's not concrete enough evidence for the police, but it's enough for me, man. Liana is capable of anything. There's no way Ice took ketamine. Sophia sure as hell didn't touch any drugs willingly."

"I'm. Going. To. Fucking. *Kill*. Her." I can barely speak. I can barely breathe.

"And *that's* why I didn't tell you sooner. Ice has it handled. You going all hulk about it isn't going to do shit," he says with a roll of his eyes.

I don't know how he's being so calm about this.

"Why didn't they go to the police?" I demand.

I can hear the blood in my veins whooshing in my ears. I'm so filled with rage.

I've never hit a woman in my life, but if Liana were in front of me right now, I think I'd have a hard time not snapping her neck.

"I just told you. Ice thought Liana would just get away with it since you can't actually see her putting the drugs in, or prove it's actually her in the footage – it's just a blonde in a blue top with her hand moving towards the bottle. Then the two girls drank that drink not long after, and next thing it was lights out. It adds up, but not enough for the police to be able to charge her, if I had to guess. Berlin said something about trying to get her to confess. I dunno, man, it was a lot of girl politics, and I was out numbered."

"And you didn't think to involve me in this?"

"She made me promise I wouldn't say anything yet. She said she would tell you when the time was right. Whatever that means."

"I can't fucking believe this. Liana has lost the plot."

"Who could have seen that coming?" he says, sarcastic as fuck.

"Don't start with me," I warn him.

I'm twitching. I need to do something to make this right.

"Mark my words, bro, you go in there all guns blazing, throwing this information around, and you're going to fuck things up for Berlin. You need to take a minute, make sure you're thinking straight, and worry about your girl. Liana will get what's coming to her... we're all going to make sure of that."

"Fuck this, I'm going around there."

He pushes me hard, catching me off guard, and I fall back into my chair.

"No, you're not. You're going to chill out, sit the fuck down and write the rest of that letter, then you're going to go around to see Ice and give it to her. You can't fix this. Do you seriously think if there was something we could do, I wouldn't have already done it? I wanted to skin the bitch, but that gets us nowhere, Cull."

For what is quite possibly the first time in my life, I stop, think, and listen.

He's talking a lot of sense.

Every muscle in my body is dying to get up and do something about this – do *anything* about this. But I can't. I don't have all the information. I don't have the power.

That's what kills me the most and keeps my ass in the chair.

I don't have the power to fix this.

I don't know how to be the solution to this problem.

All I want to do is protect Berlin, but my behaviour is what keeps hurting her the most. That's the only thing I can control right now.

"Okay." I nod.

"Well shit. Didn't think you'd actually listen." He runs his hand through his hair, a shocked look on his face.

I smirk at him.

He smirks back. "Mum's keys are on the bench."

I BANG on the door again. "Come on, B, I know you're in there, just let me say what I came here to say. *Please*," I call out loudly.

I don't even give a fuck that all the neighbours can probably hear me. I just want *her* to hear me. I could just leave the letter behind for her, but I'm fairly sure she'd torch it. I need her to see how sorry I am, maybe then she'll read it.

I step back in surprise as I hear the bolt on the door unlocking from the inside.

I've been out here for ten minutes, and even though I know she's definitely in there, I didn't think for a second that she would actually come out and talk to me.

My heart pounds as the door starts to move. It's felt like the longest few days of my life, not being able to see her.

The door opens wider and Cole steps out.

Fuck.

I didn't think he was home.

"Cole, I –"

He silences me with a wave of his hand.

"You're making a scene on my front porch."

"Ah... yeah," I reply sheepishly. "Fuck, I'm really sorry."

All of a sudden, I feel like a total dipshit. I shouldn't have come here. I look like an idiot. It's embarrassing.

"I just wanted her to know I tried. And that I'm sorry."

He crosses his arms across his chest, and honestly, I'm a little intimidated. I'm a big guy, but he's a bigger guy.

"You knock that blonde girl up?"

My eyes bulge. I guess Berlin really went all in on the dad chat this week.

"No, Sir. I mean Cole. No. Excuse my language, but she's a lying piece of shit."

He gives me a look that makes me think he can relate in some way.

"Did you know she was going to fuck up B's work?"

"Fuck no," I breathe. "I'd never have let that happen if I'd known. I swear to God. She's insane."

He nods his head, and it seems like he's staring into my fucking soul with the amount of eye contact we've got going on here.

Hopefully he's getting the answers he wants out of me – the dude could probably crush me like a coke can if he didn't like what he heard.

"I can appreciate what you're trying to do here, kid, I really can, but she told me to tell you to leave – in a slightly more colourful manner, I'll admit – and I'm not going to force her to do something she doesn't want to do."

I huff out a laugh. I can imagine it was delivered a hell of a lot less politely than what I'm receiving.

"I wrote this for her." I hold out the sealed envelope in my hand to him. "It's your choice if you give it to her or not, and it's up to her if she decides to read it, but I have to try."

He looks between the letter and my face a couple of times before taking it from me.

"I think you're a good kid, Cullen, I do. A little full of yourself maybe, but I was the same at your age." He mulls over his words. "And I don't know where Berlin's head is at or if I've even got the whole story, but for what it's worth, I think you made her the happiest I've ever seen her."

She made me the happiest I've ever been too.

I know we're fucking young and everything feels so important at this age, but her and I, I really think we have something.

Had something.

I step back off the porch. "Thanks for talking to me, Cole."

"No worries. Stop banging on my door and go and sort your head out for tonight. I want you focused on the team."

I nod. "Do you know if she's coming to the game?"

He shakes his head. "She's grounded."

That *sucks*. Even though I'm at least eighty percent confident she hates me, I was still hoping to spot her face in the crowd.

He smacks the envelope into his hand a few times while he stares at me. "But you know... making her go might be a more effective punishment than letting her stay home," he says, his expression unreadable.

I can't be sure, but I think maybe, just maybe, I might have her dad on my side.

THIRTY-TWO

Berlin

I shut the door to my room and seriously contemplate just ripping this thing in half and never looking back, but I'm pretty sure I'm too nosey for that – which Cullen knows all too well.

Bastard.

He knows I won't be able to resist opening this. The kid's as smart as he is pretty.

Asshole.

At least he's stopped banging on the front door like some type of desperate teenage heart throb in a tragic movie. Talk about fucking embarrassing.

I was hoping Dad was going to drag him away by his ear, not turn into his own private mail man, but here we are. Bros before hoes, I guess.

I turn the letter over and over in my hands.

I'm tempted to call the girls over here right away, but I know once I involve them, there's no going back – if I don't open this thing, one, or all of them will do it on my behalf.

I still don't know if I can trust Pax, or who or what I believe anymore, but that's not going to stop me from calling him up anyway.

It only rings a couple of times before I hear his voice.

"*Ice*, you called," he answers warmly.

Damn him. He sounds like my best friend.

"Hi," I say.

I hear him moving around and then the sound of a door shutting.

"What's going on, Ice? You all good?"

"Did you know he was going to come over here and make a scene in front of the whole neighbourhood?"

He chuckles. "Did he look like a tool? I hope you got it on video."

Part of me wants to laugh too. Part of me wants to cry. The biggest part – the part that's about to win, wants to get angry.

"You think it's funny that he came here, practically stalking me?"

I hear it as I say it – the absolutely unreasonable attitude that I'm giving, but I'm nothing if not stubborn, so I'm going to roll with it.

"We're barrelling towards a misunderstanding here, just chill the fuck out, stop being so dramatic, then read the letter and never tell me what it says because I'll give him shit for the rest of his life if you do."

I can picture him rolling his eyes at how extra I'm being.

"What if I don't want to read it?"

"Then don't read it," he replies, not missing a beat, "but we both know you're going to. I don't know who you think you're kidding, Ice, you love him. He loves you. Just get this shit straightened out so you two can go back to being all in love and disgusting, and I can have my friend back. Not talking to you sucks. I have *so* much tea to spill."

That does get a laugh out of me. Pax gossips like a little old woman. It's hilarious.

I miss him too. I want our friendship back as much as I want what I had with Cullen back. But the reality is that it might not have been real. I just don't know anymore.

"Stop being dramatic. Read it," he says, reading my mind again.

"*Fine.*"

"Fine you'll read the letter, or fine you'll stop being so dramatic?"

"I'll read the letter. I make no promises about the rest of it."

He laughs. "Wouldn't be you without your antics."

"I gotta go," I tell him softly. I want to stay right here – talk to him, catch up on everything that I've missed, but I'm not ready for that yet.

I still feel hurt... angry... unsure.

"I was waiting for that," he says with a sigh. "Alright, I'll let you go, but the sooner you figure out he's not a total cunt, he's just a bit of a meathead, the better. I'll admit, I'm a little insulted you've made me guilty by association, but I don't blame you, Ice. You're one of the smartest people I've ever met. You'll figure it all out."

"Thanks, Pax," I whisper, my voice thick.

"Anytime. Okay? I mean that."

My head's a mess, but it's hard to deny that he really does seem to mean it.

My life might be a total shit show, but maybe, just maybe, I can trust him after all.

"WELL, what does it say? The suspense is kiiiiiilllllllling me."

Holy shit.

What *doesn't* it say? That would be an easier question to answer.

Cullen has literally spilled his guts in this letter. He said everything I laid awake at night thinking – *hoping* – he'd say to me. I lay there, staring at my ceiling, fantasising about him saying all these things, but knowing that I'd probably never give him the chance to.

But when my dad handed me this unexpected letter and with it, a stern word about 'giving the kid a shot', I knew I was going to have to read it.

An hour later, and here I am, with my girls in my

room, ready and waiting to dissect every last line of it. I was too chicken shit to do it on my own. I needed the power taken out of my hands, so after I got off the phone to Pax, I called the girls and they all turned up within five minutes.

Small towns have their perks after all.

I clutch it in my hands. "It says *everything*," I breathe. "Every word of every conversation with Liana, every feeling he's had, his feelings for me... he's acknowledged all the fuck ups he made, and held strong in his defence of everything that was out of his control."

"Do you think it's genuine?"

I can't deny this feels like the most genuine piece of literature I've ever read in my life.

I don't know how to feel about it. Part of me felt comfort in hating him – it's less scary, not so vulnerable, but believing the words on these sheets of paper... and possibly giving him a chance to make things right... that scares the absolute shit out of me.

I hand the letter to Carissa. "He doesn't even like writing, and that thing is just..." I sigh, unable to find the word to explain it.

She takes it from me, and the girls crowd around her to read it over her shoulders.

I fidget nervously while they read.

"Oh man, if you don't take him back, I'll have him," Mel says.

"Holy shit," Sophia adds.

"Girl, there is no way you're not giving him another

shot. That's the cutest shit I've ever read, it makes me want to puke." Carissa covers her mouth.

"If Cullen Carrington said even *one* line of that to me, I think I'd just simply die," Laura says dramatically.

I laugh at her; she's seriously lost it.

The girls are laughing at her too, except Carissa, who's looking at her like she needs to get a grip.

"I'm not even joking. I'd stop living." Laura grins. "Times up, over."

"You're *insane*," I say through laughter.

"You're the insane one, if you don't give that boy a chance to fix this," she tells me, serious now.

I close my eyes and let my head fall back.

I want to – so badly, but I'm scared. I don't want to be that dumb girl who puts up with some dickhead's bullshit and sticks around to go another round of it.

But I miss him. I miss him so fucking much I don't know what to do with myself.

I feel exhausted even though I got a solid eight hours last night and I just downed my third coffee of the morning.

My brain hurts from thinking. Over thinking, under thinking... so much thinking.

"We'll support you, no matter what you want to do. You know that, right, B?" Sophia says softly as she takes the letter from Carissa, folds it up and hands it back to me.

I take it from her, nodding.

I know they will; they're better friends than I deserve. I could be a ten point five on the crazy scale and they'd still be there telling me I was totally sane. They'd be liars, but they'd be here.

"I just want to be able to trust him and not end up looking stupid for it."

They all look at me sympathetically. I think they can all understand where I'm coming from.

"Give him a shot, B. You don't have to take him back, but I think you should talk to him. I know you're still worried it's all a big game, but we've seen the way that boy has behaved for years. He's never been like this – not until you."

That's something I never really thought too hard about, but they have known Cullen, or at least witnessed his behaviour from a distance for a long time. A lot longer than me. They know what's normal for him and what's not.

Maybe it's time I trusted that.

"I'm going to do it."

Carissa lets out an excited squeal, and Mel and Laura look like I just made their year. I really need to work on getting those girls a life, this is just getting plain sad.

"We need to get you two laid," I tell them.

Surprisingly, they don't look like it's the worst idea they've ever heard.

Maybe there's hope for them yet.

"I'm home!" I hear my dad yell from downstairs.

Truthfully, I'd forgotten he even went out for a run. His exercise habits are so far from the top of my priority list right now.

"In my room!" I call back.

I hear him walk up the stairs before he opens my door. I grimace at how sweaty he is. I don't need that smelly shit soaking into my carpet.

He looks at us all sitting on my bed and frowns.

"B, what the fuck? You're grounded."

It takes me a minute to figure out what he's talking about.

"Am I not allowed to have people over when I'm grounded?" I ask, genuinely confused.

I've never been grounded in my life; I don't know what the rules are. I'm not entirely sure why this particular form of punishment has started now – part of me thinks Dad just wants me home safe while this whole mess gets straightened out, but I haven't had the balls to ask him when I'm allowed out yet.

One problem at a time.

He goes to speak, but then frowns even deeper and closes his mouth again. "Ah, I don't actually know..."

"Well, if you don't know, how am I meant to know, old man?" I shake my head in mock outrage.

"Girls?" he questions, looking to my friends for feedback.

Carissa shrugs, Mel and Laura almost pass out, and Sophia replies, "I think it's fine, Uncle Cole, she didn't leave the house... so..."

"I can Google it if you want?" Carissa offers.

His eyes dart down to the opened letter in my hands, and I think I see a hint of approval.

Dad chuckles. "I don't think that'll be necessary. I guess I'll let it slide."

He pointedly looks between my face and the paper in my hands.

I give him a nod.

I love that my dad approves of Cullen – and I appreciate the push to read the letter, but if I'm going to give this boy another chance it'll be because *I* want to, sure as fuck not because my dad thinks I should.

"I'll leave you girls to it."

I salute him. The legend himself.

"I'm leaving for the game after I've showered," he reminds me.

"Alrighty, you do you."

He looks at me for a few beats, then around the girls before coming back to me. "You know, B, if you wanted to go to the game, well... I guess that'd be alright – since you'd have parental supervision there and all."

"You want me to Google if that's allowed too?" Carissa says, grinning. Cheeky bitch.

Dad just shakes his head, in amusement or exasperation, I can't be sure which.

"Stay out of trouble, girls," he says as he backs away slowly – he's probably grateful to be getting out of here without getting his leg humped. He shuts the door behind him, and I can practically feel the excitement coming off the four of them.

"Oh, you are *so* going to that game." Carissa beams.

"If you think I'm going to show up there with some

big sign confessing my love for him, you're sadly mistaken," I warn them.

I'm getting a very rom-com type energy coming off the lot of them right now, and I don't like it.

I'm not Heath Ledger, I won't be singing a song to Julia Stiles from the stands or any of that shit. There will be no grand gesture or Hallmark moment.

I look at each of them, one by one, giving them a hard stare. They all grin back at me expectantly.

Absolutely fucking not.

THIRTY-THREE

Cullen

"Seriously, can you two get your fucking heads off those girls and into this bullshit game before we take our first loss of the season," Pax growls. "I get it, you're both all in love and whatever, but can we just play some footy for a few *god damn* minutes? Jesus Christ, it's like being out here with a couple of girls on their periods."

Prick.

"Actually no, you know what? That's insulting to girls' special times. They'd still have more composure than the two of you."

Wanker.

He jabs a finger in the direction of the score board. "We've got shit all time to finish this thing off. Pull your fucking heads in, we need you," he snaps before running off to his spot on the wing.

I don't think I've ever heard him so passionate about the game. I'm as proud of him as I am disappointed in me.

I'm playing like shit by my standards, and he's right – it's not good enough.

I'm the captain, it's up to me to lead the team.

Berlin, Liana, destroyed art boards, and spiked drinks – that'll all still be there when the final whistle blows... but for right now, I need to channel my inner Troy Bolton and get my head in the game.

"If you're singing that song in your head, so help me God..." Bry warns me, a rare smile on his face.

He knows I am. Just like I know he is too. Pax cranks it and dances around like a total dipshit before every single game. It's quite possibly the lamest thing I've ever experienced, but it's tradition now, and you don't fuck with tradition.

We're in a time out; one of their guys is down after a young weapon from our team put him on his ass, so we both need to come back swinging if we're going to walk away with a win. I fucked up the last play, and Bryson shanked the one before that with a pass my two-year-old cousin could have done better, so things can only get better from here. There's two minutes left on the clock and the score is all tied up. We need to make something happen, and we need to make it happen now.

"Let's crush these fuckers' dreams," I say, holding my fist out to him.

He presses his knuckles into mine. "I'm going to make them wish their mums had swallowed them."

I almost choke on my mouthguard as I shove it back into my mouth. Fucking Bryson; you never know how the guy is going to behave next.

He chuckles at my reaction as he runs off.

I don't know what the fuck has him so chipper all of a sudden, but I'll take it over the brooding bullshit he's had running lately.

"We're on, boys. Whistle blows, take no prisoners," I yell out to the team as I take my position at the back where I can see the whole game in front of me.

We're about to hit play again. Their player has been taken off the field by the medic.

"Let's get this shit done, boys," Bryson calls out from his position in the middle of the field.

The Oak Hill High guys have the ball, so we're running defence.

I don't know whether it's having me and Bry checked back in or what, but the boys all start to rally. They're communicating, calling out to each other, pointing out gaps in our line. Warms my cold heart to see it.

The whistle blows and everyone is in action. Oak Hill send the ball down field, with a well-placed kick that should see the ball just go out of touch and send us into a lineout at the twenty-two. At least that was the plan, but it seems that Pax has other ideas. He's in a flat-out sprint for the line, one eye on the ball as it hurtles through the air.

Tonksy is going with him, and fucked if I know what they're planning, but I hope it's something good.

Pax leaps in the air as the ball crosses the sideline, his fingers *just* make contact, the tips scraping the ball enough to send it back into field and keep it in play. It lands in Tonksy's hands and he's in motion, ploughing into full sprint downfield.

I'm moving too, and I can see Bry ahead of me, on his game.

The Oak Hill boys are scrambling, rushing across the paddock to try and cover this unexpected turn of events.

The crowd is screaming as we move downfield. Tonksy's slipping through defenders before getting caught and offloading the ball to Bryson in spectacular fashion.

Bryson puts the hammer down, flying downfield at a pace I don't think I've ever seen him move at. I'm fucking fanging it to catch him. I can see he's going to get cut off by two or more of their guys up ahead, but if he can get a pass off to me, I'll only have one dude to contend with before I get over the line.

"Open!" I yell at him.

His head tilts my way; his tell that he's about to pass. He waits until the last second, drawing the guys right in, and then flicks the ball out the back from under his arm to me. It's one hell of a trick pass, so tricky I almost don't see it coming, and it's not exactly right to me, but I scramble, fumble, and then grip the ball tight.

I sail down the remainder of the field, effortlessly outrunning the one guy who could have had a shot at catching me, all the way to the line.

Try time.

I touch the ball to the ground, and it hits me then, just how loud the crowd is screaming and cheering for us.

I look up into the stands and see a sea of black and silver before I'm almost knocked to the ground by the team running and jumping all over me.

The ref blows the final whistle. Thank fuck that's over without a loss. I don't need another disappointment right now.

Pax arrives, whooping and hollering, and I pull him in for a hug, slapping his back.

His move is what got us here. Without him becoming a champion high jumper out of nowhere, we'd still be at the other end of the field, fending off their attack.

He's the man of the match in my eyes.

Fucking legend. Tonksy too. It was a stellar effort all round.

Bryson takes the ball and kicks the conversion, which sails over easily, not that it matters now. We've won.

We're all celebrating, clapping each other on the shoulders, rubbing each other's heads. I can tell we're all pretty proud of this win. It wasn't our best game, not by any stretch of the imagination, but we pulled it together at the end and the boys can feel that me, Pax, and Bry needed this.

"About time I saw you smile, you sour prick." Pax grins at me.

"About time you played like you actually give a fuck," I fire back.

He laughs, loud, throwing his head back.

"You can fuck off and go see your girl now," he says, and my heart skips a beat.

"*What?*"

He smirks, the smug little prick clearly knows something I don't.

"You heard me. Go get your girl."

He turns and points to the bottom of the crowded stands. It takes me a minute, but there she is.

Every stunning fucking inch of her.

"You knew she was here?"

"Yeah, Cole told me before the game. Made an executive decision not to tell you though, ya whipped piece of shit." I can hear in his tone that he thinks he's funny as fuck.

Can't even blame him.

I would have done the exact same thing if roles were reversed.

"You're an asshole," I tell him, my eyes never leaving her.

"Yeah, yeah, love you too, bro."

Someone is probably about to tell me that 'Saturdays are for the boys' or some shit, but I don't give a fuck. This moment right here is for her. Hopefully it's for *us*.

"Oh, fuck off already," Pax says, shoving me in the direction that she's waiting.

I don't need to be told again.

I make my way over there; people move to get out of my way. Even the cheerleaders don't try to stop and distract me. I must look like a man on a mission.

I can see her searching the field. My ego fucking hopes she's looking for me, and when she finally sees me, I know I'm right.

Carissa taps Berlin's arm and points in my direction. We're still half the width of the field apart but our eye contact is so strong, everything else fades away.

The people patting me on the back as I pass them, the calls of my name, the cheers from the crowd... none of it matters.

I pick up my pace, striding towards her. I'm in such a hurry all of a sudden, I want to run.

I'm trying to read her expression and failing hard. I don't know where we're at.

Did she read the letter?

Does she hate me? Love me?

Do I get her back?

I have so many questions, but she's here, and if nothing else, that has to count for something.

A smug grin settles on her lips, and she crosses her arms across her chest as I get closer. I'm vaguely aware of her girls surrounding her, whispering to each other, but I can't gauge the vibe.

I could be about to get a drink thrown in my face for all I know. I'd probably deserve it. That'd give the crowd something to really yell about.

Scoring the game-saving try and being the captain of the team isn't going to help me – not with this girl – not if I'm not treating her right. She's not impressed by my 'rugby bullshit', as she so diplomatically puts it.

She's no brainwashed cheerleader who would cut a bitch to be the girl on my arm. Not *my* girl.

"New girl. You came."

Fuck it's good to see her. I've got photos and memories, but they don't do her justice. Not even close.

"Golden boy." She tugs her bottom lip between her teeth as I stop right in front of her, only the metal barrier separating us.

She's on a platform that makes her taller than me.

I look up at her. She's so fucking beautiful.

"Did you get my letter?"

She nods, her long, dark hair falling into her face.

"Did you read it?"

"I read it."

The girls are all staring, watching the interaction closely, but none of them are giving me any indication whatsoever of whether or not this is going to go in my favour.

"Do you have any feedback?"

Fuck I'm nervous. This could be it – the last conversation I ever get to have with her.

Fuck I hope not.

I don't want this to be the end.

The silence stretches, and it's killing me more and more by the second.

A hint of a smile graces her lips. "I guess it was pretty well structured for a rugby meathead. I'd probably give you an eight out of ten."

"An eight out of ten, and a second chance?" I push, fucking hopeful as ever.

She makes me wait for an answer, heart racing. She's wound me up like this and kept me guessing from the minute she walked through the gates to West Lake High; I should have known she wouldn't go easy on me now.

The silence stretches, painfully.

Carissa gives her a shove. "Put him out of his misery already, I'm getting second-hand embarrassment."

Berlin just laughs. This *fucking* chick – she's enjoying this.

"I guess I could consider it," she says, but the smile on her face is telling another story – one where she's already considered it and decided I'm in with a grin.

Fuck yes.

I reach over the barrier and grip her waist, lifting her over the metal rail and into my arms. She shrieks as her feet leave the ground. She wraps her legs around my waist, tight as hell.

I kiss her like I'm starved. I may as well be; it's been days since I've felt these pouty lips and inhaled the smell of her.

This torture is not something I want to repeat, ever again.

No more secrets.

No more bullshit.

Just me and her.

"Everyone is staring," she whispers when I pull away for air.

"Let them stare," I growl.

"I swore there was going to be no big dramatic moment."

"Tough fucking luck." I chuckle.

I can hear Pax yelling and cheering, giving me shit, along with what sounds like half the team and the stadium.

I couldn't care less.

I'm nothing but proud.

THIRTY-FOUR

Berlin

One week later

"You're a straight-up savage. Fuck I love it."

Me, Pax, Cullen, Carissa, and Sophia are all hanging out at my house in the downstairs living room, because apparently, I'm still grounded. The old man did end up Googling a set of rules and decided I could have friends over, but only for two hours a day, and no boys in the bedroom.

Eye roll.

I still don't know what kind of power trip he's on, but for now at least, I've decided to just go with it. He's never grounded me before, so it's ironic to start when I'm legally an adult, but that only makes me think he's just trying to look out for me more than anything. And I'll seriously think twice before I shove a bitch again, so I guess that's something.

It could be worse. Thanks to him and my boyfriend, I have a darkroom here and I can make everyone come to me over the holidays. *Winning.* It's too cold in this shit hole of a town to be too cut up about having to stay home.

"Still can't believe you've been catfishing my ex for months and you didn't think to tell me until a week ago." Cullen scowls.

"Oh, get your hand off it," I say with a roll of my eyes. "I didn't know if I could trust you then – just be grateful that I trust you now."

To be fair, I'd forgotten I still hadn't told him that part – but he knows now.

Pax cracks up laughing.

"Yeah, Cull, quit being a little bitch."

I sigh as I watch Cullen launch a coaster from the coffee table across the room; his impeccable aim landing it right in the centre of Pax's forehead.

"Ow," Pax complains, rubbing his head. "You're a prick."

"You're a fucking loudmouth."

"*Children,*" Carissa mutters.

She's not wrong.

They really are brothers. Bickering and all.

I watched them wrestle over the last can of Sprite

the other day. It went on far longer than it needed to. I drank the Sprite while they fought. Dangerous game that was.

"Can we talk about the video and what we're going to do about it?" Sophia asks, exasperated.

I grin as I think about it again. It was almost too easy.

Jaxon hasn't managed to get Liana to confess to the drugging or destroying my photos, not yet anyway, but she *has* sent through the footage her and her stupid friends took of them cutting up my PE uniform *and* the footage of me prancing around the gym wearing the scraps of clothing – much to Pax's delight. I swear that day was the highlight of his year so far.

Everyone is pretty pumped about it. It's not everything I want, but it's something, and something is better than nothing.

"So, what's the plan, Ice?"

"Let's take this to the school and get this bitch expelled," Sophia suggests.

"Nah, fuck that. I'm going to make her pay, and it's not going to be by tattling to a teacher. And it's not going to be until we've got her for *everything*."

I'm feeling theatrical, and there's a plan brewing in my mind that is *so* drama-filled it almost makes me sick.

Nothing but the best for the queen bitch.

Carissa grins.

Sophia groans. "Come onnnnn, B, how long are we going to let this play out?"

"Until she hangs herself out to dry completely." I

shrug. "The chick is a sociopath. I don't want to give her any wiggle room to talk her way out or have daddy buy her way out of it – I want to have it all sewn up in a nice little bow."

"I curse the day you moved back here," Soph grumbles. "My life was peaceful before you arrived."

"You pronounced *boring* wrong."

She narrows her eyes at me and mutters something under her breath.

I know she loves me really, she's just in a situation with this whole Bryson and Tonksy mess, and I have to admit, I am somewhat to blame for that, but it's not exactly my fault the guy we arranged to make Bry jealous actually turned out to be cool. Apparently, that's not helpful. Sue me for thinking it doesn't hurt for her to have options.

"She hasn't got us into too much trouble," Carissa tells Sophia.

"There's still plenty of year left, give her time," Cullen teases.

"She wouldn't be playing these games if it weren't for your bunny boiling ex," Pax points out.

"Thank you, Paxikins, a valid point." I stick my tongue out at Cullen.

"So, we're just going to keep going to school like normal next term, waiting for demon barbie to strike again?" Sophia asks, her total outrage obvious.

"No," Carissa says at the same time that I say, "Sure."

We exchange a look.

"If she wants to keep giving us more fuel, I'll burn the bitch to within an inch of her life. Doesn't bother me," I say.

"Sweet Jesus," Cullen says on a heavy exhale.

I think he's quietly on team *run to the teachers now*, but he knows he's wasting his time.

We spent all night talking after we made up at his game last week – we talked about every little Liana related detail, so he knows I'm not going to let this go without a bang. I don't just want justice, I want revenge. I don't even care how childish that makes me. I want it, and I'm going to get it.

Sophia points a finger at me. "I don't like that look in your eye."

"And I don't like your lack of commitment to the cause."

"We could talk to Cole," Cullen suggests.

"No way." I shut it down quickly. "Dad will over-react – especially about the drugging. Like, he'd probably murder her and hide her body in a well or something."

"Morbid, but I'm kind of here for it," Carissa mutters.

Same. But I can't let the old man ruin his no-violence streak for me. I'd have to ground him for the rest of his life.

"You just need to trust me. She's going down, and she'll be doing it in style. Are you guys with me or what?"

"Fuck yes," Pax says, while the other three agree somewhat less enthusiastically.

I grin gleefully.

I may have never wanted to move here, to this country, this town, but now that I'm here, with these four boneheads, I actually can't remember a time that I felt this happy and content.

I've got a boyfriend who belongs on the cover of a sports magazine and best friends I know I can trust with anything.

Everything is so good with me and Cullen, and for the first time, I have every reason to believe it'll continue for a long time.

What a time to be alive.

"PAX, what the fuck are you doing in here? Get out!" Cullen snaps as he drags the cover up his bed to better cover me in my totally undressed state.

"Shhhh." Pax hisses. "They'll hear us."

"What do you mean 'shhh'? Get the fuck out of here!"

"*Pax.*" I groan. "I'm tired."

"Your dad is here," he says in a whisper shout, like he's got some right to be up in arms, as though he's not the one who just busted into Cullen's bedroom without knocking.

That gets my attention.

"*What?*"

"My dad is dead, bro. Are you high?" Cullen demands.

"Not *your* dad, you fuck stain, Ice's dad. Jesus Christ, sometimes I have serious concerns about your intelligence."

"What the fuck?" I ask, a little bewildered. I was half asleep when he burst in, and I honest to God have no idea what the fuck is going on right now.

"*Cole* is *here*?" Cullen asks, flicking his bed side lamp on.

"Yeah. I was just going to get a drink – and a break from listening to you two," I feel myself blush, "and I heard a dude's voice. I snuck down and had a look and it's Cole. His car is in the drive."

I glance at the clock. "It's eleven at night. What the fuck is *my* dad doing at *your* house?"

"Your guess is as good as mine, sugar plum."

"Who's he talking to?" Cullen demands. "Ma or Mum?"

"Ma *and* Mum."

That's not good news.

"He must know I'm in here." I groan. "The old man is cool, but I'm grounded, so he's probably trying to teach me a lesson."

I snuck in Cullen's window, like I have several times over the past week, and he in mine, but it sounds like maybe we've finally been caught. It was bound to happen, to be fair.

"Well, I dunno about you guys, but I'm going to go find out what they're talking about," Pax replies.

"Me too." I nod. There might still be time for me to make an escape, but I won't be holding my breath.

Cullen rubs his hand over his face. "I guess we may as well make it a party."

Pax stands there, waiting for us to get out of bed.

"Dude, I'm naked and so is she. Give us a fucking minute."

Pax grins and waggles his brows at us.

"Oh, go away you pest." I throw a pillow at him.

He catches it and throws it back at me before ducking out of the room.

"I swear to God, sometimes I wish I could just knock him out," Cullen grumbles.

I huff out a laugh as I climb out of bed and get dressed. I'm tempted to just throw on one of Cullen's t-shirts but second-guess it. If I'm going to get caught red-handed, I should at least have my underwear on.

He throws me my bra from the other side of the bed – apparently that gained some distance in the undressing-each-other process.

We both hastily throw on enough clothes to be respectable and sneak out into the hallway to meet Pax.

He tips his head in the direction of the living room before holding up a finger to his lips, telling us to be quiet. We stop just shy of the doorway that leads into the living room and stand silently, listening.

I can hear the three of them talking. Small talk by the sounds.

No one sounds mad. And no one has come looking

for me in Cullen's bedroom, *yet*, so maybe I haven't been snapped sneaking out after all.

But then why is he here?

"I have to admit, I was surprised to get your call. It's been, what? Eighteen years?" my dad says.

I can hear someone mucking around in the kitchen; Hannah making tea, if I had to guess. It's her speciality.

"It's been a long time," Julia says.

"You were very secretive. I don't know why you asked me to come over here so late, but it's good to see you, Julia. You look good."

"Your dad is DTF my Ma," Pax hiss whispers.

I shush him.

Gross.

I don't need to think about my dad and him being DTF anyone.

"Thanks, Cole, it's good to see you too. You look... it's good to see you." She fumbles over her words.

Cullen rolls his eyes.

Poor bitch. I can feel the heat coming off her cheeks from here. The Cole Davids effect is obviously in full swing.

"Get a grip, Ma, for the love of God," Pax whispers to us.

"So, what's going on? Is it the kids?" my dad prompts.

I don't get it. It sounds like Julia and Hannah have called my dad over here, under the cover of darkness, to have some type of secret conversation.

I don't like it.

This can't mean anything good for me and Cullen. Or me and Pax. Straight up, it's probably not good news for *any* of us.

"Thanks, Hannah," my dad says.

I peer around the corner. Cullen's mum is handing out mugs. I was right – the woman sure loves making a cup of tea.

Sad? Have a hot beverage.

Celebrating? Hot beverage.

Any time of any day... you guessed it. Hot beverage.

She takes a seat next to Julia. The pair of them are sitting facing my dad like they're about to double team him in a job interview like a couple of office sharks.

I have a *real* bad feeling about this.

Hannah and Julia exchange a look. And it's not a good one. I know that look. Bad news follows *that* look.

I pull my head back. I don't want to watch anymore.

"Do you think we should mind our own business?" I whisper to the boys. I've got a bad feeling in the pit of my stomach, like whatever it is they're going to discuss – maybe we shouldn't hear it.

There are things you cannot unhear once they've hit your eardrums.

"Nope."

"Fuck no."

I sigh. Apparently, I'm on my own. Eavesdropping it is then.

"I ah... I wanted to talk to you about Berlin," Julia finally says after a long, awkward silence.

I can literally feel my heart slamming against my rib cage.

Me? Why does she want to talk about me?

"What about Berlin?" Dad asks, his tone wary. Poor old man, it really could be anything when it's about me. Props to him – he's put up with a fair bit of shit and he always takes it like a real champ.

"I'm sure you're aware how much time she's been spending with both Pax and Cullen."

"Yeah. The three of them seem very close."

I don't know what they're getting at, but I don't like it. In fact, I like it even less now that it's clear this *is* about the three of us in some way.

Cullen wraps his arm around my middle, and Pax grabs my wrist. I must look as nervous as I feel. I realise I'm bouncing my knee – a tell-tale sign.

"Is that a... problem?" my dad asks, his tone showing his confusion.

Julia and Hannah both like me – or so I thought until this very moment. Now I'm not so sure. I don't know what I'll do if they don't want me hanging around Cullen and Pax.

I mean, we're all eighteen now, so technically they can't stop us, but I like this family – I *love* them. I want to be accepted by them.

"It's not a problem... it's just *complicated*," Hannah replies. She's nervous too – I can hear it in her voice.

"Complicated how?"

There's an awkward silence before my dad speaks again. "I don't know what's happening, but if you could tell me what's going on, I'd really appreciate it... clearly I'm missing something here."

Aren't we all?

"Tell him, Julia," Hannah says. "It's time."

Time for what? I'm so filled with dread I can barely stay upright.

"I'm worried with the kids spending so much time together... that something might... that *they* might... there's something you don't know..." Julia is stuttering; she's very clearly panicked.

I peek out and watch my dad reach across the table and take Julia's hand in his. "Breathe," he instructs. "It's okay. Just tell me what you need to tell me."

She takes a deep breath, just like he said, and when she speaks again, her voice is clear. "It's Pax... he's your son, Cole. Berlin and Pax are siblings."

Son.

Siblings.

"*Berlin and Pax are siblings.*"

Pax is my brother...

I kissed my brother.

I hear myself gasp.

ALSO BY

<u>Love like Yours Series</u>

Rushed – Book 1

Pierced – Book 2

Hunted – Book 3

Chased – Book 4

Love like Yours Box Set – Books 1-4

<u>All Access Pass Series</u>

Paper, Scissors, Rock – Book 1

Hide and Seek – Book 2

One for the Money – Book 3

<u>My Heart Duet</u>

My Heart Needs

My Heart Wants

Every Last Beat – The Heart Duet Box Set – Books 1 & 2

<u>Calendar Boys</u>

Mr. January

Mr. February

Mr. March

Mr. April

Mr. May

Mr. June

Mr. July

Mr. August

Mr. September

Mr. October

Mr. November

Mr. December

Calendar Boys Box Set – Books 1-4

Calendar Boys Box Set – Books 5-8

Calendar Boys Box Set – Books 9-12

Master Manipulator

The First Rule

Royals of Westlake
The King of Black Diamonds

ACKNOWLEDGMENTS

Thanks to everyone that helped me get this one over the line, who know who you are.

Please refer to the last twenty-something books because honestly, I've run out of new things to write in this section.

ABOUT THE AUTHOR

NICOLE S. GOODIN is a romance author and mother of two from Taranaki in the North Island of New Zealand.

In mid-2015, she started to write about a group of characters who wouldn't get out of her head. Her first book, Rushed, was published in mid-2016.

Nicole enjoys long walks on the beach, pillow fights and braiding her friends' hair. She dislikes clichés, talking about herself in the third person, and people who don't understand her sense of humour.

Please feel free to contact her either via her website, email, Instagram, Twitter or on her Facebook page, she would love to hear your feedback. If you're feeling really game, you can even sign up for her newsletter.